RICK PARTLOW
THE
HUNTER
DROP TROOPER: RECON | BOOK TWO

aethonbooks.com

HUNTER
©2023 RICK PARTLOW

This book is protected under the copyright laws of the United States of America. No part of this publication may be reproduced, stored in a retrieval system, or transmitted, in any form or by any means, without the prior permission in writing of the publisher, nor be otherwise circulated in any form of binding or cover other than that in which it is published and without a similar condition including this condition being imposed on the subsequent purchaser. Any reproduction or unauthorized use of the material or artwork contained herein is prohibited without the express written permission of the authors.

Aethon Books supports the right to free expression and the value of copyright. The purpose of copyright is to encourage writers and artists to produce the creative works that enrich our culture.

The scanning, uploading, and distribution of this book without permission is a theft of the author's intellectual property. If you would like to use material from the book (other than for review purposes), please contact editor@aethonbooks.com. Thank you for your support of the author's rights.

Aethon Books
www.aethonbooks.com

Print and eBook formatting by Steve Beaulieu. Art provided by Luciano Fleitas.

Published by Aethon Books LLC.

Aethon Books is not responsible for websites (or their content) that are not owned by the publisher.

This book is a work of fiction. Names, characters, places, and incidents are the product of the author's imagination or are used fictitiously. Any resemblance to actual events, locales, or persons, living or dead is coincidental.

All rights reserved.

ALSO IN SERIES

RECON
THE HUNTER
THE MERCENARY
THE OPERATIVE

1

The wet grass at the crest of the high hill coiled beneath us, a carpet of discomfort that soaked through my shirt in the chill dampness of the autumn morning. I tried to ignore it, tried to keep the camera steady as I panned across the breadth of the massive herd of elk. They covered the rolling hills below us, shifting this way and that at the insistent bugling of their horned lord, the brawny bull with a fire in his eyes and wickedly curved antlers arching over his shoulders like sabers.

"You think we're far enough away?" I asked Sophia, not whispering but speaking in a normal, low tone that carried much less distance. "He looks crazy with the rut."

"We're just under a hundred meters," she responded in the same tone, shrugging slightly, not looking away from the binoculars. "He won't notice us."

Sophia's dark brown hair was pulled back into a long ponytail, gathered away from the soft curves of her high cheekbones except for a few strands that had escaped and clung tenaciously to her ears. I caught the corner of her mouth turning up slightly. "Besides, he's going to have other things to worry about in a couple minutes."

She tapped me on the arm and pointed off to the left, where the trees skirted the river. I turned the small camera in that direction, just now noticing the black, white and grey shapes slinking up between the trees.

"Four greys, a white and three blacks," Sophia listed off, almost in a mnemonic chant. "That's the Twisted Creek pack. They had twelve until this last winter, when the Round Hills killed their old Alpha Male and three of the females went over to the White Crest pack."

"You know," I said, not for the first time, "you could have the drones take footage of this instead of making me run the camera."

"I sure could, sweetie," she agreed, smile broadening. "But then I wouldn't have an excuse for bringing you along, would I?"

"Good point," I acknowledged, leaning over to kiss her on the cheek. "Between your job and mine, we don't get much downtime, do we?"

"No one said you *had* to go work for the planetary constabulary, love," she reminded me. "I know the Demeter Ecological Survey would have let me hire you as a strong back. It's been almost three years since the war ended and we're *still* understaffed."

"What I know about genetics, zoology, and ecological engineering could fit in a pamphlet," I said. "Carrying a gun and being intimidating, that I know how to do."

"Shhh," she hushed me, lowering her binoculars, and pointing again. "Here they come."

The wolves went straight for a calf only a few months old, born in the late spring. The mother tried to run them off, but their packmates circled back around to corner the young animal while the other elk edged away like a school of fish scattering before a shark. I looked over the top of the camera's display screen, wanting to see it through my own eyes and not through the filter of the device. This was too real, too raw for that. This was why I loved living here. The Revenant Forest on Demeter was like stepping back in time tens of thousands of years and watching an Earth before humans built their cities.

Here, animals that had been extinct for millennia, mastodons and saber-tooth cats and megatherium and dozens more, stalked and grazed and lived alongside wolves and elk and deer, all of them engineered and incubated here for the Revenant Project. Demeter was one of the oldest colonies in the Commonwealth, and when we'd found it, it had very little in the way of complex life. There was enough of an ecology of fungi and lichen to keep the atmosphere breathable, but not much more. It had been the perfect place to introduce Earth life without worrying about destroying an existing ecosystem, and it had been the perfect place to start the Revenant Project.

DNA samples had been harvested decades before and preserved and later duplicated; and here, they'd come to life. The Revenant Forest had been the first area they'd been reintroduced, and was still the densest concentration on the planet, but the ecosystem had been spreading across the temperate zones of this world for decades now, and there had been other introductions in the polar zones. If we didn't screw it up and the Tahni didn't invade again and force us to eat a bunch of the herd animals again, this place would be even cooler in a century or so.

And it was all playing out in front of me. The bull elk was rushing in now, but three or four wolves were snapping at him, trying to keep him distracted while the others finished off the calf. The poor thing was bleating in terror, blood running down its flanks from the wolves hanging off its haunches, sinking in their teeth. It was ugly and brutal and depressing, but I'd seen worse. I'd done worse.

In the year I'd been trapped here during the Tahni occupation, I'd done a lot worse. Left for dead in a failed attempt to take the colony back from the enemy, the rest of my Marine Force Recon platoon ambushed and slaughtered, I'd joined up with Sophia and what was left of the human resistance and did what I could to fight the Tahni with what we had. By the time the Commonwealth military had come back into the fight and given us hope we could win this thing, I'd developed an affinity for those wolves and the merciless efficiency they showed towards their prey.

"You ever see this before," Sophia asked me softly, leaning into my arm and settling in to watch, "back on Earth, before the war?"

"I saw wolves a few times with Gramps," I told her, eyes still locked on the sight of the cow and the bull trying to chase off the pack, wearing themselves out as the wolves dodged away nimbly. "In the Canadian Rockies, and again in Arizona. Different sub-species in Arizona, the Mexican wolf. I was never around when they made a kill, though."

"Gramps?" Sophia repeated. "That was your great-grandfather, right?"

I nodded, realizing I hadn't thought about him, or any other part of my former life, for most of the last three years. "Master Gunnery Sergeant Cesar Torres," I said proudly, "old United States Marine Corps, back when there was a United States."

"Jeez, how old was he?" She blurted, actually looking away from the kill.

"He'll be 203 in a month," I said, "if he's still alive." I shrugged. "Mom seemed to think he was."

"You haven't heard from him since you joined the Marines?"

I snorted at the understatement. "I haven't seen him since the night my mother sent an assassin after her own grandfather," I corrected her, "and I killed the guy, then changed my identity and went on the run to the Marine Corps."

"I was *trying* to be judicious," she said. Then she frowned, her eyes narrowing. "Do you ever miss that life? I mean, your mom was at the top of the Corporate Council totem pole. You guys were on top of the world, almost literally. This," she waved around us, "seems like a pretty big comedown."

Down in the river valley between the hills, the calf was kicking fitfully as the life ran out of it, the wolves hanging on patiently.

"No," I said flatly. "I don't miss it at all."

After the feeding began, we started making our way back to the rover; we'd been there to capture the hunt. The road back to the main research facility was muddy and treacherous this time of year, but the utility vehicle was built for it and Sophia had driven these trails since before I met her. I didn't even look up when the wheels lost traction for a heartbeat or I felt the rear end slide.

It was getting late in the morning and my stomach was growling; I was digging in the center console for a protein bar when my 'link chimed for attention from my jacket pocket with the tone I'd assigned to my boss, Constable Nunez.

"Shit," I muttered, fishing for my ear piece and pushing it into place. "This is *supposed* to be my day off."

"Maybe Amity's being hit by yet another crime wave," Sophia murmured sarcastically. The tourist town was *just* getting back on its feet as the post-war recovery began to make its way out to the colonies little by little, and street crime wasn't a major problem.

"Munroe," I answered tersely.

"Munroe," I heard Nunez' deep bass rumble vibrate in my ear, "we got a…situation here." He paused as if he wasn't sure how to say it.

"What's up, boss?" I asked him, frowning curiously.

"We had a registered bounty hunter land at the port," he told me. "Big guy named Roger West, landed in his own private ship. Got all his clearances from the Patrol and everything."

I felt the corner of my mouth curl into a sneer. Bounty hunters were a nasty reality of our interstellar civilization. There were too many jurisdictions, too many places to hide, and too few Patrol ships to keep track of all the criminals. The only way to ensure that people didn't kill someone or steal a ship in one system and run to another with impunity was to allow licensed bounty hunters to bring them in for profit. No cop I knew liked it too much, though.

"What's he want here?" I asked. Did we have a fugitive hiding out in town?

"You," Nunez said and I felt my blood run cold. "He wants to talk to you."

I fidgeted, tightening the chest fastenings of my uniform vest and checking the looseness of my pistol in its chest holster over and over as I watched the muddy road slide underneath the wheels of the rover. The pistol was comforting; it was the same model I'd carried in the war as a secondary weapon. We'd stopped at our house---Sophia's house, really, the one the Ecological Survey provided---and picked the gear up on the way into town.

"Are you sure you're not overreacting, Munroe?" Sophia asked me, eyes darting away from the road to watch me play with my weapons and armor yet again. "It might be nothing."

"And it might be that my mother has put a bounty out on my head and this guy tracked me down," I said, more harshly than I'd intended. I sighed, reaching out a hand to squeeze hers where it was tight on the wheel. "Either way, the uniform reminds him that I'm local law enforcement, and maybe the armor and the gun will keep him from trying anything."

"I'm going in with you," she said.

"I've got the Constable with me and…"

"I'm going in with you," she cut me off with a look that many a Tahni soldier had seen just before he died, and I stopped objecting.

"Did you bring a gun?" I asked her instead.

She shot me an annoyed glance. "Of course I brought a gun. Why the hell would I go in with you if I wasn't armed?"

I couldn't help it; I laughed. She chuckled too, the tension broken for just a moment.

"We'll get through this, Munroe," she said.

Some of our friends thought it was funny that she called me by my last name, but the false identity the street surgeon in Vegas had picked for me all those years ago was Randall Munroe. I'd gone into the Marines immediately after, and nearly everyone there, including your friends, called you by your last name. I sure as hell didn't want anyone calling me "Randy," so Munroe it stayed.

Amity came into view once we'd cleared the Revenant Forest. The city had been rebuilt since the war, and it had grown past its original boundaries as new hotels and restaurants had opened up to cater to the reinvigorated tourist industry. They were growing a little *too* fast in my opinion, and I'd begun to worry about the new resorts and vacation villas eating into the preserve's land.

I let my eye wander to the sonic fences designed to keep wildlife out of the city, noting they were almost a kilometer farther out than they'd been when I arrived here, on that ill-fated mission four years ago. Just past them, a small herd of deer wandered, grazing on the lush grass and taking advantage of the greater discomfort the sonic barrier caused for predators.

There wasn't much traffic this morning; it was a holiday, technically, Founders' Day. It was a century and change on this day, local time, since the first Commonwealth Survey ships had passed through the wormhole jumpgate into the Cronus system and landed on the one habitable, Demeter. The resorts were still open because tourists didn't take holidays from their vacations, but government offices were closed, other than emergency services. The Constabulary was an emergency service, of course, but I'd had the day off anyway since I had seniority over the rest of the deputies by all of three weeks.

The Constabulary was near the center of town, across the street from the offices of the Colonial Governor. Those had been rebuilt since the war; there'd been too much blood spilled in and around the old offices. I knew, because I'd been responsible for much of it. I was of the opinion that the new offices had less character than the old ones and tried too hard to look anachronistic, but Sophia assured me that was just me being prematurely curmudgeonly. The Constabulary was a utilitarian building that didn't pretend to be anything but a police station, boxy and plain with a garage for a half dozen rovers and a couple ducted-fan hoppers. We *really* needed a flyer, but VTOL jets were still pretty expensive out in the colonies and Constable Nunez hadn't been able to convince the Governor to approve it.

Sophia parked the rover just inside the Constabulary garage, in a space for visitors. She pulled a compact handgun out of the center console and tucked it into the pocket of her jacket before she slid out the driver's side door. I steeled myself with a deep breath and got out of the car.

Mother knew about this identity. She'd found me at the military base on Inferno when I'd returned from Demeter after the Fleet and the Marines had freed it, and it had only been some very quick thinking by my Company Commander, Captain Yassa, that had kept me from a quick flight home to Earth. It wasn't at all unlikely that she had people looking for me still, despite the deal I'd made.

I took Sophia in through the employee entrance to avoid the weapons detectors at the front door, walking through a narrow hallway that led up through the break room and into the offices. The station wasn't fully staffed today, but there were a couple other deputies in the break room when we passed by and they mumbled hellos, barely looking up from the administrative work they were doing on issue tablets. Sophia was a regular fixture around here, and neither of the deputies was paying enough attention to notice I was strapped.

Constable Nunez was sitting on the edge of my desk in the main office, dressed in our everyday blue utility fatigues, with his rank on his sleeve and the Constabulary seal on his breast pocket. He was a short, thickly-built man probably twenty years older than me, with forearms as thick around as my calves. No one fucked around with Esteban Nunez twice, which came in handy in our line of work.

He looked me up and down, his bushy, black eyebrows shooting up at my load-out.

"There something you want to tell me, Munroe?" He asked, deadpan, not getting up.

I glanced around the room, seeing that all of the other desks were empty and we were alone. I wondered if that was on purpose.

"Boss," I said, trying to work up some moisture in my mouth, "there's a possibility this guy might be after me."

"Are you telling me you're a fugitive from justice, Deputy?" He was half joking, but I could see a hint of concern in his dark, hooded eyes.

"Not from justice," I clarified. I hesitated, wondering how best to say it. "It's a family thing. I left on pretty bad terms, and my mother has enough connections to maybe set someone like this bounty hunter on me." That was honest enough to not make me feel bad about lying to Nunez.

"You want me in there for backup?" He stood from the desk, hand going automatically to the spot on his belt where his gun would be if he'd been carrying it.

"I got his back," Sophia said, hands in her jacket pockets. Nunez grinned at her, but with respect. He was a post-war immigrant, but everyone knew what Sophia had done with the Resistance during the war.

"He's in interrogation," he told us, jerking a thumb over his shoulder at the door leading out of the offices. "He was strapped, but I made him store it in a locker."

"Thanks, Boss."

I clapped him on the shoulder as I passed.

"What if I have to run?" I asked Sophia very quietly as we passed into the broad corridor that led out of the offices, past the interrogation room and the holding cells and up to the lobby. "What if she's found me and I have to leave?"

"I always wanted to travel," she said, grabbing my hand and squeezing it tight for just a moment before she let it go.

Then we were at the interrogation room. I thought for just a moment about slipping into the adjoining observation room for a second and observing this Roger West on video before I confronted him, but I shook the idea off. Might as well get it over with. I put my right hand over the grip of my pistol, then palmed the ID plate of the door and stepped through.

The bounty hunter was sitting on the table, arms crossed. He was a big man, tall and rangy, wearing vat-grown leathers and heavy spacer's boots. He had shaggy, light brown hair and a drooping mustache and gunmetal grey eyes with faint lines at their edges that showed the weathering of a life spent outdoors. He grinned at me and saluted casually with two fingers.

"Nice to see you again, Munroe," he drawled with a strong Southwest accent.

"Shit," Sophia breathed softly, her eyes going wide.

I let my hand drop away from the gun; it wouldn't do any good against him.

I nodded to him, shutting the door behind us.

"Hi Cowboy."

2

Three and a half years ago, on Loki:

I had my helmet off; even with the cold, I wanted to take advantage of the opportunity to breath in fresh air, not recycled shipboard crap. That's why I didn't register the ship coming in until it nearly landed on top of me. It was quiet for a ship the size of an Attack Command missile cutter, maybe a hundred meters long and half that wide, but this was no missile boat. It was flat black with mind-bending curves and no markings at all, and I'd only seen the like of it once before; it belonged to the Glory Boys.

I rose from my seat and watched as it touched down on the tarmac, its landing jets whining and sending out the hot breath of a dragon that was a relief from the cold, until its treads hit and it settled into their suspension. The whining roar died away along with the hot wind, and a ramp opened up from the ship's belly, just behind her cockpit. The man who walked down it was tall and rangy and wearing utility fatigues instead of the camouflaged combat suit I was used to seeing.

Cowboy met me halfway between his stealth ship and my

improvised chair and offered a hand. I shook it warily; I respected the hell out of what this guy could do, but I didn't know if I would have considered him an acquaintance, much less a friend.

"Hey, Cowboy," I said. "Where's Kel?"

"He had things to do at the gas mine," the Fleet Intelligence agent told me, waving in the general direction of the gas giant, invisible behind the grey cloud cover. "But I saw on the Fleet manifests that you were over here on Loki and thought I'd stop by."

I raised an eyebrow. That was a not-insignificant waste of time and fuel. "Well thanks for thinking of me, but that seems like a long way to go to just say hello."

He crossed his arms and regarded me silently for a moment with a flat, neutral stare that made me feel like an exhibit on display.

"It would have been a long way to go just to say hello to Staff Sgt Randall Munroe," he admitted. "But it's not that far at all to apprehend Tyler Callas."

I felt my breath quicken unconsciously and I tried to keep it under control. A mad desperation made me think about going for my pistol, but I knew that was a waste of time. Cowboy could disarm and incapacitate me before my hand twitched. This was it. There was nowhere left to run and no way to fight. Mother would win the way she always did.

"I didn't know you were working for the Corporate Council," I said bitterly, trying to keep my hands away from my weapons.

He laughed at that, a long, slow chuckle that sounded genuinely amused.

"Mr. Callas, we all work for the Corporate Council one way or another," he told me. "But I'm not here to arrest you."

"Then why *are* you here?" I asked him.

"You gotta' know by now," he said in a Texas twang, "that you can't run like this forever. They *will* catch up to you, probably sooner than later. Unless you have someone running interference for you...someone with a few more connections than your Company Commander."

"Why would you do that for me?" I felt a slight lightening of the blackness closing in around me. I didn't want to give into that feeling because I still wasn't sure if this was a trick.

"Two reasons, Mr. Callas," he said, and I noticed his stance relaxing, as if he'd decided he wasn't worried about me pulling a gun on him anymore. "For one thing, despite what your mother thinks, you aren't ready to step up and take a Council position. It's not who you are now, but I think you might be in a place where you'll want to do it one of these days, after you get the chance to live your own life for a while. And maybe I want a Corporate Council Executive who owes me one."

I wanted to laugh at that notion, but I kept my face as stony as I could, nodding to encourage him to keep going.

"Second," he went on, "you're too valuable an asset to stick away somewhere locked up while they scramble your brains."

"An asset?" I repeated, cocking my eyebrow. "For who?"

"Right now, for the Marines," he said, gesturing around at the military aircraft. "I know the Corporate Council leadership doesn't consider the Tahni to be a major threat to their interests, but I respectfully disagree. Maybe that's because I'm closer to the problem." He smiled, a genuine smile. "Anyway, we can use every level head and straight shot we can get right now. But I was thinking more after the war." He shrugged. "I expect to have a position of responsibility by then, a position that might require, let's say, independent contractors to do work for me from time to time."

"What kind of work?" I wanted to know.

"Just the occasional favor," he said, his tone minimizing words that seemed pretty ominous to me. "Nothing that'll interfere with whatever life you choose to lead. And I swear…" He pronounced it "aah sware." "…your mother will not find out where you are. You don't have to deal with her until and unless you decide you're ready to."

I faced away from him, staring out into the grey gloom, feeling the snow flurries that were all that was left of last night's storm teasing coldly at my neck.

"This feels a lot like making a deal with the Devil."

"It may be," he admitted readily enough. "But as devils go, am I better or worse of one than Patrice Damiani?"

I realized that there was no point in debating this. I had the choice between immediate punishment or some odious duty in a hazy, distant future. At twenty-one, the future seemed pretty far away. I turned back and nodded in fatalistic acceptance.

"All right, Cowboy. You've got a deal." I snorted humorlessly. "Do we sign it in our blood?"

He laughed at that, and despite the fact that it sounded genuine and homey, it was a chilling sound.

"Deals like these," he said, "always get signed in other people's blood."

NOW:

Cowboy was the only name I'd known him by. He was...he *had been* a commando in a top-secret unit working for Fleet Intelligence during the war. He had also been a sleeper agent for the Corporate Council. He had landed on Demeter along with his partner, Kel, and we'd worked together to prepare the planet for the Fleet offensive that retook it. That was when he'd met Sophia. She hadn't been around for the deal we'd made on Loki, months later, but I'd told her about it since, and she didn't look any happier to see him than I was.

"So," I said, feeling a sense of fatalistic acceptance settling deep in my chest, "is Roger West your real name?"

"Close enough," he replied with a shrug.

"It sounds fake," Sophia said sharply. "And if you're a bounty hunter, I'm a fucking hairdresser."

He chuckled, as seemingly unconcerned with her angry disapproval as he was with the gun I carried.

"Being a hunter's a good cover for sticking my nose in some odd places." He cocked his head, eyeing me with an amused self-satisfaction. "I told you I expected to have a position after the war, and I do. I take care of problems for someone...very significant in the

Corporate Council. Someone even more significant than your mother."

"That's a short list," I said, a bit impressed. "What problem are you taking care of currently?"

"What do you know about the Predecessors, Mr. Callas?" He asked me. I frowned, feeling my fingers flex of their own accord, as if they wanted to go for the pistol.

"My name's Munroe," I reminded him, trying not to grind the words out.

"Of course it is," he said drily. "So, Deputy Constable Munroe, what do you know about the Predecessors?"

"What everyone knows, I suppose," I said with a shrug, trying to relax. I moved over to the table and pulled out a chair, falling into it easily, as if his presence here didn't concern me. I felt more than saw Sophia moving behind me, her hands on the back of the chair. "They were around sometime tens of thousands of years ago, and they left us the map in the Edge Mountains on Hermes of the wormhole jumpgate network." I paused and went on. "Some people *think* they actually *created* the network, and I guess they might have. I don't know enough about physics to say for sure. And some people think that most of the habitable planets we've found were engineered to be that way tens or even hundreds of thousands of years ago by the Predecessors."

"But nobody *knows*," Cowboy agreed. He pushed himself off the table and pulled out a chair opposite mine, sitting down with a lithe agility that belied his height. "But we *want* to know. The Corporate Council Executive Board has had its eye out for any possible remnant of Predecessor technology pretty much since they formed back during the First War with the Tahni. They examine every archaeological report, they chase down every rumor and they don't fuck around. Anyone who got their hands on Predecessor technology could destabilize the economy and maybe even challenge the Commonwealth military."

"So, you're chasing a rumor?" Sophia asked from somewhere above me. "What do you need Munroe for?"

"This particular rumor," Cowboy said, his hands flat on the table, "is out of the Pirate Worlds, on a planet called Thunderhead."

I didn't have to ask where he meant. The Pirate Worlds, inhospitable and barely habitable planets out at the edge of Commonwealth space, had been settled by criminals and anti-government types right after the Teller-Fox Transition Drive had gone on the market and opened up dozens of new systems that weren't connected via the Jumpgate Network. It was technically illegal, but by the time anyone thought to try to stop them, we were at war with the Tahni again. Now, the Pirate Worlds were the headquarters of a half dozen criminal syndicates and the fodder for every action movie and ViRdrama that had come out for years now.

"How would someone out in the Pirate Worlds get their hands on a Predecessor artifact?" I asked him.

"And what do you need Munroe for?" Sophia repeated. "Why can't you check on this rumor yourself?"

"If I knew how, I wouldn't need to investigate it," Cowboy said with obviously strained patience, eyes flashing between the two of us. "I just know that Abuelo has been hiring any scientist with ties to Predecessor research who'll take his money."

"Abuelo?" I repeated, squinting in confusion.

"That's the man who runs Freeport, the largest city on Thunderhead," Cowboy supplied. "No one knows much about him before he arrived on the planet sometime during the war. They say he killed the old boss, a miserable bastard named Crowley, and took over his syndicate...and the fairly extensive anti-spacecraft defense system that allows him complete control over planetary orbital traffic." He looked up at Sophia, who was still standing just behind me. "And I need Munroe because there are people on Thunderhead who know who I am. If they saw me nosing around, they'd warn Abuelo and he'd dig himself a hole and pull it in after him."

I laughed and shook my head. "What the hell do you think *I'm* going to be able to do that you can't? I don't know shit about the Pirate Worlds, and I'll stick out like a whore in church trying to ask questions about Predecessor artifacts on Thunderhead."

"What I expect you to do, Munroe," Cowboy said, pointing a single, gloved finger at me, "is recruit yourself a squad, people who can handle themselves in a fight, people who served in the war with the Marines, preferably, and take it to Freeport. Abuelo is always looking to hire veterans with combat experience. You're going to go to work for him, and then you're going to find out where he has this Predecessor artifact." He smiled broadly, in a look that would have seemed friendly on a real person.

"Then you're going to steal it for me."

———

"I'm going," Sophia declared flatly, in a tone that would brook no argument.

And yet I had to argue, and I had to do it well.

I rested my hands on the hood of the rover, letting my head hang for a moment as I tried to collect my thoughts. Cowboy had headed back to the spaceport, giving me instructions to meet him at his ship in three hours, and I'd gone to Nunez and let him know I was going to need an emergency leave of absence for a few weeks. I'd told him it was to deal with family problems, which I guess was true, in a way.

Sophia had barely been able to contain herself while I talked to Nunez, and she'd confronted me the moment we were outside in the parking garage. I looked around carefully, checking to make sure there was no one else around to overhear us.

"No. For three reasons," I went on before she could break in with an objection. "First, there's no one else who can do your job, not yet. If you leave here for weeks, what do you think's going to happen to the research? What are the glorified janitors you hired out of Amity going to do if the sonic fences break down and a fucking mastodon needs to be herded back into the reserve? Or a saber-tooth? Is Nunez going to bother to hunt down a stunner from your locker at the facility, or is he just going to shoot it?"

I could see the cracks in her resolve, but she wasn't even close to giving up.

"You're more important to me than the Revenants," she said, slamming a fist into the side of the car. It felt good to hear, because the Revenant Forest Preserve was her whole life.

"Reason number two," I went on, grateful that I'd actually managed to think up a reason number two, because neither one nor three would have done it alone. "What about your family? If anything happens to me, the only person I care about knowing it is you, and I think I can count on Cowboy to come and tell you. But if we both wind up getting killed, your parents will never know where you went or why you never came back. Do you really want to do that to them?"

"Munroe," she insisted, grabbing me by the front of my jacket and pulling me around towards her, "*you* are my family."

That felt good, too, but I could see more chunks falling away.

"That's the last thing," I told her, putting my hands on her arms and pulling her against my chest. "I'm a selfish prick," I admitted. "Because I know how much it's going to hurt you if anything happens to me, but all I can think about is how I would feel if you got killed because of me, because of a debt I owe."

Her head sagged against my shoulder, the breath going out of her in a sigh. I could feel a shuddering go through her, and I realized with a start that she was sobbing. She hadn't cried in front of me since the war. I kissed her forehead, stroking her hair.

"I'm sorry," I whispered. "I'm sorry, Sophie."

Then she hauled back and hit me *hard* in the shoulder, rage and ferocity etched into her face beneath the tears.

"If you fucking get yourself killed, I'll dig up your corpse and kill you again," she growled. "Do you fucking understand me? You are *not* leaving me alone here."

"I love you, too," I said, rubbing the spot she'd punched.

She was still crying, and still angry, when she kissed me. I wanted to promise her I'd come back, but I'd never lied to her, and I didn't want to start now.

3

The inside-out world of Belial stretched out before me like a twisted wonderland of human debauchery and I remembered all in one rush why I'd left my old life behind. I stepped out of the lift I'd ridden here from the docking bay, moving aside to let others by behind me, staring like a tourist up the hub of the "blown" asteroid that was now the largest man-made construction in all of human space.

Some independent investors---back before the Corporate Council, when there had been such a thing---had taken a basically spherical, nickel-iron asteroid, drilled a narrow hole down its center, filled it with water and then exposed the thing to sunlight amplified by large mirrors. The resultant steam pressure produced a hollow tube of compressed ore, in this case nearly thirty meters thick. Spin was imparted to produce near one gravity at the lowest levels. The "open" ends were sealed by transplas, with reflectors mounted to provide natural sunlight, and a pair of huge docking rings were connected through the core with a non-spinning transport tube.

They'd left gaps between the hub and the innermost ring, so you could see basically all the way from one end of the station to the other in a mind-bending and balance-challenging view. The gravity this close to the hub was fairly light, and I saw thin, impossibly tall

Belters and low-gravity natives striding quickly with their long, skinny legs as they searched out places to eat or do business or get their lightweight rocks off. I idly wondered if the sex dolls and prostitutes on this level were just as tall and skinny as their clients.

I shook that thought and the uncomfortable mental images that accompanied it out of my head and walked carefully to the next lift station, the one that went outward towards the lower levels. I'd been here once before, just after the war's end, when I'd been searching out discreet and untraceable transportation back to Demeter. This time, I already had the transportation; Cowboy had left a ship docked for me here. What I was looking for now were passengers.

"You have room for maybe eight or nine on the boat," Roger West had told me hanging on to the railing beside me as I'd taken a look at the small, delta-winged starship just a few minutes ago.

It had been one of the first generation of missile cutters from the Fleet Attack Command, produced just after the Battle for Mars had shown the weakness of our capital ships to assaults from Transition Drive warships. Superseded by more advanced models later in the war, it had been stripped of its armament and sold for surplus a year later, and there were hundreds more like it all over the Commonwealth. It was barely bigger than a cargo shuttle at a hundred meters long and half that wide, and it had the name "Wanderer" stenciled on its rounded, armored nose.

"If you want, you can fill her up with that many," Cowboy had continued, "but I want you on Thunderhead in five hundred hours, whether it's you and eight other people or just you. I transferred the files you asked for to your 'link."

"I saw that a couple of the people are right here on Belial," I'd said, eyeing him suspiciously. "Did you know who I'd ask for, or was storing the boat here just a happy coincidence?"

He'd just grinned at that, in that not-quite-pleasant way of his. "The clearance codes for the *Wanderer* are on your 'link too." He'd glanced around to make sure no one else in the docking bay was close to us. "There's another set of codes in there too. I'm leaving a little insurance policy in orbit around Thunderhead for you, geosynchronous over Freeport. It's a kinetic strike package, totally stealthed so their anti-spacecraft sensors won't pick it up. The atmospheric conditions make communications problematic though, so you'll need a tight-beam laser uplink to use it, and you'll only be able to do it once. Once it fires, the anti-spacecraft system will blow it out of orbit."

He'd fixed me with a harsh glare. "This is a last resort only. The people I work for want what's down there intact." Then he'd shot me a wave as he headed back to the berth where his own ship was docked. "Five hundred hours," he'd reminded me. "Good luck."

I felt the apparent gravity of centrifugal force begin to increase the farther towards the outer shell the lift descended. I didn't have a problem with microgravity, but I saw some of the others in the lift car let out relieved breaths as their weight increased to closer to what was normal for them back home.

They were a mixed lot, from business travelers in vat-grown suits to cargo crews in stained coveralls. Belial was a gathering place for all types: Belters from here in the Alpha Centauri belt and the one back in the Solar System congregated on this station for recreation, along with Corporate and private freighter crews and some off-duty military on leave from the small base on Hermes out at Proxima. Not to mention the lower-tier Corporate Council people who came here to live out their own private sexual kinks in a place where it couldn't come back to haunt them as they climbed the ladder.

And then there were the ones who were here for business instead of pleasure. Belial was legendary as a hotbed of corporate espionage, shady black market deals and fugitive criminals. Security here didn't put up with people killing each other indiscriminately, but they pretty much turned a blind eye to anything else, and were insistent that since they were a private entity not affiliated with the Commonwealth government that its rules didn't apply. Most legal scholars had doubts as to how that argument would stand up in court, but it had never been tested, thanks to money greasing the right palms.

The establishment I was heading for couldn't have existed anywhere that operated under Commonwealth laws; and even on Belial, it was stuck pretty far back in the ass-end of the shadier parts of the station. I got off the lift car about three levels from the outermost ring, emerging into a district of the station that was dimly lit by design, a world where it was always night and the businesses and storefronts were mostly labelled with simple, uninformative names like "Klondike" or "Dunkel Nach Hause," whatever the hell that meant. You weren't in this section of Belial unless you knew what you were looking for and where it was.

I tried not to pay attention to what went on in the places I passed on those streets, but I couldn't help but register the glimpses through curtain doors as they parted for people who seemed to look over their shoulders instinctively, even in a place like this where no one cared. It was in places like these that you could practice the habits that broke you, either physically or mentally. Fantasies that weren't tolerated anywhere else, that would land you in involuntary psych counseling and a law enforcement watch list, could be indulged with Virtual Reality, or for a bit more, with pleasure dolls nearly indistinguishable from the real thing. Or, for enough money, with real people just as desperate as their customers.

Once in a while, when a soundproof door was opened at just the right time, you could hear screams. I wondered if they were from a pleasure doll or a human. Either way, a human was causing them and it would have made me think some very dark thoughts about what we were capable of as a species…if I hadn't already known.

This whole area seemed to be devoted to those who derived pleasure from pain, and my destination was different only in execution, and in size. This establishment dwarfed the smaller shops around it, taking up three times the number of lots and stretching from the ceiling ten meters above down to the rough, stone floor. "Lucha" was the name above the large double-doors and, unlike anywhere else I'd seen on this street, those doors were manned by private bouncers and a sign on the wall proclaimed "No Weapons Allowed."

The station didn't allow guns or projectile weapons of any kind, but you could bring in knives, shock gloves, mono-wire whips and basically any other sort of deadly device you wanted that had to be used one-on-one. But not in this place. There was a line of people in front of me, varied from the stylish Corporate Council types to the ragged ship crewmembers or towering Belters struggling against the .8 gravities; and every once in a while, one of them would produce a weapon from a concealed sheath or pocket and deposit it in a locker for which they'd get a code so they could retrieve it when they left.

Everyone also had to deposit a rather hefty entrance fee, usually in actual, physical Tradenotes. Luckily, Cowboy had foreseen the need for a good supply of untraceable funds on this mission and I had a few hundred in my jacket pocket, plus more on the *Wanderer*. It's always nice spending someone else's money, particularly when it was some Corporate Council asshole. I tipped the bouncers.

Through those doors was a bar, with dozens of stools and tables, but it was only lightly populated; the real business was beyond it, through a curtain entrance that stretched all the way to the ceiling. I stopped to pick up a shot of tequila from the real, human bartender---always a sign of a class establishment, in my experience---then moved through to the main event.

Either the curtain was made of some soundproofing material or they were engaging in some very elaborate and expensive acoustic dampening; the second I stepped through it, I was assaulted by the roar of the excited crowd, the slap of flesh on flesh and the unmistakable grunts of someone being hit very, very hard. I could see it immediately; the floor was sloped gently downward, to let you view the show from every level. There were no seats, but the place was so packed, it would have been standing room only even if there had been.

The match was being held in a square, mesh cage about five meters on a side, with a floor of flexible polymer, once white but long since stained with dried blood, among other things. There were four men inside it, all dressed in tight-fitting singlets, one pair colored white and the other two black. The ones in white were older, weathered and scarred, one of them shaved bald and both with amber skin darkened under alien suns not that long ago. They were traveling champions, pursuing this illegal sport in the undergrounds of a dozen colonies.

The other two were newer to the game, from their youth, and had been here in Belial for a while from their pallor. They were brothers, obvious from the likeness of their squared-off features and the common blond color of their long, braided hair and beards. Yet new or not, they were solid, corded muscle and there was a cold, deadly frost in their shared blue eyes that seemed totally bereft of fear. Besides their singlets, each man had tight gloves of hard leather and the brothers' were already stained with the blood running from their opponents' faces. Even as I watched, leather hammered into flesh and each of the brothers scored a punishing body blow almost simultaneously.

I made my way downward, closer to the ring, through throngs of screaming fans, their hands in the air, chanting "lucha!" Their faces seemed transfixed, transported with an almost sexual excitement. Inside the cage, the older fighters attempted a gambit that I was sure was well practiced by its smoothness of execution, probably one that had served them well in a dozen other fights on a dozen other worlds. Each ducked aside, under the guard of the man they were fighting, and slipped around to take the other's opponent unaware from the rear.

I tensed, expecting disaster for the brothers; they were vulnerable to any number of attacks, from a rear naked choke to a debilitating strike that could break a bone. Instead, both of the brothers spun into matching back kicks and their opponents walked straight into them. There was a crunch of cracking ribs that I could hear above the chanting and yelling, and both the older fighters were down, the bald one on a knee, struggling to breathe, and the other man flat on his back and unmoving. One of the brothers moved behind the bald man and put him into a choke hold, and I wondered for a moment just how far they were going to take it. Was this to the death? Would they go *that* far, even here on Belial?

But he stopped once the bald man was unconscious and let him fall limp to the canvas. Then the brothers raised arms spattered with blood and absorbed the cheers and screams of the crowd, their faces twisted into grimaces that seemed less satisfied and more enraged. Medical technicians dressed in white opened the gate into the cage and rushed over to the unconscious men, while the blond, hulking brothers stepped out behind them and headed up a walkway back up to the dressing rooms.

"Victor!" I yelled after them, rushing up towards the cage. "Kurt!"

A very tall, very unpleasant looking bouncer took a step to block my way, one hand raised palm out and the other poised in a fist by his chest.

"Sir, you need to stay away from the ring." His voice was calm and professional, but his demeanor was more along the lines of a barely-restrained psycho killer.

"Sure," I acquiesced, raising my hands in surrender. "But you need to tell Kurt and Victor that Munroe is here to see them."

"The fighters do not socialize with guests," the man said flatly. He was so tall and broad-shouldered, I couldn't see past him, and I cursed under my breath, sure they were already through the door into the dressing room by now.

I debated briefly and internally whether I'd be better off bribing him or hitting him; I wasn't sure either would be effective, but I was leaning towards bribery.

"Holy shit, I don't fucking believe it!"

The voice was familiar, deep and booming, maybe a little harsher and harder-edged than the last time I'd heard it. Victor Simak stepped around the bouncer, putting a restraining hand on the man's shoulder.

"Is that really you, Munroe?" Kurt asked, wonder in his eyes as he came around the other side of the guard. Kurt had a cut on his cheek oozing blood, but he didn't seem to notice it.

Back before I'd been able to remember their names, I used to call them the Viking Brothers, and that name suited them now more than ever. They'd been college kids when they'd joined the Resistance on Demeter, and they'd looked older and more hardened than they had any right to be when it was over. Now, though, they were beyond hardened into…feral.

"It's really me," I said, and tried not to grimace when they both swept me into a group hug that smelled of blood and sweat. One or both of them pounded me on the back hard enough to drive the wind out of my lungs and I heard them laughing wildly.

"Good God, we haven't seen you since the night of the assault on the fusion plant!" Victor whooped. "What the hell are you doing here?"

There was still the roaring of the crowd around us, and I was beginning to see people moving forward out of their seats, maybe emboldened by my presence outside the normally acceptable areas for spectators. The bouncer was frowning and I saw him touch an earpiece and mutter something inaudible as he began to get visibly agitated.

"Is there someplace we can talk in private?" I asked them, having to yell to be heard over the din.

"Yeah, follow us," Kurt said immediately, waving towards the door to the dressing room.

Glancing back at the cage as we jogged towards the exit, I could see that the two older fighters were both sitting up and conscious now. The fight had been brutal and brief and I was impressed how good the Simak brothers had become at this game just two years after leaving Demeter.

The bouncer opened the door for us with his palm on the ID plate, then stayed on the other side of it when it closed, guarding it against any incursion by insistent fans. The hallway back into the dressing room was almost obscenely bright after the insistently dim lighting everywhere else in this district, and it felt like we were going backstage at one of the old-time theaters favored by the rich tourists on Demeter. Kurt and Victor bypassed the first few open locker rooms and led me to a private door keyed to their palm-prints. The dressing room inside was spacious and well appointed, with a massage table, a couch, two reclining chairs and a shower stall.

"It's nice as all hell to see you again, Munroe," Victor said, leading the conversation as always; Kurt was the more shy and reticent one, always willing to let his older brother spearhead conversations. "But I can't think you tracked us down to this God-forsaken pit just to grab a drink."

He was changing as he spoke, peeling off the sweat-soaked one-piece and pulling on a robe that had been hanging from a hook on the wall. Kurt just sat down as he was on one of the chairs, grabbing a bottle of water out of a holder in the arm and taking a long drink.

"No, honestly I didn't," I admitted. "But I did want to ask you something first. After the war, I went back to Demeter. I live there now with Sophia."

"Congratulations!" Kurt said, his hard mask of a face cracking into a smile. "I'm glad you guys made that work."

"Thanks," I said, nodding to him. "But when I came back, I looked for you two, and no one could tell me why you'd left or where you'd gone, not even your parents. How the hell did you wind up here," I waved a hand around us demonstratively, "doing this?"

The brothers shared a look, like this was a conversation---or maybe an argument---they'd had with each other many times before.

"We tried to fit back in after the Fleet took Demeter back from the Tahni," Victor began.

"We got jobs with the reconstruction," Kurt cut in. "They were hiring any warm body that would work, and going back to college classes wasn't an option in the short run. There wasn't any college, there weren't any courses, there weren't any professors alive even."

"But after a while," Victor went on, "it seemed kind of…"

"Empty," Kurt supplied. "Meaningless."

"Yeah," Victor agreed.

He walked over to a refrigerator set in the wall and pulled out a beer. He held one out to me, but I shook my head. I'd never liked beer, which made me the odd man out as an enlisted Marine. Kurt nodded and Victor tossed him a bottle, then grabbed one for himself and sat down, popping it open.

"After what had happened during the occupation," Victor said, swallowing a sip, "after what we'd done and seen, running buildfoam dispensers and pouring concrete felt like the most boring thing in the galaxy. So, we both went and tried to join up with the Marines." He looked over at me and shrugged. "We figured we could do some good that way, maybe help end the war."

"But it ended before we got the chance," Kurt said bitterly, taking a long gulp of the dark beer. "We were waiting for our flight to Inferno when the local Fleet office got the word that there wouldn't be any more recruiting classes accepted for the next six months because they were throwing everything they had at the Tahni homeworld and there weren't resources left for training."

"Yeah, I remember," I said, nodding. Inferno had been one giant buzzing hive of activity, as everyone with a trigger finger got shipped out for the last, big push.

"So we just watched while guys like you won the war and killed the Emperor," Victor took his turn. I was glad I hadn't accepted a drink, because I would have spit it up right then. I actually *had* killed the Tahni Emperor, almost by accident, because he'd been behind cover I'd wanted to use when we hit the Imperial Palace. I'd made sure no one had found out about that, though, with Cowboy's help. "And we finally couldn't take it anymore, so we begged for work on an independent freighter heading anywhere else. They dropped us here, and we'd just about ran out of money when a fight agent found us."

"It wasn't too hard at first," Kurt put in. "The war was just over and not that much tourist travel was happening, so we were mostly fighting locals who wanted the purse. By the time competition got tougher, well," he shrugged, "so had we."

"And have you found this more satisfying?" I wondered.

They shared that same look as before.

"No," Victor admitted. "Not anymore. At first, maybe. It was…" He shrugged. "What's the word? Something you feel in your gut?"

"Visceral," I suggested.

"Yeah, that. But lately, I feel like we're just going through the motions."

"What are we gonna' do if we leave here, though?" Kurt demanded, his reaction seeming like something he'd repeated before. "We don't have enough money to get anywhere except Hermes, or maybe somewhere in the Solar System. It's not like we're qualified to do anything other than kill people or beat them up."

"I have a job, if you two want it," I said. They looked at me, with a mix of curiosity and hope and for an instant, I felt like a total shit. These people had been my friends, once upon a time. "I've got to tell you right up front: it could get you both killed, and we'll be so far up the ass end of nowhere, no one will ever know."

"Doing what?" Victor asked me.

"I can't give you the details here," I said. "But you're going to be out in the Pirate Worlds, killing people who probably have it coming. And you'll get paid enough that you can buy a ticket anywhere you like when it's over."

"Who are we working for?" Kurt wanted to know. His squared-off face was worked into a thoughtful frown.

"Someone high up in the Corporate Council, that's all I can tell you." Hell, it was all I *knew*. "But the go-between who's been dealing with me is Cowboy."

"Cowboy?" Kurt repeated in disbelief. "That Fleet Intelligence guy who was on Demeter with us?"

"Yeah. He's working for the Corporates now and he looked me up because he needed help and thought I could do the job." I felt bad misleading them, but I didn't especially want to expand the pool of people who knew about my past.

"Do you believe this is on the up-and-up, Munroe?" Victor asked me, and in his eyes, I saw a trust that I knew I didn't deserve.

"I think the money is on the up-and-up," I said, trying to be as honest as I could. "The job…" I shrugged. "I can't say whether he's telling me everything, but maybe I don't need to know everything."

Victor looked over to Kurt and the younger brother nodded.

"All right, Munroe, we're in," he said, standing and offering me a hand. I shook it, my own hand swallowed up by the slab of meat.

"You guys are the first, then," I told them. "Pack your stuff, we leave as soon as you're ready."

Victor laughed softly, staring into nothing. "You know, Munroe, we've been here two years, and I don't think there's a damn thing besides the clothes on my back that I'd want to bring with me."

"He's right," Kurt said. "Give us ten minutes to clean up, then we can get the hell out of here."

"Meet me at docking slip A243 in two hours," I told them. "I still have one more stop to make."

And I didn't think this next one would be anywhere near as easy.

4

Belial wasn't just a world, it was *many* worlds, each nearly as distinct from each other as any of the human colonies, as different as my mother's penthouse in Trans-Angeles and the shack Sophia and I shared on Demeter. It was the matter of a short ride in a lift car from the brutal, Dantean hell where I'd found Victor and Kurt to brightly-lit, cheerful playgrounds full of fantasy characters where those willing to pay the price could engage in ViR worlds so immersive that you could feel and smell every detail without the need for surgically implanted interface jacks.

I walked through clouds of hypnotic holographic advertisements, offering the chance to lose yourself in never-never lands of dragons and elves and flying horses and unicorns, the gravity just light enough that it combined with the colors and images to buoy your spirits to the point where those fantasies seem delightful instead of banal. It seemed surreal to me, after coming from the land of pain, as if I'd stepped from the night side of a world to the day side in one stride. The faces there were smiling and hopeful rather than guilty and titillated as they'd been in the land of the dark, and I even saw some children here, despite the fact that Belial was not a place to bring them.

I didn't know why he'd asked me to meet him here, but I found the place easily enough. It was much like any of the others, except in this one they advertised that they catered to people with 'face jacks. With military vets, professional net-divers, and more and more spaceflight crews sporting the implant jacks, it was a growing customer base. And with the jacks, you could *really* immerse yourself, the way you never could with stimulator suits or neural halos.

Inside the studio, there were individual bays you rented by the hour, with a four-hour limit to keep people from becoming so lost that they forgot to eat, drink or take a dump. They were sealed until the time was up, but each had a small, two-dimensional screen on the door to show you what adventure the person---or, in some cases, people---inside the room was having. I passed by knights riding powerful horses through battlefields turbulent with clashing orcs and humans, under skies darkened with arrows; past elves watching fairies playing in shadowed meadows under trees that towered hundreds of meters overhead; and past a man and woman swimming without equipment a hundred meters beneath the surface of an impossibly blue ocean, surrounded by a pod of narwhals.

Then I was at the door whose number I'd been given, and I paused in front of it, watching the video playback. Rugged mountains towered high above the spires of a medieval castle and the small village built up around it. Forks of lightning crackled through the sky and the mountaintops were hidden in black clouds. Out of those clouds, from somewhere high above the tree line, a dragon descended like an aerospace fighter, bat-like wings spread and carrying an impossibly massive, dinosaur-like body with a spiked tail and dark red skin, scaled like a snake.

Down on the grey, crenelated walls of the castle, I could see the horror in the eyes of the human soldiers guarding the battlements. They were dressed in chain mail and carried halberds; some dropped them and ran screaming in fear for the stairs to the lower levels, while others ran to the heavy ballista set in the battlements. Bolts two meters long shot outward into the night, searching for weak spots in the gigantic reptile's armored hide, but the dragon was moving way too fast for them to aim accurately at night. The bolts arced away and were lost in the darkness, and then it was too late.

The gigantic beast slammed into the castle tower with a shoulder as massive as a small starship and the whole structure shook and cracked and began to buckle. Men screamed as they pitched off the top and went tumbling twenty meters to the ground, and then the dragon was standing in the courtyard of the castle, ignoring the bricks and debris still falling around him. Dozens of armored warriors rushed at him, clutching spears and halberds like talismans; but the beast reared back and sucked in a breath, then spewed out a raging stream of fire that engulfed the whole courtyard, playing over the humans and setting them alight.

The dragon ignored the dying warriors running or writhing as the flames consumed them; he spread his wings, threw back his head on his serpentine neck and roared into the night, sending out a flare of billowing flame. Then the screen went dark and the timer above it went to all zeros. The door opened automatically with the click of a lock sliding away, and swung outward towards me. I stepped back to let it by, then blinked as the light inside the little room flickered to life.

The man standing in the center of the chamber wasn't a dragon, but he also wasn't entirely human anymore. He reached up to unplug the leads from the interface jacks implanted in his temples with fingers of shining, bare metal, as supple and articulated as metal could be, but bare silver all the way to his shoulders, where they disappeared under a black, leather vest. More bare metal climbed up the back of his neck, stretching all the way up to where the left half of his face should have been. The eye on that side was a glowing, red ocular, the ear a round, concave disk. He wore shorts just to make it more visible that his legs were cybernetic as well, again bare silver metal rather than the flesh-toned prosthetics they could have been.

The flesh that was left was pale white, baby-smooth and hairless, a sign it had been transplanted in a crude clinic. The biological part of the face had been handsome once, with a strong jaw and a straight, narrow nose, and a single, green eye like a jewel set in a twisted mask. That eye fixed on me as he turned, and he nodded.

"Sergeant Munroe," he said, his voice raspy from damage to his vocal chords. "Been a while."

"Ensign Kane." I returned the nod. He didn't offer a hand and neither did I. "Or did they make you a LT-JG before you mustered out?"

"Never checked," he admitted, his tone dismissive. "People call me Kane."

"And people call me Munroe," I said. "I haven't been a Sergeant for almost as long as you haven't been an Ensign."

"Fair," Kane acknowledged, brushing past me as he left the studio and headed for the exit with long, swift strides.

"I haven't seen you since you got my ass off the Demeter," I said, walking quickly to keep up with him. "How did it happen?"

He stopped then, impossibly abrupt, and I nearly stumbled as I tried to avoid walking into him. He stared at me with an unnerving, bisected glare of red and green.

"Most people are afraid to ask," he said, the rasp making it sound harsher than it might have. I shrugged in return.

"If you were uncomfortable with it, you wouldn't flaunt it like this." I nodded at the way he was dressed.

He nodded, half his mouth turning up in a smile. Then he started walking again, and I followed.

"It was during the push to Tahn-Skyyiah," he said, referring to the Tahni home-planet. He seemed uncomfortable speaking about it, I thought at first. Then I changed my mind. He seemed uncomfortable speaking at *all*, and particularly in long sentences, as if he were out of practice.

"I was with a task force sent to take out a Tahni outpost that controlled a key jumpgate hub that we wanted to open up lines of FTL communications for the Fleet." He didn't even breathe hard despite I was having to nearly jog to keep up with him. "I was taking a squad of Marine battlesuits down to take their base dug into a moon around a gas giant. We were hit by a missile and went down, the whole flight crew was killed except me, and I got messed up…bad."

We were heading for a lift bank, but not the main one. This one was stuck into a corner of the level, away from the businesses, near the restrooms and showers. It also required an ID scan, and he had to use his retina for that, since he lacked a palm for a DNA read. I stepped in behind him, and we were alone in the car, the first time that had occurred since I'd been on Belial.

"Most Fleet ships have med bays equipped with auto-docs," I said. "They should have been able to at least fix you up enough for cloned transplants."

"Problem was," he said, "the cruiser hit a mine. Destroyed." He caught my eye and smirked. "Marines took the Tahni base, but all I had was a Corpsman with a medical kit until relief arrived." The green eye blinked, but the red one didn't. "Twenty days."

"Shit," I murmured, trying to imagine what that must have been like for him, with those sorts of injuries and limited medical supplies.

"Fleet med-techs did the best they could," he went on in his uncomfortable rasp. "But I needed a full clinic, weeks in biotic fluid to fix me. By then, I'd stopped wanting to." He held up a metal hand, flexing it. "This is who I am now."

The lift doors slid aside and I felt, to my surprise, what seemed like over one gravity weighing me down. The farthest out I'd been towards the rim was the Earth-normal section spun to one apparent gravity. This had to be beyond that, in the very outer edge of the station, up against the water tanks, just inside the meters-thick nickel-iron walls. I didn't even know there *was* an inhabited level that far out.

The hallways were narrow and dimly-lit, though not as dark as the level where I'd found Victor and Kurt. There were no markings, no advertisements and no guiding voices in your 'link's ear bud suggesting where you might want to go next. The people walking by in those corridors didn't seem happy or festive, just tired and annoyed, and some perhaps resolute on reaching a bed.

"You work here," I deduced quickly. That hadn't been in his file, but then it hadn't contained much about him at all.

"Data security," he said. "Twelve hours on, twelve hours off. Gets me enough for room, food and the game once a day."

"You like it here?"

"No," he answered immediately. "Need more money."

"For what?" I wondered. "To go home?"

"Don't have a home," he declared, as he stopped with a metal clomp on the bare rock of the floor in front of an apartment door. Another retina scan and we were through it.

The apartment was basically an empty room. There was one table and one chair in the kitchen, beside the food processing unit, and that was it; just bare, white walls and a single light. He waved at the chair and I sat in it. He stood; I had the sense that he didn't *need* to sit to relax.

"So, what do you need money for?" I asked him again.

He was silent for a long moment, and I thought maybe I'd pushed things too far. Then he answered me.

"I want more." He motioned at his arms, his legs, his eye. "More metal, less flesh."

"Why?" I blurted, feeling my eyes go wide. It wasn't the answer I'd expected.

"Flesh is vulnerable."

I didn't know what the hell to say to that, so I got to the point.

"I need a good pilot," I told him. "One who can double as a net-diver at need, and handle a gun in a fight. The job is in the Pirate Worlds, and it's dangerous as shit, but the pay's enough to get you wherever you want to go and…" I trailed off. "Replace whatever you want replaced."

"Yes," he said immediately, without a trace of hesitation in his face or his voice.

I didn't ask if he was sure, didn't ask him to reconsider. He hadn't asked who he'd be fighting or what he'd be fighting for; it was obvious he didn't care. I wasn't comfortable with that, but I also wasn't in a position to be choosey.

"Can you be ready to leave in an hour?" I asked, pushing to my feet with the flats of my palms on his table. It creaked beneath me, cheap plastic.

"I can leave now," he said. He walked to a closet and pulled it open, revealing a small shoulder bag, open and stuffed with clothes. He zipped it shut and slung it over his shoulder.

I looked around the room, barren and impersonal.

"Yeah, I guess you can."

———

"Who the hell's this?" Victor asked as he and Kurt floated into the utility bay of the *Wanderer*, duffle bags hanging off their backs. They were both staring at Kane, who was wedged into the small Engineering station that was in an alcove between the utility bay and the passage to the cockpit, plugged in via his interface jacks as he ran systems checks on the reactor and the drives.

"Kurt, Victor," I introduced, catching myself against the bulkhead as I floated back to make room for them, "this is Kane. He flew a Marine lander in the war, and he's going to be our pilot."

Kane nodded without looking, his one biological eye unfocused as he concentrated on his work.

"You look like one of those Skingangers," Kurt blurted out.

I frowned. "What the hell's a Skinganger?" I asked. Kane said nothing.

"I heard about them from other fighters," Kurt said. "They're getting to be a problem on some colonies. They replace their shit with bionics, like that," he nodded towards Kane. "They think that they're the next step in evolution...they call it Trans-Humanism, I think it was."

"They've muscled in on a lot of the existing criminal gangs," Victor said, moving over to a locker against the bulkhead and opening it to stow his gear. "They're dealing Kick and black-market

ViR, and I've even heard they've started RipJacking to fund their replacements."

I scowled. RipJacking I'd heard of, but I always thought it was just hype and scaremongering. It was kidnaping transients and selling their organs off to street clinics to transplant into people too poor to afford cloned replacements.

"Well, Kane isn't a Skinganger," I informed them in a tone that I hoped told them that was all the talking we were going to do about it. "He's our pilot and he's one of the crew. Any problems with that?"

"You're the boss, Munroe," Kurt acknowledged, taking the locker next to Victor's. He slammed it shut on his duffle. "Where are we headed now?"

The hatch sealed behind them and I saw the brothers startle at the sound, Kurt seeming to forget his question as he looked around, wondering who shut the door. Kane stirred from the Engineering station, yanking the 'face plugs out of his jacks.

"I notified Traffic Control," he told me. "Docking fees are paid."

"Thanks," I said to his back as he headed for the cockpit. I watched him for a second, hoping I wasn't making a mistake. Then I turned back to the brothers. "Go get strapped in," I told them, motioning the way Kane had gone as I headed after him. "We're going to be moving out in a couple minutes."

I paused and looked over my shoulder at them. "We're going to Hermes," I said, answering Kurt's question.

"What's on Hermes?" Victor asked.

"Old friends."

5

"You sure this is the right neighborhood?" Sanders asked me, squinting around at the trash-littered streets of Overtown.

I glanced over at Ian Sanders and wondered again if I shouldn't have brought Victor and Kurt along instead. Sanders was a year or so younger than me and had been a team leader in my squad back on Loki and Tahn-Skyyiah near the end of the war, but that had been almost three years ago. The mild, almost soft civilian walking next to me on that street didn't seem like the same man who'd walked point into the Tahni Imperial Palace. His brown hair hung shoulder length and his clothes were expensively fashionable, out of place in this section of town.

But this was his world and his city, and he knew the Captain. The others didn't. I'd found Sanders in his uncle's construction office in Sanctuary's industrial district, bored out of his mind and desperate to do almost anything else. He'd been almost as easy to recruit as Kane, though he'd taken longer to pack. He'd even led me to two other former Marines who'd been stuck in boring jobs and missed the action enough to sign up for something this sketchy. I'd even known one of them: her name was Bobbi Taylor and I'd gone through Recon Qualification with her.

Maybe I should have brought her, I thought. She'd looked and sounded as hard and tough as I remembered from hand-to-hand combat training, maybe a bit more seasoned from her experience in the war. But again, she didn't know the Captain, and if the file was accurate, it would be better to have someone along who did.

Overtown was unimaginatively named; it was in the hills above Sanctuary, a fairly recent and mostly unwanted addition to the oldest and largest city on Hermes, our oldest and largest colony. The city proper sprawled out below the cheap, pre-formed buildfoam tenements of Overtown, gleaming in the afternoon sun like a jewel set for the poor to covet. There were a lot of refugees from the war, their homes destroyed, travel to the colonies where they'd lived cut off for years. The buildfoam and concrete apartments had started out as temporary housing for them, but they'd turned into something much less benevolent. Some refugees had never left, and others had moved in to take advantage of them and their appetites; if you couldn't have the shining gem of Sanctuary, you could at least have drugs and illegal ViR to make you stop thinking about it.

Dull, glassy eyes stared at us from doorways and alleys, sunken in faces lean not from lack of food but from lack of interest in eating. Some were leaning back on the steps to their building, drug patches on their necks and their eyes closed in the chemical rapture, while others huddled like predators planning a hunt. Their clothes were the cheap, colorful flash you could get free from the city's public fabricators, their hair done in fashions that imitated the gangs of Trans-Angeles. I glanced back over my shoulder at the rental vehicle I'd parked in the lot at the end of the street. It was Cowboy's money, but I hoped the car's security system was good enough; I didn't feel like walking back to the port.

The numbers had been painted over on most of the buildings, but my 'link still led me to the correct one. It looked like all the rest, down to the junkies on the steps, semi-conscious. I saw three ferallooking children, none older than eight, staring at us from where they gathered around a mangy cat. They'd been taunting it, poking it with sticks and blocking it from running away. I shivered a bit at the deadness of their gaze, the hopelessness and worse, the acceptance, like they'd never known anything different and never would.

Sanders was right behind me, so close he almost bumped into me as we walked up the steps, past a man who could have been eighty but was probably forty, the lines in his face etched by malnutrition and inactivity and despair. I pushed open the cheap, plastic door and it squeaked on its hinges, throwing light into the unlit hallway. There were stains on the walls and floor that could have been blood, gouges that might have been made by knives or clubs, one that might even have been from a bullet. There was a short, skinny teenager squatting against the wall at the end of the corridor, watching us as we stopped at the door.

Like the building, it lacked a number, but it was where the map in my 'link had led us. There was no ID plate or call button, so just I pocketed my 'link, looked around carefully and knocked. I waited, listening for a moment, but heard nothing. I looked at Sanders. He shrugged, reached past me and knocked louder and longer than I had. We waited another ten seconds and heard nothing.

"Maybe there's nobody here," Sanders suggested, the look on his face telling me he wished I'd accept that so we could go.

I pounded on the door with the flat of my hand.

"Captain Yassa!" I yelled. "Are you here?"

There was more silence…and then a barely-audible groan. At first, I wasn't sure I'd actually heard it, but then Sanders locked eyes with me. He'd heard it, too.

"Captain Yassa, can you hear me?"

Another low moan. I cursed under my breath, then hauled back and slammed the heel of my boot into the latch. The door looked flimsy, and it was; it exploded inward at my kick and the light from the front door of the building leaked into the darkness of the room.

I waited a moment for my eyes to adjust, and slowly the dark blobs inside became visible in the filtered, grimy light. This apartment wasn't as unfurnished as Kane's had been; that would have been an improvement. There was a kitchen so small it could barely hold the cheap, government-handout food processing unit crammed onto the counter, a bathroom without a door and with stains of mysterious provenance all over its ancient tile, and a single, small, ragged futon.

The woman lying on that bed wasn't quite skeleton-thin, but she was getting there. Her face, once rounded and pleasant, now seemed slightly sunken and gaunt, and her light brown hair was ratty and knotted and much longer than I'd ever seen it. Her clothes were cheap and basic, not the gaudy and colorful styles most of the chawners wore, but they were worn and ragged and stained, like they hadn't been changed in a long time. Her lips were dry and cracked, her eyes wide open and bloodshot, lost in a haze of unreality. Her skin, which I remembered as perpetually light pink with sunburn and dusted with freckles, was pale and taut, and pinched slightly at her neck where the drug patches were affixed. Three of them. That was enough for an overdose.

Former Marine Captain Brandy Yassa had been a woman full of life, in command of it. Whoever this was barely showed a sign of life at all. I bit off a curse and felt for a pulse; it was slow, but it was there.

"We have to get her to the ship," I decided. "There's an auto-doc in the utility bay."

Sanders didn't say anything. I looked back over at him and saw his face slack with disbelief, distraught that someone who was as much of a rock in our lives as Captain Yassa was in this condition. I sympathized, but I'd been prepared for it; I'd read Cowboy's files on her. I hadn't believed it at first, but I'd read it.

"Sanders," I said sharply and his eyes snapped towards me. "We have to get her back to the car. Can you carry her?"

"What?" He blinked, then seemed to come back to himself. "I mean, yeah, sure."

I helped him get her up. There was still some tone to the muscles of her arms, which meant she hadn't been this bad for long. Sanders grunted as he put her over his shoulder in a fireman's carry, but seemed to settle into it. He was a bit bulkier and more broad-bodied than I was, even if he'd been sitting at a desk too much lately. Once I saw that he had her, I took a quick look around the apartment, making sure there was nothing she'd want to take with her.

Something caught my eye: a small, hand-carved wooden box maybe seven or eight centimeters long and three or four thick. If it was real wood, it was pretty valuable, which meant it had to be something significant to her or she would have sold it already. I grabbed it, then led Sanders out of the front door and into the hallway.

The kid was gone from the corner. That should have been my first clue that something was wrong, but I didn't catch it right away. Then a long shadow fell over us as a tall, long-armed man stepped into the front entrance to the apartments. He wasn't common street trash, you could tell that by his clothes. They were expensive, either cloned leather or a good enough faux that you couldn't immediately tell the difference, and tailored to his form by a laser scanner. He wore a waist-length jacket and matching pants, with holograms of dragons weaving over the arms and legs in a hypnotic pattern.

His face told me that he was dangerous. There was no drug haze to it, no longing or envy. He had what he wanted and he was smart enough to know not to taste the merchandise. It was a long, horsey face, not pre-planned from the genes up, and not particularly good looking, with a slightly crooked nose where it had been broken once too often. There were deep lines around the eyes and mouth, but I didn't peg him as being that old. Those lines came from pain, from privation. The lined mouth was turned down in a scowl.

"You don't belong here," he said. His tone was deep and pleasant, like one of those computer-generated voices they use for directions in your 'link, a voice of confidence and authority.

"No, we don't," I agreed, keeping my voice calm, despite an incipient trickle of sweat down my back. "That's why we're leaving."

"You can leave when you put her back where you found her." He barely moved his head, but I could sense as much as see the motion.

"She's my friend," I told him. "What's she to you?"

"She's a steady customer," he said. "And an occasional contractor, when the need arises. And it arises enough," his voice became just slightly more strident, "that I will have to insist that you put her back where you found her."

My eyes were adjusting to the brighter light outside, and I could see the shadows on the steps out front. There were two more people out there. I didn't figure someone like this would come alone.

"I can pay," I told him. "I have $3,000 in Tradenotes on me, and I can get twice that much in an hour."

"Or," he suggested, "I could take what you have now and be satisfied with that *and* my customer."

He took a step closer, through the door, and the two men behind him moved into view. They weren't as well dressed as he was, but they shared the same confidence in him. This wasn't going to end easy.

"You could *try* to do that," I told him, feeling the words come out naturally, without thought. I felt myself relax as I said them and I wondered where they were coming from. "But first, let me tell you a story. There's an animal called a wolf. It hunts in packs, and it sometimes takes on prey twice or three times its size. But it takes a big risk when it does that, because prey that big can hurt the wolves, maybe kill them, and they have to be sure the meal they're trying to get is worth that risk. That's what we call the risk-benefit ratio. Ever hear of it?"

"You don't seem like that big of a risk," he commented, smiling with white, even teeth.

"If you don't let us out of here," I said to him, trying not to send threatening, just matter-of-fact, "someone is going to wind up dead. If it's one or more of you…" I shrugged. "I have a ship to catch; I'll be gone before they find the bodies. If it's any of us… Do you really want the heat that would bring from the Constabulary?" I gestured down the street. "We rented the car; it's keeping track of our location so they'll know where we went missing."

He laughed at that, far too comfortable for my liking, and I felt the hackles rise on my neck. He took another step forward, less than a meter away from me now. I could smell the strange, herbal scent off of him, either some incense he'd been burning or maybe something he'd been smoking recently.

"The Constabulary doesn't come here," he said. "This is my town…"

I didn't let him finish. One of the first things Gramps had taught me about fighting was to hit someone while they're in the middle of trying to sound like a badass. I leaned my upper body back away from him, and he lunged forward instinctively, hand snaking out to try to grab me and keep me from getting away as all of his weight went to his forward foot. But only my upper body had rocked back; I snaked out with a left round kick that took him in his forward knee cap.

There was a crack that almost made me wince in sympathy and the big man grunted as his kneecap dislocated and suddenly there was no strength in his plant leg and he began to pitch forward. He was a tough son of a bitch, I'll give him that; he tried to grab me on the way down, to take me down with him, but I yanked his arm towards me to give him some more momentum, and he pitched forward down the hallway, head over heels.

The muscle he'd brought with him lurched into motion, hands reaching under their shirts for weapons, but I was expecting it. My old roommate in the Marines, Johnny Pacheco, had been from the barrios in San Jose, and he used to tell me stories about the gangs there. I'd laid hands on their boss, and he'd want them to kill me for that; that was how this sort of operation went. They'd at least have blades, maybe even guns; they were illegal in the city, but you could fabricate one from a black-market pattern in an hour or two, and ammo was even simpler.

My gun had been fabricated in the *Zwischenwelt Waffen Herstellung* factory in Earth orbit, bought by the Commonwealth Military Procurement system, then probably stolen or smuggled out or just sold outright by some twisting of regulations to the Corporate Security Force, then acquired by Roger West, given to me and holstered under my jacket. It was very familiar to me; it was the same one I carried at my job, the same one I'd been issued during the war. It was capable of synching up with a battle helmet or commercial enhanced vision glasses or even the contact lens I wore in my right eye that displayed a Heads-Up Display for my 'link.

I saw the targeting reticle hanging in front of my vision the second my finger touched the trigger, and everything seemed to slip into slow motion the second it appeared. I had an uncanny feeling like I was back on Demeter again during the war, and a harsh, deadly cold seemed to settle in across my nerves. I shot the bigger of the two men first, the one closer to me. He was almost ten centimeters taller than me, and probably ten kilos heavier, but it was the monowire whip he'd pulled out of his pocket that worried me more than his size. It dropped from nerveless fingers as pieces of his skull exploded backwards into the face of the shorter one.

The second man rammed into the back of the first, unable to check his rush towards me, and went off balance, reflexively firing a round from his fab'ed handgun into the floor of the hallway. The sound was loud and percussive, a contrast to the hiss-bang of the rocket-propelled round I'd fired, and it echoed painfully through the entryway and my head. I followed him as he fell and put a point-blank shot through his head. Two men. I'd killed two men. I felt nothing.

One left. The one in charge, the dealer, the boss. He was trying to get up, trying to draw his pistol. He didn't look scared, but I didn't think he would, not him. Instead, his lined face was determined, intent on survival and victory. He would have been hell on the Tahni during the war, but now he was the one who'd kept a woman I'd liked and respected hooked on Kick and Spindle and God knew what else, and taken her services in trade. I looked at him and didn't feel cold anymore, suddenly didn't feel nothing. I felt rage.

He had his gun in his hand when I shot him in the forearm. The stamped metal, black market gun flew away with a spray of blood. I kicked him in the face. More blood, and teeth. He went down, the breath gushing out of him in a wheeze. He tried to get up and I broke his good leg with a vicious stomp, feeling the tibia crack, sending him back to the ground. I went down to a knee beside him and put the barrel of my pistol against his forehead.

"Don't get up," I said. He went still, his dark, intelligent eyes narrowed and staring at me. "Do you know why I don't kill you?"

He shook his head, not speaking. I might have broken his jaw with the kick.

"Because I *want* to," I said. I jerked my head at the other two. "Those two, I *had* to kill. I don't have to kill you, but I want to, for what you did to her." I motioned to Yassa, still unconscious on Sanders' shoulder. Sanders was stock still, like a deer in a spotlight, a look of horror and disbelief on his face.

"After I do what I have to do," I told him, "I'll come back here. When I come, I don't want to see you. If I see you, if anyone in the neighborhood has even *heard* of you, I'll finish what I started and beat you to death. Nod if you believe me."

He nodded. He wasn't scared, but he was a survivor, a predator, and he knew when he'd come across another.

I walked over and picked up his gun, sticking it in my belt, then grabbed the other from the dead man before I headed for the door again, my own weapon in my right hand, the metal stampings of the street pistol pressed up against the box I'd taken from Yassa's apartment in my left. I'd get rid of their guns in a storm drain I'd seen back near where we'd parked the car.

"Let's go," I said to Sanders. This time, he didn't need me to say it twice.

There were no watching eyes or playing children on the walk back to the car; the streets and doorways and windows were empty. I could see from fifty meters away that the car was unmolested. People here, I thought as I dropped the guns into the open storm drain by the side of the road, knew when to duck and cover.

"You killed those guys," Sanders said. It wasn't an accusation, nor a gasp, nor a complaint. It was more of a...realization, maybe. As if he'd just realized what he was getting into.

"If you want to go back to your uncle's company," I said,

unlocking the doors and helping him lay Yassa across the back seat, "now's the time."

He didn't say anything at first, pushing the woman's legs inside and shutting the door. She didn't move, barely breathed.

"No," he decided, getting into the passenger's side. "I'm in. I just…" He shook his head. "It's been a while."

"Yes, it has," I agreed, pulling out of the grass lot and heading down towards the spaceport. "But the rules are the same."

6

Brandy Yassa slowly blinked awake, a hand going to her face and rubbing it vigorously, as if she expected it to be coated with mucus or vomit. Instead, there was nothing and she stared at her hand in confusion. Then she looked down at the grey utility coveralls she was wearing, and then down further to the cot on which she was lying, and her confusion deepened.

Then she looked up at me.

"Munroe?" She forced the words from a dry throat in a hoarse murmur.

I handed her a cup of water and she downed it without thinking.

"Hey, Cap," I said quietly, not moving from the chair beside her cot. The cabins on the *Wanderer* were all basically closet-sized, but I'd given her the largest. "How do you feel?"

"I feel like shit," she said frankly, her voice sounding more normal now. She pushed up to a sitting position on the cot. "Where in the hell am I? And what are you doing here?"

"You're on my ship," I told her, "in Transition Space." Which was the reason we had artificial gravity; the Teller-Fox warp unit could create it, but only in T-space, for some reason.

"What the hell did you do to me?" Her hands went to her head, digging into her long hair, cleaner now than it had been.

"You OD'ed on Spindle. Maybe Kick too, I don't know, didn't have time to stick around and find out. I popped you in the autodoc." I shrugged. "We have a couple females on the team, I had one of them wash you and dress you. I tossed your old clothes into the airlock and spaced them."

"Shit!" She slammed a fist into the cot and glared at me. "Get me back to Hermes, now!"

"You want to go back to Overtown?" I asked her. "You're going to need another dealer then."

"Goddamn it, Munroe, what did you do to Barry?" She was standing now, unsteady, balancing herself with a hand on the bulkhead. I stood to keep on her level: she was a tall woman and we were almost eye-to-eye.

"If Barry is the guy who showed up to try to keep me and Sanders from taking you out of your apartment and getting you treatment, then he's going to have to spend a little time in an autodoc himself. And the two goons with him who pulled weapons on me..." I shrugged. "Well, let's just say an auto-doc won't do them any good."

She screamed in pure rage and swung at me wildly, but spun to the deck and hit hard on her shoulder. I stayed standing, not trying to help her up.

"You need to take it easy," I cautioned her. "You were in the auto-doc for over twenty hours. You need to eat something."

"Why the fuck did you stick your nose into my life?" She was on her hands and knees, her face down, and her voice sounded like a sob.

"Because I have a job offer," I said to her. "After you get something to eat and get your shit together, I'll tell you about it." She didn't look up, didn't try to stand up. "If you aren't interested, I can drop you off at Loki or even one of the Pirate Worlds. If you want to kill yourself with Spindle and Kick there, you could probably do it without the Constabulary throwing you into rehab every six months."

I took a step towards the door, but she stopped me with a hand on my ankle. She looked up at me, tears streaking down her cheeks. I paused, but it took her a few minutes to work up to what she had to say.

"I wish I could pretend it was the guilt." Her voice was calmer now. "I wish I'd done it because I couldn't live with all the Marines I'd lost, but that's not the truth. I tried to stay in, after the war, but I was stuck on Tahn-Skyyiah in garrison duty, and it was boring as hell. I got out, and went to Hermes to try to get a job in security consulting, but I sucked at it and they let me go after three months. I couldn't hold down a job, and I couldn't sleep, and I couldn't handle civilian life…and I thought I was too much of a hard-ass to get psych counselling from the Military Separation Center."

She took a deep breath and pushed herself up to a seated position, legs crossed. "Then I went to a club in Sanctuary, trying to have a little fun, to lighten up. Someone offered me some Spindle. It made me feel…less stressed. For a while. Then I took the Kick to get myself going again, then the Spindle to come back down. Then I ran out of money, Overtown was cheap, but not cheap enough to keep up a habit, so…"

"You don't have to say anything else." I didn't want to hear it. She'd been a respected superior officer, and a friend, and I didn't care to think about her that way. "The auto-doc ran you through a detox, but that's just physical. We'll be at the node to drop into Loki in twelve hours. If you still want, I can drop you off there. If not, there's this thing I'm doing, and you can be my second in command."

She looked up at that, eyes going wide, but I was already opening the door

"Twelve hours," I reminded her. "Oh, and I brought your box, the one from your apartment." I nodded across the compartment. "It's in the drawer next to the cot."

I let the hatch shut behind me. The passageway was very narrow through the waist of the ship, but Sanders was waiting there, his arms crossed, an uncomfortable expression on his bland face. I wondered how long he'd been waiting there, afraid to come in.

"How is she?"

He seemed genuinely concerned. He was the only other person on the ship who'd served under the Captain; I was the only one who'd been in her platoon when she was a Lieutenant.

"She'll be okay," I told him, hoping I was right. I nodded towards the cabin he and I shared. "Go get some sleep while you have the chance."

I left him there, not waiting to see if he took my advice, and moved up to the cockpit. I expected to find Kane there; he hadn't left except to eat and use the head since he'd boarded the ship. He'd told me he could sleep sitting down, or even standing up if he needed to, which was handy since it freed up a cot. I didn't expect to find Bobbi Taylor, but there she was, sprawled out in the acceleration couch at the navigator's station, reading something on one of the ship's tablets.

She was broad-shouldered and hard-edged, her blond hair cropped short and her muscular arms bare past the sleeveless sweatshirt she wore with her utility fatigue bottoms and a pair of soft-soled ship shoes. She didn't look much different than I remembered her from Recon Qualification training; maybe a bit rougher around the edges, but living through an interstellar war will do that to you. She regarded me coolly with water-blue eyes.

"So, you wound up stuck on Demeter," she said out of nowhere. "That's a stone bitch."

I nodded towards the tablet in her hand. "What, you've been looking up my life story?"

I sat down in the copilot's seat, hitting the release latch to free it and swiveling it around to face her.

"It's not like there's much else to do on this trip so far," she replied, shrugging. "Why didn't you get the damned Medal of Honor, Munroe?"

I laughed. "What, the Silver Star isn't enough for being lucky enough to not get killed?"

"You organized a bunch of half-assed civilians into a real resistance," she said, not taking my bait. "You tied up the Tahni garrison for a year and pretty much made it possible for us to retake the planet without pounding the shit out of it from orbit first." She snorted. "If that doesn't deserve a Medal of Honor, I don't know what the hell does."

"There were...complications," I said, knowing I was being cryptic but not willing to say more.

I didn't want to get into explaining how my mother, Patrice Damiani, had found me on the Fleet base on Inferno after I'd returned from Demeter, and I'd had to jump out of a flying hopper to get away from the Corporate Security team she'd assigned to escort me back to Earth. Cowboy had managed to keep me hidden from her after that, but the media coverage a Medal of Honor would have brought would have made that impossible.

"Anyway," I went on, "it's not like I did it myself. There were a couple DSI agents they sent down after a few months, and then we had some Fleet Intelligence operators who weren't officially there." I waved a hand dismissively. "I made some bad calls. Did some things that wound up getting people killed. I'm not saying I didn't do some good..." It had taken me a while to admit that, to really accept that I hadn't totally fucked things up. Sophia had to basically pound it into my head. "...but a lot of Marines could have done what I did."

"A lot of Marines would have crawled into a fucking hole and cried," she shot back. "You were a leader, you did what you had to do." She slotted the tablet into a sleeve attached to the cockpit bulkhead. "And I knew you were a squared-away Marine by the time we finished Force Recon training. That's why I'm not going to come out and tell you that you're a fucking idiot to bring that strung-out junkie onto the boat." She rolled her eyes. "But I *want* to."

"She was the best combat officer I ever served with," I said, maybe a bit defensively. "And if she commits to this job, I know she'll pull her weight. If she doesn't, we'll cut her loose."

"You're the boss, Boss," she said. "You got anything to drink on this tub that isn't processed soy?"

"Check the cooler," I told her, nodding towards the mini-refrigerator built into the bulkhead over on her side of the cockpit.

She spun her seat around and pulled it open. Inside were a few bottles of a locally bottled beer I'd found on Hermes. I'd bought them for the others, not for myself. She smiled as she pulled one out and twisted the top off.

"Excellent," she said, taking a swig. "It's even my brand."

I glanced over at Kane, who was so silent that he could have been a piece of furniture; I'd almost forgotten he was in the compartment with us.

"Would you like a beer, Kane?" I asked him.

"No."

I didn't wait for him to elaborate. I'd learned during the short trip from Belial to Hermes that the man didn't say any more syllables than were absolutely necessary.

"Give me one."

I looked around. It was Captain Yassa, looking straight-backed and composed, more like the woman I'd known three years ago than the one I'd left a few minutes ago.

"Someone told me I needed some calories," she added, the corner of her mouth turning up slightly.

I chuckled and looked over to Bobbi. She grabbed another bottle from the cooler and tossed it underhand to Yassa. The older woman caught it one-handed, then twisted off the cap and took a long, gulping drink. She sighed as she brought the bottle down away from her mouth and looked me in the eye.

"Tell me about this job."

I looked around at the faces squeezed into the utility bay, the largest room on the boat. On my left were Victor and Kurt, blond and bulky and happy to be there. Next to them was Kane, standing stock-still with an indifferent expression, only interested in the money that would let him achieve his goal of not being human anymore.

Then there was Carmen Ibanez, petite and skinny, smiling and bubbly with wild, curly hair, but tough as banded steel; she'd been in another company in my battalion on Inferno, and I think I'd met her once before Demeter but I wasn't sure. She'd had drinks a few times with Sanders and Bobbi at the local Veterans' watering hole in Sanctuary and they'd swapped stories. I wasn't sure if that was all she and Sanders had swapped, but if they were involved before, they weren't now.

Sanders was still next to her, seeking out someone familiar I suppose. He hadn't looked comfortable since our little foray into Overtown, and I hoped I hadn't made a mistake bringing him along. Bobbi was on the other side of him, fists planted on her hips, looking like she believed she could take anyone in the room. Maybe she could.

Finally, my eyes travelled to Brandy Yassa, Captain, Commonwealth Fleet Marine Corps, First Force Reconnaissance Battalion, Delta Company, Retired. She looked better now than when she'd woke up a few hours ago; I'd insisted she get a full meal down and rehydrate before we had the mission brief. Her eyes looked brighter, more intent, and her stance was steadier and well balanced. But I thought I saw a quiver of doubt in her expression; maybe it was just me seeing in her what I felt in myself.

"Any of you ladies and gentlemen heard of Thunderhead?" I asked them.

"Yes," Kane said. All of them looked at him, expecting him to elaborate; they didn't know him as well as I did.

"It's in the Pirate Worlds," Bobbi Taylor said. "I audited a news report on the Pirate Worlds once, for a report I did in NCO school."

"They're just like nearly worthless, barely habitable, right?" Sanders asked her. "Right on the fringes of Commonwealth space and not worth the effort for the government to try to crack down on?"

"Some think," Kane spoke up, surprising me, "the feds do nothing because the cabals pay them off."

I looked at him, but he volunteered nothing else, and his green eye was as cold and unrevealing as the red one.

"Or maybe," Yassa interjected, "the feds don't do anything because the pirate cabals have a deal with the Corporate Council."

"Either way," Bobbi Taylor cut in, looking a bit irritated at the interruption, "Thunderhead is way out on the periphery, far at the end of one of the last Transition Lines in the Cluster."

"What's 'the Cluster,' anyway?" Victor asked, face screwed up in confusion.

Bobbi's ears started to turn red from being interrupted again, so I answered quickly. "The Transition Lines," I told him and Kurt, "the ones that run between star systems, that we use the Teller-Fox warp unit to travel along, they're like fault lines in the structure of space-time caused by the gravitational interactions of stars. But they only connect a few hundred systems in our immediate area. That's called the Cluster. It's all the stars we can reach with the Transition Drive. As far as anyone knows, there are no Transition Lines that lead out of the Cluster, and we've been looking for them for decades now."

Victor nodded his understanding. Kurt still looked confused, but I figured Victor could explain it to him later, so I waved at Bobbi to go on.

"Thunderhead's got a big moon," she went on, "and a fast rotation---I think the days are only like eighteen hours long there. And it's got a hell of an electromagnetic field and a lot of background radiation, which makes communications hard and isn't that great for humans to live in, either. Last I heard, the whole planet was run from the only real city, Freeport, by a cabal under some toad named Crowley."

"It was till a couple years ago," I agreed. "Then he was replaced by someone they call 'Abuelo.' He supposedly killed Crowley and took over his operations. Our job is to go to Freeport and pretend to be a bunch of vets who're dissatisfied with civilian life and want to try being mercenaries."

"Not much of a stretch there," Carmen Ibanez drawled, chuckling.

"No," I said, smiling back. "The best lies have a lot of the truth in them. We need to get hired on by Abuelo and brought into his operation."

"Why?" Yassa asked me, and for a moment, I could see my old Company Commander in that face. "What's the objective?"

"Abuelo has found something," I told her, and all of them. "Or at least there are strong rumors he's found something; an artifact that might be Predecessor technology."

Bobbi Taylor's mouth shaped a soundless whistle.

"Something like that," she said with awe in her tone, "would be basically priceless."

"It could also be damned dangerous," I pointed out. "Our job is to steal it from him, if possible, and deliver it to the people we're working for."

"And who might that be?" Yassa again. She was probably the only one among them who cared.

"That's where things get complicated," I admitted. I hesitated, knowing the reaction I was going to get. "We're working for someone high up in the Corporate Council Executive Board. I don't know who, exactly; the go-between who hired me wouldn't tell me."

"Not your mother..." Yassa's eyes went wide and her hands came down to her sides like she was getting ready for flight or fight.

"No," I assured her. "That's why it's even more complicated. Mother and other members of the Executive Board might also know about this, and they might have people on the ground as well."

"Wait a second," Victor held up a hand. "What the hell does she mean about your mother? Who's your mother?"

"It's not important or relevant," I told him. Then I watched the eyes of all the others staring at me, even Kane's, and I sighed, rubbing my hands over my face.

Shit. I *really* hadn't wanted to tell the others any of this.

"Okay," I said, leaning back against a locker set into the bulkhead. "My mother is a very highly placed Corporate Council Executive Board member. We had a disagreement about me joining the military…which ended with her sending one of her people to kill my great grandfather, because she felt he was trying to lead me away from her and what she wanted for my life."

"What the *fuck*?" Bobbi muttered, her expression scrunched up in a look of disbelief. "Is this your actual life or are you ripping off the plot of one of the drama serials on Commonwealth HoloNet?"

"I killed the guy," I said, unamused and showing it. "I had the choice of letting my mom cover it up and being her puppet for the rest of my life or taking off and changing my identity. I ran." I gave them a truncated version of the events that had happened after that, and of Cowboy's involvement. "That's why I'm here. I owe Cowboy, and this is how I have to pay him back."

"You'd rather risk dying in the Pirate Worlds and no one ever hearing of it," Carmen said slowly, smiling hugely, eyes beaming, "than living the life most people only dream of and winding up a high level Corporate Council executive? That's so damned romantic." She laughed. "And absolutely nuts, of course."

"And I thought my relationship with *my* mom was fucked up," Sanders muttered, still seemingly bemused by the story. At least something had taken his mind off Overtown.

"The money's still real, right?" Bobbi asked, looking a bit concerned.

"The money's very real," I told them. "You all get half in advance in your accounts the minute we Transition into the system. If you die, you get the full amount sent to whoever you want."

"I'm not sure there's anyone I like *that* much," Yassa commented drily.

"If anyone wants off," I said, "I'll make you the same deal I did Captain Yassa. We'll be at the Transition Node for Loki in a few hours. If you don't tell me by then, you're in and I'm in charge. No backing out and no trying to make any side deals." I caught each of their eyes and made sure they understood me. "This is a military operation, and we're going to be pretty far from any laws or any backup. The Chain of Command is the law. Everyone good with that?"

There was a lot of surreptitious looking around as everyone tried to see what everyone else was going to say, but in the end, they all nodded, or said some version of "yes," or "I'm in."

"Okay, then. I'll be handing out weapons before we land. You're going to need one there, just walking around, if what I'm told is accurate. We aren't going to have the luxury of run-throughs or tac-lanes, or training, because we have no idea what the ops we'll be pulling will look like until we get some intelligence; so I hope none of you have forgotten how to shoot-n-scoot since the war."

Again, nods all around. I was only really worried about Victor and Kurt, who hadn't had any formal military training, but I figured I could go over a few things with them before we got there.

"There's no set jobs and no rank," I reminded them, "except Kane is the pilot and the net-diver, for obvious reasons. I'm in charge and Captain Yassa is my second. If anyone has a problem with that, say so now and I'll leave you on Loki."

Bobbi and Sanders both looked at her sidelong, but said nothing. If Yassa noticed it, she gave no sign.

"Like I said before," Bobbi piped up, "you're the boss, Boss."

"Okay then," I concluded. "Get some food, get some sleep, do whatever you need to do to be ready. From here on out, you're on the clock."

They dispersed, except for Yassa. She waited until the others were out of the compartment before she stepped closer to me.

"Are you sure you trust me with this?" She asked me quietly.

"You trusted me once," I reminded her, just as softly, "when you had no reason to, when the MPs and the DSI and every fucking body on Inferno wanted my ass arrested. I owe you one."

"What if I fuck up?" She wondered, just a hint of a tremulous note in her voice.

"We're going to the Pirate Worlds, Cap," I reminded her. "We're going to be surrounded by criminals and spies." I forced a grin. "If you fuck up, you'll be dead. And so will the rest of us." I moved toward the passageway, intent on getting some sleep. "So, don't fuck up."

7

I'd traveled through T-space at least a couple dozen times in my life, starting when Mom had hauled me to Hermes for a "vacation" that mostly involved her schmoozing with other executives when I was about eight years old. They'd let me onto the command bridge of the Corporate transport for the conversion and I remember the ship's Captain had told me about the computer negotiating our course and orbit automatically with the traffic control systems in orbit around Hermes. I could see on the ship's sensor display that there were hundreds of other ships in orbit, some heading to the civilian or military stations, some carrying cargo to or from the orbital industrial plants, all dancing to the complex tune that the computers played for them.

Arriving at Thunderhead was nothing like that. The universe had unfolded around us and deposited the *Wanderer* just past the orbit of Thunderhead's major moon, Stormbringer, and I was adjusting to the return of microgravity and getting my first look at the blues and greens and angry, swirling whites of the planet when Kane glanced over and touched a control on the communications panel.

"This is Freeport Control," a human voice said, sounding annoyed at the interruption. "Who are you and what do you want?"

I glanced over at Captain Yassa, the only other member of the crew who'd come to the cockpit for the landing. She shook her head and raised her hands palm up in a clear "I have no clue" gesture.

"This is the independent freighter *Wanderer*," I said into the audio pickup, improvising. "We're here on business, looking for work."

"There's a $200 landing fee, payable in Tradenotes or Corporate Scrip," Freeport Control informed us. "You'll pay it when you land or you won't be allowed to take off again. You're currently being targeted by a laser defense system that can reach anywhere between the surface and lunar orbit, so you will stay in the approach corridor I'm sending to your navigation system. If you deviate, you'll be blown to vapors. Is all that clear, *Wanderer*?"

"Read you five by five, Freeport Control," I assured him. "We will stick to the prescribed flight corridor. *Wanderer* out." I cut the connection and looked over at Kane. "You got the flight plan?"

He nodded once.

"Then take us down."

"See those clouds?" Kane pointed to the display, where quickly spinning storms of angry skull-white swirled over the major continent of the Northern Hemisphere.

"That's where we're going?" Yassa demanded a bit too loudly.

"This is Munroe," I said over the ship's intercom. "Everyone strap in, and grab a motion-sickness patch if you're so inclined. It's going to be a rough ride down."

I felt acceleration press me back into the cushion of my seat as the fusion drive ignited, and I cursed as I slipped my arms into the restraints hurriedly.

"I *just* told them, Kane," I grumbled. "You could have given everyone a second."

He said just what I expected him to, which was nothing at all, but I was already grabbing a motion sickness patch from the supply in a pocket of the acceleration couch. Peeling the backing off, I slapped it onto my neck. I had a sudden thought about what memories that the sights of the patch might dredge up in Captain Yassa, and I shot her a worried look.

"It's okay, Munroe," she assured me, smiling grimly. "I don't get motion sickness."

The drive took us along the approach corridor at a steady one gravity of acceleration and it wasn't that long before we slipped around to the night side of the planet, darkness swallowing us as the primary star fell out of sight behind the midnight blue of Thunderhead's largest ocean. No one lived on the coasts, I'd read in Cowboy's files. The size and proximity of the moon caused tides that bashed at the shore like sledgehammers, leaving bare, naked rock in its wake. Sea farms or undersea mining was impossible with the storms, and the frequent windstorms made the open plains a nightmare. The only cities, such as they were, were nestled in isolated valleys between the largest mountain ranges, sheltered from the worst of the storms.

We had to fly through that.

The ship shuddered as the atmosphere thickened around us, from a wisp of baby's breath to a soup of turbulence that battered the *Wanderer* mercilessly. My fingers dug into the soft, malleable plastic of the acceleration couch's armrests as my stomach did flips and the seat kept trying to jump away from me. I could hear the whine of the turbojets through the bangs and jolts of the winds that assaulted us, and while I knew on an intellectual level that the cutter had enough power to force its way through anything in that atmosphere, what I knew in my head wasn't quite making its way to my gut.

Thank God for motion sickness patches.

The turbulence didn't let up until we emerged from the lower level of clouds only a few hundred meters over the spaceport. Well, to call it a spaceport was stretching the truth; it was a landing field, nothing more, and you could see that even at night, from three hundred meters up. It was packed with ships, but they were mostly heavy lift cargo craft and orbital shuttles; the only other starships were two cutters like ours, military surplus or maybe stolen, given where we were. Floodlights illuminated the field from poles set every fifty meters around the perimeter, and there was a building of some kind set up on the only paved road out of the field.

Then the view disappeared in a spray of steam and sand as the *Wanderer* descended on columns of fire from the landing jets, the whole boat shaking with the effort and then touching down with a jolt on five massive skids. I felt the slight bounce as the ship settled down onto the landing gear, then the fading whine as the turbines spun down and I let out the breath I'd been holding. The display went dark and Kane swiveled his seat around to face me.

"I can stay here," he volunteered. "For air support."

I thought about it for a moment. It wouldn't be a bad idea to leave someone with the ship, but would it be smart to leave a guy who was the only one who could possibly crack the encryption codes to fly it without my permission *and* had a big incentive to go sell it somewhere and use the money to fix his body up with bionics?

"No," I decided. "With all the EM interference here, we wouldn't be able to call you even if we did need help. It's better if we stick together." He shrugged, and I couldn't tell if he was disappointed or not.

Everyone was waiting in the utility bay, gathered around the weapons locker like kids at a toy box. I shook my head slightly. Well, the kind of people willing to go get shot at for money because they were bored with their lives probably weren't the ones I could expect to have a mature attitude about being issued a gun.

I touched the ID plate on the locker and the door popped open, revealing a double rack of firearms, handguns across the top, carbines on the bottom, ten of each with cases of loaded magazines stacked on a shelf above them and a loose collection of belt and shoulder holsters jammed in-between.

Bobbi pulled out one of the carbines and gave it a cursory inspection, racking open the grenade launcher affixed under the barrel. It was a Gauss rifle, standard issue when the two of us had been Recon Marines, a bit dated now.

"Just sidearms for now," I said, slipping off my jacket and shrugging into a shoulder holster before grabbing one of the pistols for myself. I stuffed a few spare magazines into the pockets, then zipped the coat up. "We can come back and get heavier weapons if we need them." I motioned to a smaller locker off to the side. "There're commercial enhanced optics glasses in there that'll synch to the gun's sights if you need them."

I didn't; I still had the contact lens. It wasn't as versatile as the enhanced optics, but it also couldn't get knocked off your face and kill your night vision in a fight.

Bobbi scowled as she put the carbine back in the rack and grabbed a handgun. "What do you think we can accomplish with these popguns, Munroe?" She asked me, popping the magazine out of the ZWH pistol and checking its load. The variable-warhead, rocket-assisted round straining against the feed lips gleamed a dull silver in the stark light of the bay.

"We're here to get hired," I reminded her, trying to summon patience I didn't ever recall having, "and gather intelligence. When the time comes for breaking shit and blowing things up, you'll be the first in line for the big stuff."

Once everyone had got what they needed, I sealed the locker and led them over to the boarding ramp. It was raining outside, and a few drops blew in as the ramp lowered, cold against the bare skin of my face. I let the others go ahead of me, and when I closed the ramp, I activated the security seal. That meant that only Captain Yassa or I could open it, though I hadn't actually told her about it yet. Walking out from under the nose of the *Wanderer*, I felt the rain and wind smack me in the face and my boots nearly slipped out from under me in the thin coat of mud on the fusion-form landing field.

I stared up into the roiling clouds and saw lightning forking across the sky, its glow illuminating the slopes of the mountains surrounding the town. Thunder trailed a second later, echoing back and forth across the valley.

"That's not all ominous or anything," Ibanez said, smiling

crookedly. I grinned back at her; it was impossible to dislike the woman.

I walked through the midst of them and headed for the lone building, more like a shack, out near the edge of the field. It was about a half a kilometer of walking, and by the end I was feeling pretty glad my jacket and boots were waterproof. It was a small building, but everyone crammed into it anyway, and the skinny, unhealthy looking little man behind the single desk inside eyed us suspiciously as we dripped water and tracked mud on the plastic sheeting that lined the floor beside the single entrance. He was dressed in practical clothes that looked more hand-made than fabricated, which might cost less out here for all I knew, and he wasn't armed.

Behind me, I could hear the door creak shut as the last of us made it inside, slamming at the end as the wind gave it a final, spiteful shove.

"You off the *Wanderer*?" He asked us, looking around for someone to focus on.

"Yes," I answered, giving him a target for his stare. I reached into a pocket and withdrew a dataspike, flipping it over to him. "There's the port fees," I explained as he caught it with an awkward grab.

He made a face at the spike, but then jabbed it into a reader built into the cheap, plastic desk and nodded at the figure that came up on the display.

"Two hundred in Corporate Scrip," he confirmed. He eyed me sidelong. "You want to hire protection for your boat?"

I rolled my eyes. I guess I should have been expecting that, out here.

"Protection?" That was Victor, sounding outraged. I looked over and held up a hand to silence his protest. Arguing with the sad sack behind the desk would accomplish less than nothing. And on a place like this, maybe it was just the cost of doing business.

"How much is it?" I wondered. "And what do we get for it?"

"Three hundred per day," the little man told me, smiling so widely I knew he must get a big cut of that.

"*Local* day?" Bobbi cut in, eyebrows rising. "Those are only eighteen standard hours long!"

"We have quite a few people in our party," I mused, remembering my days haggling with the merchants in the Zocalo in Trans-Angeles. "It wouldn't be that big of a deal to leave someone behind to keep an eye on the ship, I suppose…"

"I know the people who offer the service," the little man hemmed, acting as if the savings were coming directly out of his flesh. "Maybe I can talk them down to…two hundred a day?"

"We're going to be here probably at least a local week," I told him. "How about we give you a thousand for the week, ahead of time, in Tradenotes?" I fished the roll of bills out of my pocket and peeled off ten of the twenty dollar notes, handing them over to him.

"You drive a hard bargain, sir," he said, but he nodded.

"How about arranging us a ride into town?" I asked him, handing over an extra twenty.

He looked at the eight of us, scratching at his scraggly, grey-streaked beard. "It'll cost you more with so many," he warned me. "They'll have to send a truck."

"That's fine," I assured him. It was better than walking the two or three kilometers into town in the rain, and just like in the Zocalo in Trans-Angeles, it was all someone else's money.

Freeport wasn't as ugly and primitive as I'd thought it would be. The buildings were mostly one-story, probably because of the high winds they could get even down here in the sheltered river valley, but they looked quaint and homey, built from local wood and stone instead of buildfoam and concrete, and fleshed out with the personalities of the people who lived and worked in them.

The truck had dropped us off at the heart of the hospitality district, rolling slowly through the darkened and sleeping apartments and townhouses at the edge of town, through the shops and storehouses closed now for the night, and into the part of Freeport that never slept. It was fairly crowded for that late at night and lights blinked teasingly from hotels, restaurants and clubs catering to spacers.

Smugglers, I corrected myself. Honest spacers wouldn't be out in the Pirate Worlds. They'd be smugglers, pirates, mercenaries, thieves and probably criminals whose specialties I hadn't even heard of. I watched them passing by us on the muddy streets, motley packs of individuals, more mangy and ruthless looking than any of the wolves I'd seen on Earth or Demeter. Two meter tall Belters toddled alongside squat, broad-bodied trolls from high gravity worlds, and here, bionics were a rule more than an exception; not surprising given how rare and expensive high-tech medical procedures would be out here. Weapons were also the rule, most worn openly, which was even less surprising. I kept wanting to reach under my jacket to make sure mine was still there, but I resisted the temptation and tried to look calmer and more confident than I felt.

The others seemed to be doing okay. I thought Victor and Kurt might be rubbernecking like tourists, but I guess their time at Belial had inured them to the strangeness and variety. Sanders was looking around, but he'd settled down since Hermes and was at least trying to be cool, and even looked more dangerous behind the mirrored shield of his enhanced optics glasses. Bobbi regarded everyone evenly, quite obviously calculating in her head if she could kill each of them and just as obviously deciding that, yes, she could. Carmen Ibanez seemed coolly fascinated, ready if anything happened but content just to be experiencing something new.

And Yassa...she was stiff-backed and uncomfortable, her left hand hovering around the pistol holstered high on her hip. She wasn't afraid, I was pretty sure...she hadn't struck me as someone who was afraid of much. I had a suspicion she was keyed up by the proximity of the bars, and the knowledge that inside were undoubtedly the drugs she'd surrendered to some months ago, and to which she probably still had a psychological dependency if not a physical one.

"There's the place," I said, nodding to the biggest, brightest and busiest of the joints on the strip.

It was four stories tall, which made practically made it a skyscraper here in Freeport, at least a hundred meters on a side and covered with advertising holos that offered the best food, the best liquor, the best drugs, the best ViR, the best sex dolls and the best hookers on the planet. It was called the *Lucky Bastard* and it was where Cowboy had suggested we look for Abuelo's people.

"We should split up into groups of two," I suggested, stepping out of the flow of traffic and wiping the rain from my face. It had died down but it was still drizzling, and I could feel it matting my hair. "Victor and Kurt," I said, focusing on the brothers, "you guys go get a table, order some food. If there's a human server," likely in a place like this where spare parts for automated service 'bots would be harder to come by than humans desperate for a job, "try to chat them up, find out what you can. Slip them a few bucks if you have to." I'd given everyone a small supply of Tradenotes for spending money, tips and possible bribes.

"Sanders," I said to him, "you and Taylor go try gambling. Lose a little if you have to, whatever gets the others talking." He nodded, and Bobbi Taylor shot me a knowing look, realizing I was having her team up with him because he was cautious and she was not.

"Kane, you and Carmen hit the ViR rooms. If their firewalls aren't too strong, maybe you" I looked to Kane, "can penetrate their central systems and dig up some data. Carmen, watch his back in case they twig to what he's doing."

I motioned to the main entrance, about twenty meters from us down the street and lit up like mid-day with a ring of lights. "Go on in. If you need to find me or Captain Yassa, we'll be at the main bar. If we get separated, meet at the rally point no later than 0100 local."

The six of them drifted into the place two at a time, each of the pairs pausing instinctively to put some space between one group and the next. I found myself nodding appreciatively. I hadn't had a lot of time or a lot of choice picking this team, and it was nice to see they hadn't forgotten everything they'd learned.

I offered Captain Yassa an arm and she regarded it doubtfully for a moment before she took it and we headed inside. I could feel her stiffness and hesitation, but she kept walking.

"Some paradise they got here," she said quietly next to me, almost drowned out as we got closer to the music playing inside. She was keeping her voice even and calm despite the trepidation I knew she was feeling. "Constant storms, winds, electromagnetic interference, earthquakes, and background radiation enough to give you cancer in a few years if you didn't get the prenatal nanite treatments…and most of these people didn't."

She looked at me sideways and snorted a laugh. "If I'd known this was how you treated a girl, I'd have snagged you up before that student on Demeter grabbed you first."

I was trying to think up something clever to say in return, but then we stepped through the doorway and our conversation was swallowed up in light and noise.

8

A bass beat thumped somewhere in my chest, and the lights flashed red and blue to match it in a hypnotic combination that seemed to be designed to drawn you further into the *Lucky Bastard*, like the spasms of an alimentary canal. There was no cover charge, no line of bouncers, no weapons scanners; you just walked in and there was the dance floor, pulsing from below like the building itself was alive and the floor was its beating heart.

There were maybe a dozen couples out on the floor when we walked in, and no two of them seemed to be dancing in the same style or even to the same beat. They thrashed or weaved or spun in place, often with eyes closed, oblivious to what their partner was doing; I saw more than one drug patch and wondered if that was the explanation or if smugglers just made really bad dancers. And some of them were visibly armed, including the ones with the drug patches, which made getting by them nearly as nerve-wracking as the flight through the storm.

Yassa and I stepped together through the swirling, leaping, writhing mass of them, almost dancing ourselves as we dodged and zigzagged across the flashing, vibrating floor, her hand holding my bicep loosely, ready to cut loose if we needed to move faster or fight. It felt natural, like we'd practiced it a hundred times, and she actually seemed more relaxed now than she had before, as if the possibility of physical danger was a comfort.

Then we were through, walking suddenly on a real, hardwood floor that would have cost hundreds of thousands in Corporate scrip or Commonwealth dollars back on Earth or any of the major colonies, where the only wood allowed for furniture or building materials had to be cloned in a lab. I felt a twinge of envy along with a sense of horrified wrongness at the thought of cutting down a decades-old tree just to make flooring or a desk out of it. It seemed...selfish and short-sighted to me, and I wasn't sure if it was because of the way I'd been raised on Earth. I'd lived on Demeter long enough to know that attitudes were different about things like that in the colonies, and they would sure as hell be different still here in the Pirate Worlds.

The wood floor began in a short hallway that led off to the right back to the Virtual Reality theaters and then out another exit, and on the left up a narrow stairwell. We stepped straight through it, into the bar. It was anachronistic and old-fashioned, not from a style choice like the pricey bars in Belial or back on Earth, but because here, everything was anachronistic. They didn't hire human bartenders because it meant they could charge more for the drinks, they hired them because they couldn't afford the maintenance and repair of the computer systems that would take orders and dispense them automatically. They didn't use real glass because some corporate executive expected it, they used it because no one could afford to import transplas or build a factory that could make it, or maintain that factory. Glass was cheap and made from readily available silicon.

The bar was made from local wood as well, polished and gleaming in the low light that glowed from fixtures embedded in the walls, and the stools were padded with what could have been leather---from something, I knew they had cows here, and horses. The crowd here was more sedate than the one on the dance floor, lined and weathered faces staring into their solitary drinks at the bar or groups of two or three sitting or standing at high-top tables, smoking cigars or pipes. The room was filled with a light haze of aromatic smoke that smelled vaguely of the narcotics that were blended with the tobacco.

"See anyone who looks like muscle?" Yassa asked me as we sat down at the bar, pulling the stools out with a squeaking of the plastic caps on the bottom of the legs on the wood floor.

"All of them," I commented wryly, trying to look the other customers over without staring at them. "You and I included."

"What can I get you?" The bartender almost startled me when he appeared in front of us. He was an older man and he *looked* old, with stringy, greying hair and an unhealthy pallor to his mottled and stained skin. He was dressed in plain, white coveralls and wore a net over his hair and a supremely indifferent look in his dark eyes.

"Shot of tequila," I said, "if you have it." In a place like Belial, or on Earth, my 'link would already have been displaying the menu and drink list on my contact lens, but here I saw nothing.

"It's locally made," the man told me, pulling a bottle from under the bar and tipping it into a shot glass.

"That's fine," I told him. "Cap?" I asked Yassa.

I saw her eyes flickering behind the bartender, to the shelf below the rows of glass bottles. There he had jars of the cigars and electric pipes, but her eyes were on the small, locked cases beside them. Inside there would be the patches of Spindle and Kick and Zed and whatever else they might have.

"You want something stronger?" The bartender asked her, catching the tilt of her gaze.

I didn't answer for her; instead, I waited, watching the tiny beads of sweat coalescing on her forehead.

"No," she told him, finally, though it took her eyes a moment longer to move on from the drugs. "Give me a bottle of whatever lager you serve here."

He set the open bottle in front of her and she took a long drink of it, seizing back control of her breathing as it coursed down her throat.

"That's ten dollars," the bartender told me. "We prefer Tradenotes."

I pulled out two twenties and passed them over. His eyebrow shot up.

"Tell me something," I said to him. "If you had a few people, veterans say...*Marine* veterans who'd seen combat, and they were looking for work, who would you suggest they talk to around here?"

The set of his eyes changed and he looked us both over for a second before he nodded slightly to himself.

"You should talk to Constantine." He motioned towards the large, open doorway in the far wall. The restaurant part of the club was through there and I could just see the edges of a few of the tables. "He has a table reserved over on the far side of the dining room."

I nodded to him, then slammed back the tequila shot. It burned on the way down and I felt a not-unpleasant tingle up and down my spine and a fire in my chest.

"Thanks."

Yassa brought her bottle with her as we stepped away from the bar and made our way through the tables towards the dining room. We were just past the last group of tables when we heard the angry shouting ahead of us. I shared a look with Yassa and we picked up the pace, striding purposefully into the slightly brighter light of the restaurant.

It wasn't packed, not nearly as crowded as the dance floor or the bar, but there were a few occupied tables, and all of them seemed to be staring at the confrontation at the far side of the room, just where the bartender had said we could find this guy Constantine.

I pegged the man yelling for a local, not a spacer. He wore utilitarian clothes, work clothes, not the expensive leathers or bright-colored flash freighter crews or smugglers wore dirtside; and he had the pale and slightly creepy tone to his skin people seemed to get here. He wasn't armed, not that I could see, but he was a big man with a barrel chest and a grey-shot, bushy beard that fell over it.

As we got closer, I could make out what he was saying, though his English was distorted by an accent I'd never heard; it sounded vaguely European, maybe.

"Don't hand me that bullshit about keeping up the town!" He was bellowing. "Taxes have gone up twice in just the last three months and you people *still* haven't fixed the damage from the winter storms! You are pocketing that money, stealing from us!"

"You need to calm down, Seth."

The man who spoke wasn't particularly imposing. His face was bland and rounded, his brown hair cut medium length with sideburns that grew down his cheeks to meet his mustache. He was about my height, I estimated roughly since he was still sitting, seemingly relaxed even under the onslaught. He might have had a few kilos on me, but not many; I'm not a small man and I'd been engineered from the genes up to have about as much strength and endurance as you can have and still be an un-augmented human, thanks to Mom. He wasn't even dressed to intimidate. His clothes were well made, probably by hand but still well-tailored, but they were simple, earth-toned and fashionable, but not flashy. His only affectation was a black, leather glove on his right hand, which seemed an odd fashion statement.

But he had a gun holstered low on his left hip, strapped to his thigh to keep it secure, and there was something about the way he wore it that made me suspect he had military training. And there was something about the cool, expressionless control on his lean, unlined face that warned me he wasn't someone you wanted to fuck with.

"Calm?" Seth blurted, waving his hands expressively. "I've been calm for months and all it's got me is dead broke! I have no extra money to expand my business or repair the damage to our buildings because every dollar goes to you! We barely have enough to buy food!"

There were two large, dangerous looking people standing next to Constantine's table, obviously bodyguards, but they weren't taking part in the argument. The man and woman were dressed in light body armor strapped with chest holsters, and wore enhanced optics glasses probably linked to their weapons. I had the sense, watching them, that Constantine had told them to hold back; they were watching this Seth character, but weren't in a defensive stance.

Seth, I figured grimly, hadn't thought this through.

I paused maybe ten meters away from them, leaning back against an unoccupied table with Yassa beside me. The bodyguards shot us a glance that was a warning to stay away.

"Seth, things are difficult for everyone since the war ended." Constantine's voice was cool and level. "There's been more attention from the Fleet, and the Commonwealth has even re-established the Patrol Service. We aren't getting the income we used to. That's why taxes are up, temporarily."

"Temporarily my ass!" Seth exploded. "I've had enough of this two-faced bullshit! I want to talk to Abuelo! Why is he never in town anymore?"

"Abuelo has important business he's taking care of," Constantine's tone grew even softer, and I had to strain to hear it. I had the sense that was a bad sign.

"Well you fucking well better tell him to get his ass back to town!" Seth was screaming now, his normally pale face turning beet red. "Or he'll have to find someone else to repair everyone's fabricators and food processing units because I'll fucking burn my place to the ground before I pay you bloodsucking shits another dollar!"

There was no warning. One moment, Constantine was a still life painting, sitting in his chair relaxed and unmoving, and the next, his gloved right fist was punching straight through Seth's chest. I jumped at the sudden motion, nearly falling into a crouch as I originally thought he was going for his gun. But then I saw the explosion of blood that stained that tailored jacket and splattered across the table.

Seth stood with a look of disbelief on his face, swaying like a pine in a storm for just a moment, and then Constantine's hand ripped back out with something blood red clutched in the fingers and blood sprayed with the motion, some of it hitting the bodyguards. The man stood, expressionless, but the woman wiped a droplet off of her cheek absently. The fabricator repair shop owner fell backwards, hitting the floor with a hollow thump and more blood and I heard a snarl coming from my lips as I reached for the gun holstered under my jacket.

"Don't." Brandy Yassa's mouth was so close to my ear that I could feel her warm exhalation as she said the word so loudly and forcefully that it hurt. Her hand squeezed vicelike on my shoulder. "Remember the mission."

I twisted my head around and nearly pushed her off of me before I saw the bodyguards looking our way again, their hands straying to their weapons. Constantine was still looking down at the heart in his hand...his obviously bionic hand, surely attached to a full cybernetic arm that had to go all the way into his shoulder and be attached to a reinforced spine for him to pull off that punch. He let the bloody lump of muscle drop to the wooden floor with a sickening plop, then shook the blood off of his glove, his expression still neutral.

Everything was interrupted by a scream, a wail of grief and fury and pain that echoed through the dining room so thoroughly that I wasn't sure, at first, from which direction it was coming. Then a woman rushed across the room from the entrance to the bar and threw herself down over Seth's body, convulsed with sobs.

She was young, younger than me, maybe still in her teens, her dark hair long and gathered into twin braids. She was dressed much like Seth, in work clothes that had seen better days, baggy and ill-fitting on her skinny, gangly form. She buried her face in Seth's shoulder and sobbed, keened for him, and I could see that their looks were similar enough that she must be his daughter. When she looked up from her father's body, his blood covered her and she seemed to welcome it, like it was evidence in a trial or perhaps the markings of a ritual sacrifice.

"You fucking murderer!" She hissed at him, her face screwed up into a mask of rage. She was crouched like a cat getting ready to spring. "Murderer!" She repeated, still loud but not screaming anymore.

"Shit," Yassa said, letting the pressure off my arm, her own hand trailing towards her holster. She knew, as I did, that the girl was about to get herself killed.

I was about to move for my gun when I realized I'd forgotten something: we already had two people in the dining room, the two least likely to be able to avoid getting involved in something like this. Victor and Kurt sailed across the room like they'd been launched from a cannon out of the corner behind Constantine's table. The bodyguards had been distracted by the girl, and they looked up just in time to have a combined 220 kilos of muscle slam into them with the righteous indignation of two former Resistance fighters and the skill of two cage fighters.

The guards never had a chance. There was a flurry of punches so fast and brutal that I could barely follow it, then the male bodyguard was flying over the table, clear over the top of Constantine and the girl and the dead body. He landed with a crack of wood and a louder crack of breaking bones, and stirred but didn't even try to get up. The woman lasted a heartbeat longer, before Kurt caught her between the eyes with a forearm and she collapsed, unconscious before she hit the floor.

Things had happened so quickly that neither Yassa and I had made it more than a couple steps toward the table yet, and neither of us could get there before the girl reached Constantine. He didn't bother to draw his gun, didn't even bother to use his bionics on her, just swatted her away negligently with his left hand, the flesh-and-blood hand. It took her across the chin and she spun away from him, crying out in pain.

I had my gun out now, and I trained it on Constantine before his left hand could complete the arc from the backhand down to his thigh holster. A red targeting reticle hung in the air over his chest from the pressure of the web of my thumb on the back of the grip.

"Don't," I warned him. "We're taking the girl and leaving and no one else has to die."

I *should* kill him, though. I knew it, somewhere down deep, that making an enemy of this man but not killing him was a mistake. But he was the only lead we had to Abuelo, and I clung desperately to the thought that maybe there was still some way to salvage all of this.

"You don't want to be pointing a gun at me, boy," Constantine warned me quietly, his hand hovering too near the butt of his holstered pistol for my taste.

"Victor, Kurt!" I snapped. "Get the girl! Cap, you're on point. I'll ride drag. Double-time!"

I knew with the EM interference, he couldn't call for help, but the bartender or one of the servers might have a hardwired line, and we needed to be gone before any more guards came, unless we wanted to wind up in a shootout. I kept my gun trained on Constantine as I moved over to the bodyguards and relieved them of their pistols; I didn't need one of them coming to while we weren't looking and taking a shot at our backs.

"You were military," Constantine said appraisingly, his dark eyes unreadable, his voice still dead calm. "Marines, I'd guess."

"Force Recon," I confirmed. I wasn't trying to hide it. "And you were DSI, I'd imagine."

Victor had the girl over his shoulder and he and Kurt were already following Cap back towards the bar. I backed away from Constantine carefully, dragging my feet and keeping a hand feeling behind me. I felt the eyes of other patrons on us, but none cared enough to risk a slug in the head by interfering.

"Very perceptive," Constantine allowed. "You wouldn't happen to be looking for a job, would you?"

"Actually, that's why we came here," I said, a bit ruefully as I cleared the doorway to the bar. "But even a mercenary has to have *some* standards."

"If you actually believe that," I heard his voice carry through as I moved to where the wall was between us and he fell from sight, and I turned to run, "I'm afraid you may be in the wrong line of work."

9

The rain had picked up since we'd entered the *Lucky Bastard*, and it slapped me in the face the second I made it out the door, forcing me to slit my eyes to see. I headed left, following the others, and I was happy that at least Victor was going the right direction towards the rally point. We'd designated it on the ride in, a burned-out shell of a building we'd seen in the industrial district, just after it switched over from the residential neighborhoods.

That was about the only thing that was going right.

Stupid, stupid, fucking *stupid!* I was cursing myself rhythmically in my head as I ran. That prick Constantine had been right; I was in the wrong line of work. What the hell had Cowboy been thinking sending me in here like I was some kind of damned spy? I should have acted, should have either stopped Victor and Kurt or else finished the job and killed that asshole.

Now, we were running blind through blinding rain, with what seemed like an incredibly dangerous man on our tail and four of us still stuck in the damned club. They should be able to make it out, I told myself. We'd gone in separately, and there was nothing to tie them to us. As long as they kept their heads, they'd know to meet us at the rally point and they'd be fine.

But then what? What the hell were we going to do now?

"Put me down, damn it!"

It was the girl; she'd come to, and she was squirming on Victor's shoulder, trying to hit him in the back of the head.

"Not yet!" I yelled at her over the din of the rain pounding around us. "You might have a concussion and we have to get the hell out of here before they figure out which way we went!"

"I'm gonna' puke!" She moaned, pounding futilely at the big man's back.

Victor transferred her from a fireman's carry to a cradle carry in front, which would slow us down a little but would probably keep her from getting motion sickness, and she quieted down until we finally reached the abandoned building. Even with the enhanced optics in my contact lens, I could barely see it in the downpour, but I guess Yassa's glasses worked better in the rain because she led us right to it.

Half the building had collapsed in a heap of cement block, aluminum siding and rebar, and the half left standing had a piece of plywood fastened across the doorway. Kurt ripped it down with his bare hands and I followed the others through into the shelter of what was left of the roof, feeling a huge sense of relief as the rain stopped beating down on my head and trickling down my collar.

"Put that back in place," I told Kurt, gesturing at the plywood.

Victor gently sat the girl down on the floor and she leaned heavily against a damp, block wall as she found her balance.

"Who are you people?" She demanded, looking around at us suspiciously, probably barely able to see us in the blackness of the unlit building.

I pulled a small light off my belt and flicked it on, shining it around so she could get a look at us.

"I'm Munroe," I told her. "The big guys are Victor and Kurt, and this is Cap." Yassa cocked an eyebrow at me, and I got the impression she didn't particularly care for that nickname, but I wasn't about to go into our personal bios for this traumatized kid. "We were in the dining room when your father was killed."

"I'm sorry we couldn't stop it," Victor said, his big, square face sagging. "We didn't know he could just…" He trailed off, raising his right hand like he was about to mime punching, but then obviously thinking better of it and letting it drop to his side.

The girl started to break down again, sobbing quietly for a few seconds before she grabbed at her head, wincing.

"What's your name?" I asked her.

"Natalia," she said, her voice strained, expression still twisted from the pain in her head. "Natalia Baturin." She blinked her eyes clear and looked up at me. "Are you spacers? Smugglers?"

"Mercenaries," Yassa corrected her. "We came here looking for work, but it seems as if we've just pissed off the one person most likely to hire us."

"Constantine has plenty of hired guns," Natalia said bitterly. "Though he always seems to be looking for more. Especially since Abuelo left the city."

"When did that happen?" I wanted to know. "We'd heard about Abuelo; that's why we came. We were told he wasn't a bad guy to work for, that he treated people right."

Natalia sank down to the dust-covered floor, resting her head on her hands.

"He did, once," she admitted. "Things were better with him in charge than that bastard Crowley. He actually kept the buildings repaired and kept the power on, and he kept the air defense system that kept us from being raided by pirates working. He didn't tax us more than we could afford. Then, a few months ago, he started spending more and more time away from Freeport, and Constantine started to take over running the city."

"And taxes started going up," Yassa assumed, "but the work stopped getting done."

I heard a skittering on the other side of the building and flashed my hand-light over there, catching the shadow of a rat dashing for another nook of darkness.

"Fucking rats," I muttered. "Everywhere we go, we bring those damned things with us."

There was a pounding on the plywood panel and my gun

jumped into my hand again, and I flipped off the light, moving to the side of the doorway. I saw Natalia jump to her feet and scurry farther away, taking shelter behind a fallen crossbeam.

"It's us. Open up!" I recognized Sanders' voice and grabbed the edge of the plywood, pulling it away from the door.

Sanders clambered through the opening before I even had it all the way aside, shaking water out of his hair and cursing. Bobbi and Carmen slipped in behind him, looking very wet and annoyed; Carmen Ibanez's hair reminded me of a poodle my mother had once owned after her servant had given it a bath. Kane waited until the plywood was all the way open before stepping through upright, as if ducking inside was too undignified for him.

It wasn't raining as hard anymore, I saw while I was glancing outside, but the wind had picked up and was whipping debris down the street. I pulled the cover back into place before I turned my light back on.

"Did you have any trouble getting out?" I asked the others.

"Negative," Bobbi said. "Me n' Eli heard the commotion from upstairs in the casino, so we headed down the back stairs right away."

"There were people in the street though," Sanders added. "They looked like muscle and they looked like they were hunting for someone around the *Lucky Bastard*."

"We met them out there," Ibanez said. "Kane was hooked into the bar's security by then, so he knew right away what was going on."

"What the hell *did* go on?" Sanders wanted to know. He had his gun in his hand and didn't seem in any mood to put it away at the moment. "Is it you they're after, Munroe?"

"Us and her," I told him, nodding towards the girl. "This is Natalia. Natalia, meet Bobbi, Sanders, Ibanez and Kane." I saw Natalia's eyes go wide as she saw Kane's cybernetics. "The guy we came to the bar to find," I explained to the others, "is named Constantine. He's like Abuelo's chief enforcer or something."

"Constantine Terranova," Natalia supplied, with hate dripping off the words. "He's been here since before Abuelo...he used to work for Crowley."

"Anyway," I went on, "this Constantine got into an argument with Natalia's father about taxes, and it was getting pretty hot, but no one had pulled a weapon yet so I didn't think anything of it, but then Constantine..." I shook my head. "He must have some serious bionics or some kind of augmentation, because he punched his fist right through Natalia's father's chest and killed him."

"And then," Yassa added ruefully, "the shit well and truly hit the fan, as you can imagine."

"Fuck," Sanders muttered, finally shoving his gun into its holster just so he could run his hands through his hair in frustration. "What the hell are we gonna' do now?"

"Did you find anything useful, Kane?" I asked him.

"Books are cooked," he said. "Lots of income marked outgoing but it's fake. Someone's skimming."

"That would be Constantine," Natalia said. "Everyone knows he's stealing, but without anyone being able to reach Abuelo, we can't do anything."

"We," Yassa repeated, her gaze sharpening. "Who's 'we,' anyway?"

"Most of the business-owners," the girl said, "have a kind of informal meeting." She shook her head. "We've talked about trying to do something, even something drastic like fight Constantine and his crew. But most of the shop owners are older, and their kids are either gone as far from here as they can, or they've been working here their whole lives. Constantine's men are like you, veterans, or some who've just been doing that kind of work a long time. We couldn't beat them in a stand-up fight."

"We should go back to the ship," Sanders said. "We can regroup, maybe get some heavier weapons."

"No good," I said, shaking my head. "It won't take them to long to trace us back to the *Wanderer*. They'd have people waiting for us there, and if we tried to fly out, they'd take us out with their laser weapons before we could leave atmosphere."

"We can't stay here much longer," Bobbi warned. "They'll get around to looking in this place eventually."

"I know somewhere we could all go," Natalia said. I looked over to her. She was a bit hesitant, as if she were debating whether or not she was doing the right thing by telling us. "There's this friend of my father's. He kind of runs the meeting. If you're Constantine's enemies, he'd definitely want to help you."

I glanced at Yassa and she shrugged expressively.

"It can't get much worse," she opined.

"Oh Jesus," Sanders moaned. "Don't ever say that."

"All right," I told Natalia. "I guess we haven't got much choice. Take us to this friend of yours."

Milton Amador was the antithesis of Seth Baturin, Natalia's father. Seth had been large and loud and hairy; Milton was small and bald and mouse-quiet. But if I'd been forced to pick which was the more dangerous of the two, I'd have definitely gone with Milton. He'd told us that he owned the town's soy and algae farms, which made him the largest food producer on the planet.

"I know we all grieve the loss of our friend," Milton was saying from his stool by the stone fireplace. "But this is just the cumulation of the outrages we've endured under Constantine."

"Is 'cumulation' a word?" Yassa whispered from my elbow and I shrugged my ignorance.

I saw nods from the other civilians gathered in the Spartan, almost archaic living room. There were a half dozen of the actual members of what I'd come to term "the Meeting" with a capital "M," plus a few adult children or senior employees. They were the ones who ran every major business in Freeport, and you could see that relative wealth in the quality of their clothes, not in comparison to ours but to what the other locals we'd seen wore. Handmade and homespun were the rule, rather than the exception, but they had fabricated pieces as well, and the material was higher tech than average for this place.

All of them were old, again relative to the local norm. On this world, with its background radiation and lack of prenatal nanite injections, people were lucky to break a century; and none the members of the Meeting were under fifty in my estimation. Still, they had listened intently to Natalia's story, despite her youth, and then to my telling of the rest of the tale. They'd allowed me to bring Captain Yassa into the hastily-assembled quorum, but the others had been exiled to a storage building out back, out of sight of the road and hopefully far from the minds of the goons still searching the city.

"What can we do about it, though?" The woman was sharp-faced, with high cheekbones that reminded me of Sophia. Her hair was dark but streaked with grey at the temples, and age had etched its lines and creases into her face. I seemed to recall from the introductions that her name was Ichiko and that she ran the town's only overland shipping operation. "Constantine clearly meant this atrocity as a warning to all of us, a demonstration of what he'll do if we oppose him."

"You and yours," Milton leaned towards me as he spoke, "are soldiers, mercenaries Natalia told us. If you were to…" He paused, considering his wording. "…take care of this matter for us, I know we would all agree to any reasonable price."

Shit.

"Um…" I stammered for a moment, trying to figure a way out of *that* without revealing why we were here. Yassa saved me.

"There are only eight of us," she reminded Milton, "and all our heavy weapons are on our ship, which we can't get to now since Constantine's people will be watching for us."

"Milton," Ichiko objected, standing from her stool and turning on him, face going even paler, "you can't make that kind of decision on your own! This could get us all killed!"

"Yes," another of them agreed, a pudgy and baby-faced man with dark, curly hair; I thought they'd called him Jamie. "And where are we supposed to get the money to pay them? Constantine has drained us dry!"

"Hold up for a second," I finally got my thoughts together. "Killing Constantine would probably be satisfying as hell, but what's the end goal here?" I looked around at the faces of the business owners and saw helpless shrugs. Except Milton.

"To get Abuelo's attention," he correctly surmised, confirming my first impression of him.

"Right. But if we start killing his people, it may be the wrong kind of attention. We need a plan; and for that, we need some intelligence. You guys basically make this city run, what can you tell me about Abuelo and where he might be?"

"I think he's dead," Jamie declared flatly, his tone pessimistic. "Constantine killed him just like Abuelo did to Crowley, and took over."

"You keep saying that," Devereaux scoffed. He was a slender man with dark skin and delicate features, but his tone belied them with its harshness. "It still doesn't make any sense. Abuelo didn't make any secret when he killed Crowley…hell, he had a town meeting and announced it. Why would Constantine pretend the boss was still alive?"

"That's because everyone *hated* Crowley," Jamie argued. "Constantine isn't stupid; he wants us to think that eventually, Abuelo will come back and straighten everything out because that will keep us in line."

"If Abuelo's dead," I cut in, trying to take back control of the conversation, "then we'll have no choice but to confront Constantine. But we need to find out for sure. Can *any* of you tell me anything useful about where he might be?"

"He has a place somewhere north of town," Ichiko put in. "I don't know where, exactly, but he's rented my trucks several times and the drivers have always headed north up the mountain pass." She shook her head. "He always uses his own drivers, never my guys."

"That's good," I encouraged her. "When's the last time he had any deliveries made out there?"

"A few months ago, just after the last time he was in town. A heavy-lift cargo shuttle landed at the port, and Abuelo rented *all* of my trucks. His men cleared everyone off the landing field, didn't let anyone see what they were unloading, then they hauled it up the road as quick as they could drive."

I shared a look with Yassa. That might have been the artifact.

"The road'll be guarded," she warned. "And we can't fly out there, not with the laser defense system in place."

I ruminated on that for a long, silent moment.

"The lasers," I said, finally. "They're near the town?"

"Yes," Milton supplied. "A few kilometers past the landing field. It's very heavily guarded at all times, though."

I nodded. I'd figured that. But...

"The power for the lasers," I asked him. "Where does *that* come from?"

"The same reactor that powers the town," he replied. He frowned, confused. "Why do you ask?'

10

On most colony worlds, the fusion reactors are built well outside the cities for safety reasons. Freeport's reactor was just across the Bijesan River, less than a kilometer from the center of the town, squatting in an ugly, utilitarian collection of buildfoam and concrete and surrounded by a cement block wall. It rested on blasted, black pavement in a plain of what had been forest before they'd cut down the trees there and fusion-formed what was left to flatten it for the reactor facility.

It wasn't very large as these things went, certainly not as big as the one on Demeter, nor as heavily guarded. But then, on Demeter, I'd had a company of hardened, combat-tested militia, two DSI agents and two physically-augmented Fleet Intelligence super-commandoes. I looked over at Brandy Yassa and the three former Marines and two ex-resistance fighters with her, huddled under the bridge abutment on this side of the Bijesan, none of them armed with anything more potent than a handgun, and wondered what the hell we were doing out here in broad damn daylight.

Well, broad daylight was an exaggeration; it was the middle of storm season on Thunderhead and the sky was grey and surly, darkening in the east as the sun sank lower behind the veil of clouds. But it seemed way too bright and I was sure someone was going to trip over us at any second. There wasn't any choice, though; the delivery truck was scheduled for when it was scheduled, and adjusting that would have looked too suspicious.

I tried to wish the clouds thicker and the sun further down, but it hadn't quite worked by the time I got the signal from Ibanez, who was on lookout at the crest of the river bank, that the truck was in sight. I waved to get her attention, then motioned across the river. She nodded and then leapt like a gymnast, catching the concrete lip on the side of the bridge, just in reach there where it met the road.

I held my breath as I watched her swing upward into the support framework on the underside of the bridge, finding purchase on an I-girder with her fingers and heels and scrambling spider-like to the first pier cap. She was almost inhumanly agile, swinging out with one arm to the cement cap and grabbing hold. She swung into it with a smack of impact I could just make out over the rushing of the wild river beneath her and I gritted my teeth.

But she was okay, and she quickly crawled over the obstacle and grabbed the I-beam on the other side of it. By the time I heard the rumble of the truck overhead, she was almost to the other side of the narrow, swift cataract and I'd stopped worrying she'd fall into the rocky, roiling river. This would have been so much easier if radios would work on this damn planet without a tight beam laser uplink to a satellite. Or if it had been possible to see the other end of the bridge from here without being spotted by the gate guards.

She was on the opposite bank, crawling up on her belly to the crest of the rise, watching the truck as it passed across the bridge, heading for the lone gate in the block wall around the reactor complex. I couldn't see it from where I was, but I'd gotten a good look at it when we'd been moving into position through the high grass at the edge of the river, over a three hour period from late morning to early afternoon. That wasn't as long as it sounded on a planet with an eighteen-hour rotation, but I was glad we'd brought some ration bars and water along, and that it wasn't raining that hard.

I sat there watching her watching them, envisioning the security blockhouse built into the wall, imagining the truck halted at the imposing metal barrier across the road while the guards checked their work order on computers hardwired to the systems across the river in town. I'd thought about just cutting the superconductive wires where they crossed the bridge in their polymer sheath, but that would have probably brought someone to investigate. This was riskier, but worth it.

"What is taking so fucking long?" I muttered.

"Patience, Commander," Yassa said from right next to me. I glanced over in surprise; I hadn't noticed her move, but she was crouched beside me on one knee. "Things happen when they happen."

"Yes, ma'am," I said, grinning despite the tension I felt. I was glad I'd brought her along.

Then I saw Ibanez motion for us to move.

"Go!" I hissed at the others, scrambling out from under the abutment and up the bank to the road.

The truck had already moved through into the bare, black lot beside the reactor facility's loading dock, but the gate was still up. I sprinted across, feeling the others on my heels; once I reached the other side, Ibanez popped up and joined us. The bridge was only about fifty meters from end to end, but it felt like we were out in the open forever and my eyes were locked on the closed, tinted polymer window of the security blockhouse. I slammed into the door of the guard shack with my shoulder and it popped open readily, sending me half-stumbling inside.

Kane was there, leaning over the computer console, a lead from it plugged into one of his 'face jacks, while Bobbi Taylor kept watch, pistol held down at low ready in both hands. The two men who'd been crewing the guard shack were on the bare, cement floor, unconscious, gagged with strips of cloth and secured with industrial plastic ties that were the closest we'd been able to come to flex cuffs.

"Any problems?" I asked, looking between the two of them. Yassa came in behind me, while the others crouched in the cover of the closing gate.

"Other than being stuck in the back of that truck for two hours under a load of crates?" Bobbi shot back, grinning. "No. These two didn't see a thing until Kane smacked them down, then he basically sat on them while I choked them out."

"Security vids are looped," Kane told me, unplugging from the board. "We're clear."

That was practically a soliloquy for him.

"All right," I waved for them to follow me outside. "Bobbi, you're on point." We needed to move before Ichiko's drivers finished unloading the truck. "Go, quick."

She trotted off toward the loading dock, and the rest of us followed at a regular, ten-meter interval. I stayed towards the middle of the pack and Yassa brought up the rear, taking her role as the "platoon sergeant" of our understrength squad seriously. We all had our guns out, though we would prefer not to use them; if we started killing Abuelo's people, this was going to get out of hand very quickly.

We moved up the ramp, past the drivers, who were dutifully loading crates of raw soy and spirulina onto a pallet jack. They looked at us with worried glances but didn't stop working; they knew who paid their salaries and Ichiko didn't strike me as an easy-going boss. I waved at everyone to spread out once we were inside the building, motioning for Victor and Kurt to stay and guard the loading dock entrance, then signaling Bobbi to head up the block staircase that led out of the storage bay and into the main reactor facility.

We'd gone over the layout for this place with the woman who ran the city's largest construction firm. She hadn't actually built the reactor; it had been shipped in pieces in several heavy-lift cargo shuttle loads decades ago by Freeport's founder, a woman named Aliya, who had been Crowley's predecessor. But Val, the construction boss, had been a supervisor when the cement block walls had been built around the reactor and the cooling chambers and the turbines, and she had a pretty good idea of what the layout must be still.

It was a mostly automated setup, as far as I could tell from the files we'd been able to pull up on the local 'nets, which weren't much. It wouldn't require more than a half dozen technicians on duty at any one time, maximum; Val thought two shifts might be there at once, to allow hot-swapping for breaks. That meant maybe as many as a dozen workers, and an unknown number of security guards. I was betting not too many; there wasn't any incentive for anyone in Freeport to sabotage the plant. It was their lifeline as much as Abuelo's.

In fact, we'd had that very argument when I'd explained my plan…

I moved past Ibanez and Sanders and put myself third behind Bobbi and Kane as we went up the stairs, pausing at the closed door there. I motioned for Kane to hang back, then nodded at Bobbi. She yanked the metal handle and jerked inward and I ducked through, my pistol held at low port. The hallway on the other side of the door curved off to the left, and I heard the sound of voices in a room a dozen meters down, off to the right.

"Break room," I mouthed to Bobbi as she came through behind me, motioning for her to hold up the others.

I listened for a moment, trying to get a sense of how many of them there were. I made out two voices immediately, a man and a woman talking loudly, laughing about something. I concentrated, trying to make out the words.

"…the fucking coolant stack and I said, Gordo, you can't flush the reactor just because…"

Then mumbling and cross-talk and more laughing. The man, and the woman, and one other, quieter, chuckling perhaps politely, as if he or she wasn't as amused. I turned back to Bobbi and flashed three fingers. She nodded, then turned and waved the rest of the squad up. Kane, Sanders and Ibanez moved in and I directed them to deploy up and down the hallway from the loading dock door to just short of what I figured from the markings on the wall was a break room. I'd rather have bypassed it entirely, but there was no way around without being spotted.

Yassa came in last, and I relayed the information to her silently, then motioned for her and Bobbi to come with me. I sidled up to the breakroom entrance, looked to Yassa, then took a deep breath and swung around the corner. The two talkative ones didn't even notice us at first, still gabbing away, sitting hunched over a folding table, hands clasped on the warmth of steaming coffee cups. One of them was a well-fed, squinty-eyed, pinch-faced, probably fortyish man dressed in clothes expensive enough that I knew he was a valued employee but sloppy enough that I also knew he wasn't a manager. The other was a woman, maybe a bit younger, soft-featured and doe-eyed, with a mouth that seemed a bit too large for her face and clothes similar to the other talker.

The last one at the table saw us, though, the one who'd laughed politely. *He* wasn't a technician or a manager. He wasn't soft, and he wasn't dressed like a worker. His head was shaved and he wore dark utility fatigues and an armored vest and had a large handgun strapped in a holster across his chest. His eyes opened wide, hands shifting off the table, away from the steaming ceramic mug and towards that gun.

"Don't fucking move," I said, aiming my pistol between his eyes.

The heads of the other two snapped around and I saw the man's mouth start to open in a shout. I stepped across the room in the space of a second and put a hand over his mouth. He flinched away at the touch, but he didn't cry out. The gunman glanced between me and Bobbi and Yassa and his hand didn't move off the table.

"Everyone stay quiet and stay calm," I cautioned, reaching over to yank the security officer's pistol from his holster, "and no one will get hurt. Nod if you understand."

All three nodded, the two workers jerkily, obviously close to panic.

I looked around the room. Besides the cheap, green-topped table, there was a counter with a drink dispenser and a food processing unit, partially-empty plastic crates of soy and spirulina stacked next to it. Shelves above the counter held cups and plates and a bulletin board on the wall displayed a streaming series of dates and announcements. There was one other door in the room; a bathroom maybe.

"Check there," I told Bobbi as Yassa and I patted the three of them down.

The security guy had some kind of short-range 'link in a pouch on his vest, tied to an earpiece. I figured it must be tied to an internal communications system and I pocketed it, shoving the earpiece into place so I could monitor if there were any announcements. The others had nothing but a few Tradenotes and some sort of pass on lanyards around their necks. I took those, too.

"You don't know who you're fucking with here," the gunman said in a low, soft voice. His eyes were focused on me when he spoke, and he didn't seem nearly as scared as he should have been.

"I think I do," I countered, trying to keep my voice cool and emotionless.

Across the room, there was a startled cry and then a commotion and I looked over to the interior door Bobbi where I'd sent Bobbi. She lunged inside and I heard a smack of something hard hitting flesh and a grunt of pain. That was when the bald guy made his move, and I *should* have seen it coming. The table flipped over as he moved, sending hot coffee spraying everywhere and I swung my left hand at him instinctively, slamming his own pistol into the side of his head even as his fingers closed on the collar of my jacket.

He went down with a croak, clutching at his head, and the woman worker screeched in fright and surprise, dodging away, while the pudgy male made a break for the door. He made it to the doorway before a dull silver arm clotheslined him across the throat and he went down with a thump of a hundred kilos hitting a tile floor, choking and gagging. Kane stepped across in front of the entrance, staring at the prone worker impassively. Yassa grabbed the woman around the neck and covered her mouth with a hand as she put her into a choke hold, cutting off the blood at her carotid artery, only letting go once the woman had gone limp.

I sprinted over to the bathroom and pulled the door open. Inside, I saw another guard, a blond man dressed in the same black clothes except with his pants down around his ankles, lying unconscious on the floor next to a toilet, a bleeding cut across his cheek and a silver handgun on the floor next to his outstretched hand. Bobbi covering him with her pistol, an amused look on her face.

"Well," I sighed, kicking the pistol away, "that could have gone better."

"Could have been worse, too," Yassa reminded me as she pulled out a handful of plastic ties. I tossed the handgun I'd taken off the guard onto the counter, then grabbed a few from her.

"Get them all tied and gagged and stuff them in the bathroom," I said, walking over to the bald guard and twisting his hands behind his back, then zip-tying them in place. He moaned softly, blinking his eyes rapidly and trying to struggle against me without much strength. I secured his ankles, then pulled a strip of cloth out of my jacket and gagged him.

When I straightened, I could see that Yassa had done the same to the woman and Sanders and Ibanez had come inside and were tying up the male technician.

"Not him." I pointed at the man in the expensive clothes. "Bring him over to the chair and sit him down."

While the others hauled the bound and gagged woman and the two guards into the bathroom, Sanders and Ibanez yanked the one Kane had clotheslined up by his arms and dumped him in one of the chairs next to the overturned table, his dress shoes dragging through puddles of cooling coffee. He was still coughing, trying to get his breath back, his face turned purple by the shock and exertion and his eyes fogged over with fright. I crouched down in front of him, my pistol still in my right hand.

"You," I smacked him lightly in the cheek with my left palm and he focused on me with a look of abject terror, "pay attention. What's your name?"

He didn't respond other than wheezing hoarsely, so I slapped him a bit harder and he yelped.

"I said," I repeated, emphasizing each word, "what is your name?"

"Sanford," he gasped, still trying to get his breath, his voice scratchy and pained. He smelled of stale coffee, sweat and urine. "Maynard Sanford. Chief Engineer…"

"Maynard, I need to know how many more people are at the plant tonight. How many engineers, how many more security guards?"

He hesitated and I let the muzzle of my pistol drift forward towards him.

"No one has to get killed tonight, Maynard," I assured him. "I'd rather no one did. That's why those guards," I nodded at the two security officers being dragged into the bathroom, "are still alive. If I go on into the plant and there turn out to be more people than you tell me, I might be forced to shoot someone. If you tell me the truth," I raised my left, empty hand in counterpoint to the one with the gun, "then I can arrange things so that we do what we have to do and no one gets badly hurt."

He blinked, looking at the others thoughtfully.

"Okay," he said, still breathing hard. "Okay. There are three more engineers on duty tonight, Janice, Will and Patrick." His eyes took on a pleading look. "They're good people, please don't hurt them."

There was a twisting in my guts and I suddenly felt a sense of shame.

"I'm not going to hurt them," I promised him, meaning it. "How much security?"

"Just two more," he answered. "I don't know their names, just some of Constantine's goons. Only one who ever talked to us is Joe, the bald guy." He glanced towards the bathroom again, where Joe had been deposited. "They're probably up in the control room with the crew, unless they're sneaking off to get stoned." He shrugged. "It's a boring job out here for them."

"All right." I stood and holstered my sidearm. "We're going to gag you and put you in there with them. Stay in there until someone comes to check on you and you'll be fine."

He didn't respond, just staring into space now, a tear trickling down his cheek. I waved for Sanders to come and get him.

"We need to get this done before someone figures out we're here and calls for reinforcements," I said, once the bathroom door was shut on the captives. "Speed over stealth from now on. Bobbi, get us to that control room."

Past the break room were a pair of dark, unoccupied offices, and beyond them was another door, this one larger and heavier. Bobbi looked at me for the go-ahead, then pulled it open, and with its soundproof seal gone, the whine of the Magnetohydrodynamic turbines filled the hallway. The corridor ahead was narrow and dimly lit, a passageway between the water lines that brought coolant in from the river and the turbines that ringed the reactor core.

The lines that carried power to the city, and to the defense lasers, were underground; they had to be, not for aesthetic reasons as on Earth or more settled colonies, but simply because the weather here would have played hob with anything overland. I'd seen the insulated pipe that took them across the river, and I'd briefly considered simply cutting it there, but that would have taken a lot of time, and it would have been too easy and simple to fix, as well as lacking in subtlety. This had to be done just right to deliver the message we were trying to send.

I was just behind Bobbi as she passed by the service alcove where the water pipes fed into the structure of the reactor and split off in each direction, so I saw the flicker of movement there nearly the same time she did. She acted before I could, though, lunging to the left with a single, powerful spring and swinging her pistol in a downward arc. The security guard hadn't even been facing her; he was standing with his back to the passageway, hiding the drug patch he had slapped onto his forearm from anyone that might pass by. I could see it in the shadowy gloom of the alcove as he collapsed, not even reaching for his gun.

Bobbi relieved him of his weapon and was already putting the first plastic tie in place before I covered the three steps between us.

This one was younger than the others, with a beard shaved into a zigzag pattern and holographic tattoos on his face in a style that hadn't been popular on Earth since before I was born. He looked barely conscious and I wasn't sure if it was from the blow to the head or the drugs.

The others were starting to bunch up behind us and I waved them back, signaling for everyone to keep a look-out.

"Getting stoned just like Maynard said," Bobbi murmured, gagging the man and shoving him back into the shadows. "Just one guard left."

Another twenty meters and we reached the metal grillwork staircase that led up above the turbines to the control room. Bobbi paused, crouching low in the shadows at the side of the stairs. I looked up through the open grillwork and I could see the lights shining through the transplas windows of the chamber; it was basically a large, sheet metal box bolted into the side of the buildfoam dome, with superconductive control fibers collected inside polymer sheaths running into it through a half dozen different ports.

I could see one of the occupants through the windows, sitting carelessly on top of a panel, resting his head against the window. The others were too far back for us to get a look at. There was only one door to the room and they were going to see us coming once we hit the last flight of stairs. Nothing to be done about it.

I nodded for Bobbi to go, and she started climbing as silently as you could on decades-old metal steps. The creaking was probably inaudible over the high-pitched background whine of the turbines and the gentle rumble of water through the coolant pipes, but it seemed as loud as a snare drum to me from just behind her. The head in the window didn't turn around though; my eyes were locked on it, willing it not to turn.

Then Bobbi stepped onto the last flight of stairs and the head *did* spin towards her, and a figure dressed in black fatigues stood up beside it, eyes wide and white on a dark face. I snapped my pistol up, aimed at the top of the window, just above their heads, and fired off three quick shots. Red flares speared across the ten meters between me and the window, then the warheads hit and detonated with a spray of liquid metal that melted through the light panels in the compartment's ceiling.

Both heads went down abruptly as the lights inside flickered and flared, and then Bobbi was smashing her shoulder through the door and yelling in a loud, braying voice for everyone to get on the floor. I was a few step behind her, nearly tripping on the high step up into the room, my eyes dancing around from the three technicians huddled on the floor, hands covering their heads, to the last security guard, flat on his butt, hand straying near his holstered pistol.

"Put your fucking hands on your head!" Bobbi was bellowing, her weapon trained on him, feet planted wide in a stable stance that nearly trampled on one of the prone engineers. "Don't be stupid!"

"I made a promise," I said softly, and his eyes flickered toward me and the gun in my right hand. He was young, like the other one, too young to know better. "I promised I wouldn't kill these civilians." I gestured with my left hand at the two men and a woman on the floor, cowering and in one case, crying. "I didn't make any promises about you. I've killed people who'd done less to deserve it than you."

He looked at me for a long moment, breathing hard, and I could see that he believed me. That was smart; I was telling the truth. His hands went behind his head and Bobbi darted forward to grab his weapon from its holster.

"I should start a fucking collection of these," she mused, looking at the same model of polished, silvery slug-shooter that the others had carried.

"Kane!" I yelled behind me, holstering my pistol and quickly tying the guard up. "Get in here!"

The cyborg clomped inside, his footsteps heavy and hollow on the metal. He'd worn a long-sleeved jacket, gloves and fatigue pants on this mission as a concession to the need to stay inconspicuous, and the audible evidence of his mass seemed incongruous somehow. He didn't give the engineers or the guard a second glance, just moved to the main reactor control panel. It was decades old and showed it, all the displays two-dimensional flat-screens reporting the reactor core status, the turbine speed, and a dozen other pieces of data I didn't have the training to understand.

Kane fished an interface connection from his pocket, plugging into a receptacle on the console and into the jack on his left temple. He stood motionless there for a moment, his biological eye flickering back and forth as if he were surveying a landscape I couldn't see. Then it closed and his mouth moved almost in a prayer. And every display on the control panel went dead, followed by the lights winking out together. Red emergency lighting popped on immediately, powered by backup batteries; and the guard and the engineers gaped at us in horror.

I'd almost gotten used to the whine of the turbines, and it took me a moment to realize that it was gone. There were no alarms, no indicator lights, nothing; but by the time Kane unplugged from that console, the reactor had flushed its core and every business in Freeport that depended on it for power was dark and dead. As was the laser defense system.

"You can't do this!" One of the engineers, the woman, implored us, her eyes wide, her face pale. "People will die without power!"

"The reactor systems," I told her, "are infected by a self-consuming net-worm. It will run itself out in one rotation of Thunderhead, and then you'll have control back of the system."

"But..." She shook her head helplessly. "Why? Why would you bother to do all this just to shut it down for a day?"

I gave my answer to the security guard, who was watching me with hate in his gaze.

"Tell Abuelo that Randall Munroe wants to talk to him." I motioned for the others to head down the stairs and began backing out to follow them. "Tell him I'll be waiting."

11

"So," Sanders asked, lying flat on one of the beds and staring up at the plain, white ceiling, "how long have we been waiting now?"

"About a half hour longer than the last time you asked," Bobbi replied, trying unsuccessfully to hide her annoyance. She didn't look up though, just kept playing the game her 'link was projecting to the hotel room's entertainment tank. From what I could see, it had something to do with lizards and mushrooms.

"Power's been on for a full day now," Ibanez commented. She was on the floor next to the bed in a full split. She'd been "stretching" for over an hour and I was beginning to think it was compulsive behavior.

Over in the suite's small dining room, I could see Victor and Kurt arm wrestling on the table, sweat beading on their foreheads as neither was able to make much headway against the other. I'd been timing it in my head, and they'd been deadlocked that way for over a solid minute. Kane hadn't spoken or moved from where he stood in a corner of the room for six hours, and I was pretty sure he was sleeping.

"Abuelo is off wherever, out of town," Captain Yassa reasoned. She was stretched out on the other bed, opposite the one Sanders had claimed, her boots off but her pistol still at her waist. "It's going to take a while before they get word to him and then he can get word back and then they contact the address we left on the message server at the *Lucky Bastard*. Just take advantage of the down time."

"We're lucky Mr. Amador got us a room," I said. I was sitting at the small desk the hotel provided almost as an afterthought in an establishment that didn't exactly cater to business travelers, staring at my 'link and wishing for it to chime. It was connected to the hotel's hardline datanet, so as soon as the message came through, I'd see it. "We could still be stuck in his shed, sleeping on sacks of algae flour."

"I'm not complaining about the room," Sanders assured me. "Just feels...weird somehow."

"I still think," Bobbi spoke again, sounding no less annoyed, "that we should have taken advantage of the air defenses being down and took the ship on a recon run. We could have spotted his hideout from the air and called that orbital strike down on it."

"And then not known whether or not he actually had a Predecessor artifact," Ibanez pointed out. "Isn't that the mission?"

"We could have landed afterward and done a bomb damage assessment." Bobbi's response was half-hearted. She knew she was wrong but she was antsy and frustrated and I sympathized. I wasn't going to bother to argue with her because I'd had the same thought myself.

"When's the food supposed to get here?" Victor asked from the dining room, rubbing his right arm. Kurt was shaking his out, and I realized I hadn't seen who'd won.

Damn.

The door chime sounded and eight heads snapped around, Kane's included, and Yassa and Bobbi both drew their guns. I stood and stepped quickly over to the panel next to the door, pushing the speaker control.

"Who is it?" I asked, my hand resting on the butt of my weapon.

"It's Arjun," a young, slightly high-pitched voice answered. "I brought your dinners."

I let out a breath. Arjun was the son of Dev Modi, the owner of the hotel; we'd been introduced two days ago, when Milton Amador had brought us to this place to hold up. Arjun was a young teenager, but he did a lot of gopher work for his father, including delivering meals for room service.

"Put the guns away guys," I said. "Don't want to freak the kid out."

I hit another control on the door panel and it opened with an audible click of the lock releasing. The door swung aside and Arjun pushed a wheeled cart into the room, loaded down with covered plastic trays; I felt heat coming off of it from the warming elements.

"Thanks, little dude," Victor said, grinning. "I'm starving."

Arjun smiled, a little nervously. "There should be plenty for all of you. I'll come back for the cart."

He backed away, and I was about to close the door behind him when Victor picked the lid off the largest of the trays and the world exploded.

There was light so bright that it burned out all sight, and sound so loud that it hit like a blow, like I'd been smashed in the face with a brick, and I felt the floor against my back. I couldn't breathe, I couldn't feel and the only thought that penetrated the dull, hollow ache between my eyes was that we were all dead.

But the dull ache didn't fade into darkness and the feeling started to return in waves of discomfort, and as the light flashing in front of my eyes began to settle into a blurry normality, I realized exactly what had happened. Concussion grenade.

Rough hands yanked my pistol out of its holster and patted me down for other weapons, finding the polymer knife I kept in my thigh pocket and taking my 'link as well. Then they backed off and I laid there motionless, waiting for what I was sure would be the kill shot. I tried to scoot backwards as a tall, slim form loomed over me, but I couldn't quite move yet.

"Relax." The voice was deep and gravelly, reminding me of my Drill Instructors in boot camp. "You wanted my attention...well, you got it."

That voice…it reminded me of something else besides my DI's from Boot. It reminded me of *someone* else. I gathered my strength and pushed myself upright, blinking to try to clear my eyes. The dark blob solidified, cohering into a lined, weathered face with close-cropped dark hair and piercing dark eyes.

My jaw dropped open and I sat there, transfixed, unable to form an intelligent thought.

"It's been a long time, Ty," Master Gunnery Sergeant Cesar Torres, United States Marine Corps (Retired) said to me, smiling as broadly as I had ever seen him.

All I could do was gape in utter disbelief and finally mumble one word.

"Gramps?"

I downed the tequila in one gulp, shuddering slightly as it burned in my chest and clenching my fingers against the grain of the wooden table, feeling the rough spots where it had been inexpertly sanded by whoever had made it.

"Go easy on that," Gramps cautioned. "You're still woozy from that flash-bang." But he grabbed the bottle and refilled my drink anyway, topping off his own as well.

My head swam for a moment in support of his warning and I waited till the feeling passed before I took a second, more cautious sip.

"You're the one that gave me my first drink of this shit," I reminded him, saluting with the glass.

He laughed at that, a look of nostalgia passing across his harsh, craggy face.

"On that trip to Baja for your sixteenth birthday," he recalled. "Your mother was *not* happy when she found out about that."

I took another sip and glanced around the luxury suite to make sure we were alone. He'd dismissed his guards when he'd brought me in here, leaving the others recovering in our room, but I was feeling a bit paranoid and slightly guilty for not explaining things to them before he'd hustled me out.

"You know," he went on, face clouding with memory, "when I was a boy, before the anti-aging treatments and the nanite injections, most people never lived to know their great-grandchildren. It's still so new, the idea that there's a generation that was born two hundred years ago that hasn't died yet. I wonder if anyone has thought of the implications…"

"Gramps," I interrupted him, "how the hell did you wind up here?"

He leaned back in his chair and took a breath as he directed his thoughts back to the present. I'd seen it before; it was something a lot of older people had to do. Their brains were crowded with memories, and sometimes it took them a while to sort through them.

"With Patrice and the weight of the Corporate Council after me," he explained, "there weren't too many places in the Commonwealth that would be safe for me. The night you killed Konrad and I dropped you in Vegas with the street surgeon who changed your face, I caught a private shuttle to McAuliffe Station and bought a spot on a transport to Belial."

He smiled grimly, then swallowed a sip of his drink before he went on. "I had a good deal of money stashed away in case of emergency. It cost nearly every bit of it to buy passage on a freighter heading for the Pirate Worlds. I landed here with a few hundred in Tradenotes, a single suitcase and an utter lack of any plan."

"You went to work for Crowley," I presumed. I'd heard that much.

"Cesar Torres was dead," he confirmed, "and I had no desire to spread that name around even out here. I gave Crowley a fake name, but he always called me 'Abuelo,' grandpa. So Abuelo I became." Gramps looked down into the dregs of his drink. "I was desperate, out of options. I…did things that made it hard to look at myself in the mirror."

"Been there," I muttered, feeling so much older than twenty-five.

"Finally, I'd built up enough support among the townspeople, and among many of Crowley's subordinates, that I was able to convince them that we'd all be better off without him."

"Was Constantine part of that deal?" I wondered.

He nodded grimly. "He commanded the loyalty of quite a percentage of Crowley's enforcers. It was necessary to promise him a position in my regime in order to secure his support for my little coup." He looked uncomfortable, so different than the incredibly self-assured, larger-than-life figure who'd been the closest thing to a father that I'd been allowed to have. "I was hopeful that I could keep a close eye on him and make sure he didn't indulge in the brutality I'd seen in him."

"That hasn't worked out so well," I informed him drily.

"That's what Dev Modi told me when I tracked you here. I'll deal with Constantine," he promised. "I think the rebellion among the business owners in town will be enough leverage to pry his supporters loose of him. They may not give a damn about morality, but they understand the bottom line well enough."

I had so many things I needed to talk to him about, so much I needed to ask, but suddenly, I couldn't think about any of that. It was being squeezed out by emotions I'd pushed down seven years ago and never let back out.

"I've missed you, Gramps," I said, feeling tears welling up in my eyes and not quite believing that I could still cry after everything I'd seen.

He pushed himself up from the table and walking around to me, pulling me into a hug. I did cry then, unabashedly, feeling my shoulders shake as tears poured down my cheeks, not just because I'd missed Gramps but for all that had happened in-between. I cried for Konrad, for the innocence I'd lost when I killed him, cried for Johnny and Captain Kapoor and everyone who'd died while I survived, for the innocent people who'd died on Demeter, and for Captain Yassa and the others who'd come back but never truly came home.

"It's okay, son," Gramps said, patting me gently on the back the way he had when I was eight and my first dog had died. "It's okay. I know."

"Sorry," I said, shaking my head and wiping my eyes as I slowly pulled away from him. "Sorry, it's just…a lot has happened."

"I heard about Demeter," he told me. "I've tried to keep tabs on you when I could."

"I live there now." I laughed at the absurdity of it. "Crazy, right? I spent the worst times of my life there, but it's the closest thing I have to a home."

"Not crazy at all." Gramps poured another shot. "You asked me why I was here, Ty. Now I have to ask you the same thing. You came looking for me, but you didn't know it was me you were looking for." He locked eyes with me. "So why did you want to find Abuelo?"

"Someone from the Corporate Council found me," I replied, not even considering lying to him. "They're blackmailing me into working for them or they'll tell Mom where I am."

"*Hijo de puta*," he mumbled, looking away as the implications of what I was saying sunk in. He stepped backwards, coming up against the table and resting against it for balance. "They know."

"How did you find it?" I wondered.

"I didn't," he said absently, face still clouded in shock. "Crowley had it; he'd had it stuck away in warehouse for years, didn't have any idea what it was or what it was worth. I stumbled across it after I killed him."

He said that so casually, I thought, like it didn't mean anything, like it was the most natural thing in the world. But who was I to judge?

"Gramps," I asked, "what the hell are you going to do with a Predecessor artifact?"

"Exactly what they're afraid I'm going to do with it." His voice was harsh with anger, though I was sure it wasn't directed at me. He stood straight again, looking intimidating in his black fatigues, a large handgun holstered on his belt.

"The Corporate Council has been running the Commonwealth

like a shadow government for decades now, since the time of the First War with the Tahni. No one's been able to do a damned thing about it because no one could ever put together a force powerful enough to threaten their control. Until now."

"That sounds...a bit ominous."

"They're above the law, Ty," he said. "You know that better than anyone. They have moles in the military, in the intelligence community, in the Patrol..."

"Yeah," I admitted ruefully, thinking of Cowboy. "I have some experience with that."

"The only way to stop them is to build a force they can't reach and can't interfere with. That's what I'm going to do out here, in the one place they don't control."

"You think you can do that out *here*?" I asked, not trying to hide the disbelief in my voice. "What *is* this thing anyway? What do you think it can do?"

"I've brought in every researcher I could buy for love or money." His lip curled in a derisive smile. "Some I had to smuggle out of Corporate labs. But as near as they can tell, it's some kind of weapon. And I think they're pretty close to figuring out how to make it work."

I stared at him, wondering if maybe everything that had happened had imbalanced him. This whole plan sounded like the rantings of one of the conspiracy theory loons who paid for their own show on the indie nets back in Trans Angeles. But everything that he'd said about the Corporate Council, I knew was absolutely true. And *someone* high up in their Executive Board obviously thought that what he had was dangerous; otherwise, they wouldn't have sent me.

"Show me."

12

I stared out the back of the swaying, bucking cargo truck at the cold, grey dawn hanging over the black trunks of imported Earth trees that lined the rough, rutted mountain road. I'd been on Thunderhead for nearly a week, I reflected dolorously, and I still hadn't seen the sun.

I tried not to look at the others; I knew they were staring, and I didn't blame them. We were crammed onto parallel bench seats lining both sides of the truck's cargo compartment, with a guard at the end of each of them "for our protection," according to Gramps. At least they weren't pointing their weapons at us, though they were both armed. Gramps trusted me, but that didn't yet extend to any of the others. I'd offered to ride with them to make sure there were no incidents along the way.

"This Abuelo," Yassa said from beside me, too softly for others to hear over the shuddering vibration of the truck, "is really your great-grandfather? The one you told me about on Inferno? Master Gunnery Sergeant Torres?"

I nodded. I hadn't had time to spell the whole situation out yet, but I had told them that much before we'd loaded on the truck.

"He came out here to get away from my mother."

"She makes friends wherever she goes, doesn't she?" Yassa chuckled.

Then she fell silent for a moment, frowning. I thought she'd gone off into a funk, which I'd seen her do a few times since we'd arrived. Then I felt her hand on my forearm and looked down at it.

"Munroe," she said, "have you wondered about the odds of this being a coincidence?"

I squinted at her in confusion. I was still reeling from everything that had happened and my mind wasn't working at its fastest.

"Think about it," she insisted, her grip tightening. "Cowboy must have known who Abuelo was. He had to. That's the real reason he sent you instead of going himself, because he knew Torres wouldn't kill you."

"Jesus," I hissed, feeling my gut tightening at the idea. It was just the sort of thing Cowboy would do. But… "What did he think would happen when I found out?" I objected. "I'm not going to kill my great-grandfather, and he's not going to hand over what he considers his best chance at fighting the Corporate Council just because I ask him nicely."

"That part, I don't know," she admitted. "I just think you need to keep your head on a swivel. Things aren't what they seem."

"I trust Gramps," I told her flatly. "He's the one thing I could count on when I was growing up. I'm not ready to believe he's changed in just a few years."

I noticed one of the guards staring at me and I stopped talking. I'd told Yassa I trusted Gramps, but I didn't know which of his men were loyal to him and which were still in Constantine's pocket.

I could feel the trucks shuddering in the wind as the little caravan climbed higher into the mountains, and the trees began to thin out; the ones that still remained grew shorter and thicker, huddling against the constant battering. The trees weren't native, and neither was most of the flora or fauna in the river valleys. The immigrants had brought it with them and it had taken over the places it could live, just as we had. Up here though, in the wind, only the native life remained. I could see it growing flat along the rocks, coloring them green and red and purple as it clung to them and melded with them, breaking down the outer layer and feeding on it in ways that I couldn't imagine and no Commonwealth scientist had ever had the chance to study.

Nothing moved above ground up here except us, and we were moving pretty slowly, swerving in the grip of the wind. The guards didn't seem bothered by it, but I could see Sanders, Victor, Kurt and Ibanez looking around nervously. Bobbi chewed on a ration bar with a bored expression; she never seemed to let anything get to her, but that was probably half a put-on. Kane might have been asleep for all I could tell, and Yassa...I couldn't read her well enough to know.

Once we began heading down the other side of the pass, the raging howl of the wind died to a distant whistle behind the sheltering rock and I could feel the relief like a general exhalation of a held breath from everyone in the truck. The road became rougher and muddier the lower we went, as trees grew taller and the soil thicker, until the rock walls closed in on the road from either side and we were driving through water almost a meter deep. Sprays fanned off the rear wheels on either side and I could feel a few drops touch the bare skin of my face.

"Hope it doesn't get much deeper," Sanders said, eyeing the road behind us, "or we'll be swimming back here."

The guard sitting on the seat across from me looked at him with amusement but said nothing.

The water didn't get any deeper and in fact, everything around us seemed to get dryer, the soil thinning out and turning sandier as the rock became redder and coarser. I even thought I saw a bit of the system's primary star peeking out from the cloud cover, though that could have been wishful thinking.

The road began to twist and turn with the course of an old river bed, and I was restless enough that I checked the time on my 'link. We'd been driving for nearly five hours and it was well past midday here; I realized all I'd eaten today was a ration bar and I was starving. We'd also only had one bathroom break and the pounding of the rough road hadn't helped matters.

I was about to say something to the guards about taking another stop when the truck began to slow down. Curious, I moved to the open end of the cargo compartment and hung off an inside handle as I leaned out and saw we'd stopped at what looked like a gate built of mesh wire fence across the road. Ahead of us were two other vehicles, an all-terrain rover that I knew was Gramps---he'd offered me the chance to ride with him---and another truck that was carrying Constantine and the rest of the party.

"Sit down," the guard on my side grumbled.

I ignored him, watching as the woman at the gate spoke to someone on a hardwired line, then moved aside and hit a control to lift the gate.

"I said," the guard beside me grunted, yanking on my arm and pulling me back inside, "sit the fuck down."

He was short-tempered and ugly, with a face like a bulldog and a neck about as big around as my thigh. I went with the pull and used it to spin me around into a left hook that smacked him across the temple next to his right eye. He went down heavy and hard, thumping into the metal floorboards of the truck. I shook out my sore knuckles and looked down at him with a snarl twisting my face.

I wish I could say I calculated that move, that I did it to establish my position as Abuelo's family to those who might still be loyal to Constantine. But the truth was, I just don't like being pushed around, whether it was by my mother or some mook in the Pirate Worlds who thought a gun made him a tough guy. Luckily, I have the genes and the training to keep that inclination from getting my ass kicked on a regular basis.

The other guard swore and made a move for his gun, but Kane's hand covered his and the butt of the gun and squeezed, just slightly. The man's eyes went wide and his face paled.

"Slow," was all Kane said, and he let loose just slightly.

The guard released his fingers from the gun butt and moved his hand away. Bobbi reached over and pulled the pistol out of its holster, and Kane moved his hand away from the man, sitting back as if nothing had happened. Yassa relieved the one I'd hit of his weapon and he groaned in response, hands going to his head.

I fought against a smile. It was nice knowing they had my back, particularly Kane.

I felt the truck start moving again, and I grabbed the handle to steady myself, looking down at the guards. The one I'd hit stared up at me, some rage in his eyes but more than a little fear as well.

"What's your name?" I asked him. He didn't respond and I put my foot on his chest and pressed down slightly. "What's your name?" I repeated.

"Julio," he grunted resentfully.

"Julio, I'm not here to start any trouble," I said, trying to keep my voice calm despite the surge of anger and adrenalin that was making my pulse pound in my head loud enough to drown out the truck engine. "But don't fuck with me. Abuelo wouldn't like it, and more importantly, next time I'll kill you."

I stepped off Julio's chest and he started to roll to his knees, but Bobbi nudged him with the barrel of the gun she'd appropriated.

"Stay down."

The trucks rolled on for another three or four kilometers down the road, and as they did, the walls widened out around the road, and I could tell that we were driving into what had to be a fairly large box canyon. Grass grew high in the fields beside the road, and I nearly laughed when I saw the first horse grazing on it. It was an appaloosa, spotted white on black, its legs long and powerful. Then there was another, an Arabian, all black, pure speed in every sleek line of him; then a mare, pure white.

I did laugh then. Gramps had always loved his horses; I think it was one of the few indulgences for which he dipped into the family fortune. Getting them here, though...

Yassa whistled, low and appreciative.

"Beautiful animals," she said.

The trucks curved around and parked, and out the back I could see the ranch. It looked like it took up the better part of at least twenty or thirty hectares, with the main building three stories tall and hand-built from local wood, with a brick chimney. Storage sheds and barns stretched out behind the main ranch-house and bunkhouses spread out on either side, connected with concrete pads to keep the walkways out of the mud even in the wet season.

The walls of the canyon were over a kilometer away, maybe two, but at their crest I could see the swiftly turning vanes of windmills. I figured that was what powered the place; on this planet, wind was a reliable natural resource.

I hopped down, the soft, springy soil absorbing my fall, then motioned for the guards to follow me.

"Ditch the guns," I told Yassa and Bobbi.

Yassa stripped the magazine out of hers, cleared the chamber, then tossed it into the back of the cargo compartment. Bobbi shrugged and did the same, looking as if she thought it was a stupid idea, but following orders anyway.

I could see the guards' eyes follow the arc of the pistols into the truck as they climbed down, but they kept moving away, especially when Kane dropped down.

"What do you think of my home away from home?" Gramps asked me, walking over from his rover. Behind him, Constantine stood with arms crossed, staring at me with a carefully blank expression. I wondered what it was concealing.

"It must have cost you a fortune to get those horses out here," I commented.

"Oh, it wasn't *that* bad," he demurred. "I bought them as fertilized eggs and used an incubator." He shrugged, smiling at the animals as he watched them across the pasture. "It's not home without horses." He turned to his personal bodyguard, a slender, older man with soft features and a look of hardened experience to him. "Nathan, please take our guests to the dining room and get them something to eat. They're probably hungry after that ride. I have business to discuss with my great-grandson."

"Yes, sir," Nathan said, his voice softly accented.

He waved for my people to follow, and they looked to me for confirmation.

"It's fine," I told them. "Get some food, I'll be there to brief you soon."

The rest of Gramps' party dispersed to their jobs and I followed him back around the ranch-house to the largest of the barns, a huge building constructed from sheet metal. The main doors were open at the moment, and I could see horses in a few of the stalls inside. One of them, a huge Percheron, tossed its head as Gramps entered the barn, scraping at the floor with a giant hoof.

"Easy, boy," Gramps said to the gigantic animal, reaching over the stall door to pat him affectionately on the neck as we passed.

"What are you going to do about Constantine?" I asked, following him through to a set of huge, metal double-doors set with an expensive-looking biometric lock.

"What do *you* think I should do, son?" His tone and the look he gave me were familiar; I'd heard and seen them many times when we'd been backpacking in the Rockies or horseback riding in the high desert and the time had come to make a decision about where to set up camp or which trail to take. He was assessing me the way the black-hats had in Force Recon training.

"You can't keep him around." My voice was matter-of-fact and clinical, but all I could see was Constantine's fist going through Seth's chest. "He won't put up with you slapping him down or demoting him; he'll act against you. You have to either send him out on the next ship, or kill him."

"You speak so easily of killing another human," he said, pressing his hand to the lock's ID plate. "The last time I saw you, you were near panic over killing Konrad. Have you changed so much, Ty?"

"I'm not Ty anymore," I told him by way of reply. "My name is Munroe."

The doors began to swing outward with a low-pitched hum of servos straining against the mass of the BiPhase Carbide plastrons. A light flickered on inside what looked like some sort of cargo elevator about ten meters square, and Gramps stepped inside, his footsteps hollow on the bare, metal floor.

He touched a control on the inside of the front wall and the doors shut with a vibration I could feel in my chest, then the whole compartment shuddered and began to descend.

"When the hell did you have time to build this?" I wondered. He'd only been in charge here a couple years.

"I didn't," he admitted. "Crowley built it to hold the thing over a decade ago. I just built the barn on top of it."

"What was he like?"

"Crowley?" Gramps cocked an eyebrow in surprise at the question. "He was a man who'd been playing a role so long, he became it. He started out as a businessman, but tried to keep everyone in line by pretending to be a ruthless pirate cabal leader. He was never that good at it, and in the end, he lost control."

"We all wind up becoming the people we pretend to be," I said, half to myself.

"I'm beginning to see that."

The lift stopped with a jolt and light flooded in as the doors swung aside. The chamber inside was larger than I thought it would be, probably fifty meters long and half that again wide, and the walls were bare rock; it had started as a natural cavern, and Crowley or someone had dug it out. And dumped something big right in the middle of it.

The thing was alien in a way that nothing I'd seen on the Tahni home-world ever was, something that hadn't just come from a non-human but from a mind totally different than any humanoid. It was a shape that almost seemed to shed my eyes, defying description, but if I were forced to come up with a word for it, I guess it would have been...a seed pod? It was more an idea that came to mind than a specific shape; but once it was there, I couldn't shake it.

My gaze was drawn to it, so much that I almost didn't notice the other people in the chamber. I saw the equipment first, surrounding the thing, things I didn't understand any more than the ship, but at least I could tell they were the works of humanity. I followed the wiring from the equipment back to the computers analyzing it, and from there back to the half a dozen or so people monitoring it. They all looked around at our entrance, but only one rose from her seat to meet us.

She was an older woman, but one who'd been raised on Earth or one of the major colonies, because she didn't look her age. She'd been engineered before birth to be attractive and athletic, so her family had money or power, or both; but she made no effort to accentuate those characteristics and she was out here, responding to either Gramps' offer of money or the challenge represented by the artifact. That told me that she'd either been dissatisfied with the life her status had offered her back there, or she'd disgraced them and had been kicked out to make her own way. Either way, I could empathize.

"Back again already?" The woman asked. "I thought you had problems to take care of back in town."

"Heather, meet my problem," Gramps said, waving towards me. "This is my great-grandson, T..." He stumbled over the word. "...Munroe. Munroe, this is Dr. Heather Erenreich, my chief researcher."

"Didn't know the boss had a great grandson," Erenreich raised an eyebrow as she took my hand in welcome. "Nice to meet you, Munroe."

"You too, Doctor," I said.

"Heather," she corrected me. "Everyone in here's got a doctorate in something-or-other."

"Where in the hell did Crowley find this thing?" I asked, looking back at the pod. It was hard to make myself look away for too long.

"Independent mineral scout brought it to him," Gramps said. "Figured he'd pay more for it than the mining companies."

"I still can't believe sometimes," Erenreich murmured, "that he had the only Predecessor artifact ever found sitting in a hole in the ground for twenty years."

"You've been studying it how long now, Heather?" I wondered.

"Almost two years," she said, following my gaze to the pod. "Every day of it, just about. Can't tear myself away."

"Two years," I repeated. "Do you have any idea what it is?"

"I know exactly what it is," she said, chuckling. "I wouldn't be much good at my job if I didn't." She stepped closer to the object. I felt a surge of alarm, like somehow just being close to the thing was dangerous, like it would reach out and swallow her up.

She reached out a hand and trailed her fingers across its strangely grooved surface almost lovingly.

"It's a weapon. And I'm pretty sure I know how to activate it."

13

"This thing," Brandy Yassa said softly, turning her glass round and round in her hands, staring at it like it held the mysteries of the universe, "they're sure it's a weapon?"

"That's what they think." I looked around the room again, having to remind myself where I was. It was nearly identical to the den from Gramps' ranch-house in southern Utah, back on Earth. He'd loved that place and it seemed like he'd done his best to recreate it here. "According to this Dr. Erenreich, the thing dates to much later than the wormhole map on Hermes or the message on Mars, maybe as little as ten thousand years ago, which can't be too long before the Predecessors left the Cluster to go…" I shrugged. "…wherever they went to."

"Why does that mean it's a weapon?" She demanded, setting her drink down on the bar. A painting hung behind it, done locally but of a scene that came from Earth, from a place I knew very well. A sandstone arch, blood red in the rays of dusk, with mountains visible through it in the distance.

"Dr. Erenreich's of the school who believe the Predecessors left the Cluster because they were under attack," I explained. "She thinks this is left over from the conflict, mostly because of where it was found, in an impact crater on an asteroid. She says the data the mineral scout recorded when he found it makes it look like the rock is the remains of what used to be a planet in the star's habitable zone."

"That's a little weak," Yassa muttered.

"She's in the Pirate Worlds working for a cabal boss with a bunch of other outcasts," I reminded her. "I wouldn't count on her for rigorous scientific objectivity." I sat down on one of the barstools, hands clenched in front of me. "Anyway, since she's been studying the thing, they've started bombarding it with photons, protons, neutrons, and whatever else they could manage because, hey," I waved a hand, sarcasm heavy in my voice, "when you're dealing with a possible alien planet-destroyer, why not just throw anything you can think of at it and hope for the best?"

"Did anything happen?" Yassa wanted to know, her face turning paler behind her freckles.

"They've begun to detect some kind of activity inside whenever they hit it with modulated microwaves. It doesn't last too long, but it's regular. She thinks if they increase the power, it'll make the thing…" I shook my head. "…do whatever it does."

She glanced at me sharply. "And your 'Gramps'…I mean, Gunny Torres was okay with you telling me this?"

I sighed, looking down at the polished wood grain of the bar. The one in Utah was over two hundred years old and worth a fortune by itself.

"No," I admitted. "He pretty specifically told me *not* to share this with any of you. But you're my XO, Cap."

She didn't respond to that, just closed her eyes and planted her hands flat on the bar as if she was steadying herself.

"You never asked me why I overdosed that day, back in Overtown." Her voice was so soft I could barely hear it over the whisper of the ceiling fan. "Why that day in particular."

I felt my eyes narrowing at the non-sequitur. "I figured if you wanted to tell me, you would."

"I don't *want* to tell you, Munroe," she laughed bitterly, without humor. "But I'm going to. I wasn't suicidal…yet," she amended with a shrug. "It might have come to that. But I kept thinking if I could just get high one more time, maybe I could get my head around things, get everything figured out. I hadn't given up just yet."

"Did you ever try to contact your family?"

"My mother ran out on us when I was eight," she said with brutal matter-of-factness. "My father was a Section Chief on the *Midway*."

I felt like I'd been gut-punched. The *Midway* had been destroyed in the Battle for Mars, before I'd even joined the Marines.

"Sorry," I stammered.

"It was a long time ago." She shook her head dismissively. "Shut up and let me finish. I was in a bad way, but I wasn't suicidal. Then I had a visitor. Someone I'd run into once before, when I was leading the assault on the atmosphere mines of Surtur, the gas giant Loki orbits. We'd been told he was Fleet Intelligence, but I knew he was some kind of black ops commando."

There was a cold numbness in my chest as she spoke, as I began to understand what exactly she was saying.

"He said his name was Roger West," she went on, staring at the adobe walls. "He said you'd be coming to me for help, and he wanted me to keep an eye on you. He said he'd pay me a hundred thousand in Corporate Scrip if I took the job. He never seemed to ask whether I would or not, just took it for granted."

Fucking Cowboy. I should have known he wouldn't leave anything to chance.

"And I knew I'd do it," she went on, and I heard a break in her voice. "I knew that, if you came, I'd go with you, because of all the drugs I could buy with that kind of money. So, I made sure that I couldn't."

"Jesus, Cap," I said in an involuntary hiss.

"That's why I was so furious when you saved me. I didn't want to have to face the choice and now I did. I wasn't going to tell you, but now I have to."

"Why?" I blurted.

"Because West told me some things...he left information for me on a 'link, in that box you brought from my room. I wasn't sure I believed any of it, till now. You can't let Torres fuck with this thing, Munroe. It's a weapon, all right, but it's not the kind he can control."

"What is it? What do you know about it?" My tone was harsher than I'd intended, and I found myself leaning towards her slightly, but the anger was for Cowboy, not her. Rumor my ass, he'd known *exactly* what I'd find here...

"I need to talk to Torres," she insisted, slipping off her stool and facing me. "Get me to see him and I'll tell him everything."

I debated for a moment whether I should force her to tell me first, then wondered if I had it in me to do that to someone I'd considered a friend. I decided I'd rather not find out. I grunted something barely intelligible and headed out of the room, too enraged and hurt to care if she followed.

Should I be? I wondered, somewhere above the emotion. *Did I have a right to be*?

Cowboy wasn't my friend, and he didn't owe me anything when it came right down to it. We'd made a deal, and this was how he'd chosen to collect. If he didn't trust me with everything, well, I didn't trust him for shit, either.

The Captain, though... I guess I didn't feel betrayed as much as I felt gullible. More than one person, Yassa included, had asked me whether I was right to trust her. Maybe I should have asked myself the same question one more time.

I was heading for Gramps' office, the last place I'd seen him before I'd gone to get Yassa from the bunkhouse where the rest of the team was staying, when I nearly collided with Constantine heading up the hallway. He didn't look happy to be here, and I wondered if Gramps had gone against my inclination and advice and told him off instead of waiting and killing him later.

"It's quite the coincidence," he said, stopping and eyeing me sidelong, only centimeters separating us in the passageway, "you being related to the Boss."

I looked him up and down. He wasn't armed, but then, he didn't need to be.

"What makes you think it was a coincidence?" I asked him, keeping my voice carefully neutral. "We needed a job, I knew he'd give me work." I shrugged. "I didn't know how to contact him myself, and we'd already pissed you off."

"You learn how to pull that stunt at the reactor while you were in the Marines?" He asked me, grinning with one side of his mouth. The other side didn't seem to move right and I wondered if he had nerve damage from whatever had taken the arm on that half his body.

"I learned everything I needed to know on Demeter," I told him, and immediately wished I'd kept my mouth shut. It had been my anger talking, the frustration I was feeling, and I'd knew I'd said too fucking much.

His head tilted back slightly and I saw him regard me carefully for a moment.

"No shit," he muttered. "You're *that* Randall Munroe."

He'd been DSI during the war. Of *course* he'd known what had happened on Demeter.

"You know," he went on, eyes narrowing, "I seem to recall there being an arrest order out for you when I was on Inferno. It seemed odd to me that a man who'd just been awarded a Silver Star for valor would have an arrest warrant out on him. And that the Corporate Security Force would be all up in the situation the way they were."

"Yeah, well, I'm out here, doing this, right?" I pointed out to him. "None of us are here because we were angels back in the world."

He nodded slowly, with that half-smile.

"No, we certainly aren't."

"Excuse us," Yassa said, pushing me forward past him. "We have to speak to the Boss."

I didn't look back, but I could sense the man still standing there, watching me.

"You talk too much," Yassa hissed at me as we moved out of earshot.

"I know."

The door to Gramps' office was hand-carved wood, and it was closed. I knocked on it and my knuckles thumped into the solidity of it. Not hollow, it was at least four centimeters thick.

"Come."

The knob was brass and felt cold in my hand as I turned it. The office was large, and currently lit only by a single lamp on the desk. It was also wood. If Gramps could have smuggled all the damned wood in this house back to Earth, he could have sold it on the black market and bought another ranch.

The man himself was seated behind the massive desk, watching a video report on a two-dimensional flat-screen mounted on the desktop. He paused the playback as we entered, eyebrow raising at Yassa's presence.

"What is it, Munroe?" He asked me, his voice somehow twisting around the name distastefully.

"Sir," I said, pushing the door shut behind me, "Captain Yassa has something she needs to tell you."

"Captain Yassa," Gramps repeated. "You were my son's Company Commander, were you not?"

"Yes, Master Gunny Torres," she said, respectfully. "And you were part of our curriculum in the Military Academy."

"The man I told you about," I interjected, "Roger West, the one who sent me on this job, he approached Captain Yassa before he came to me."

"I was a fail-safe," she told him. "West knew who you were and he knew you'd let Munroe into your confidence." She looked down at the floor for a second before her eyes flicked back up and she went on. "I was supposed to make sure he still did the job."

"And how were you supposed to do that?" Gramps asked her, seeming genuinely curious.

Yassa shrugged. "That was left to my judgment. I suppose I would have had to kill you."

Gramps laughed at that, a harsh, rough-edged sound. "Are you sure you weren't an NCO, young lady?"

"I was given some information about the artifact, Gunny," she pressed on, "things that Munroe wasn't told because it would have revealed how much West already knew about what was going on." She licked her lip, the first sign she'd given that she was nervous. "It's not a Predecessor artifact. Your Dr. Erenreich has the right idea; the Predecessors didn't leave the Cluster because they wanted to, they were chased out by an enemy. This is one of the weapons of that enemy."

Gramps had pushed himself up from his seat now, and was circling around the desk. I felt myself tensing, half-expecting him to attack her, but he stopped with his face a few centimeters from hers.

"And how does West know this?" Gramps demanded.

"He didn't say," Yassa admitted. "I have to think it's because the Corporate Council has found more of these things that they haven't told anyone about."

"They're that scared of this thing, are they?" His arms were crossed, his face thoughtful.

"The Predecessors created living worlds," Yassa pointed out. "These things, whatever they were, *chased* them somewhere so far away we can't reach it. You should be scared, too. That's the reason I came out and told you about this, you need to destroy this thing. It's not something you can control."

"What about you, *Munroe*?" There was that emphasis on my name again. "What do you think?"

"Gramps," I said, feeling like things were getting out of control, "I don't know if Cowboy was telling her the truth or not, but I believe she's telling the truth about what he told her. Maybe it is a weapon, and maybe they're afraid you'll use it against them. But this…" I trailed off, waving a hand around us. "This isn't exactly a government research station off in the outer planets somewhere. If you get this thing to work and can't control it…"

"That's why it's this far from the city," he countered. "It's also pretty far underground."

"It was found on an asteroid that used to be a planet. How far out of town do you think is safe enough?"

His eyes bored in on me and I wondered if I'd been a bit too flippant and disrespectful with that question. I could see deliberation behind his dark eyes, and then decision.

"Very well," he said with an almost imperceptible sigh. "Come with me, then."

I shared a hopeful look with Yassa as we followed him out of the office, through the ranch-house's spacious living room and out the large double doors in the front. It was pitch black outside, past midnight local time I judged, and there was a gentle patter of rain on the brick walkway in the courtyard. I felt it dripping cold on the back of my neck and pulled the collar of my jacket tighter.

I wondered for a second if Gramps was taking us back to the cavern where Erenreich was studying the artifact, but instead he led us across the courtyard to a tan, stucco outbuilding between the barns and the bunkhouses. It was smaller, about the size of a storage shed with a heavy, solid metal door and what looked like a sturdy if unsophisticated throw-bolt lock, and I wondered what he had locked away out here.

Then I noticed Constantine and a half dozen of his people had walked out of the house behind us, all of them armed, and they were slowly spreading out across the courtyard. I looked sharply at Gramps, distrust and disbelief warring inside me. He yanked the bolt back and pulled the heavy door open with a grunt. Inside, thrown into shadows in the dim, indirect lighting within the shed, I could see the rest of the team, laid out on a bed of straw, unmoving, unconscious or dead.

I acted on instinct, without thinking for even a second.

Gramps was between me and the only unguarded route out of the courtyard and I push-kicked him in the chest with the flat of my boot, sending him sprawling across the rain-slick bricks. And then I was running.

I didn't look back, didn't wait to see if Yassa was following, I just sprinted as fast I possibly could. I was genetically engineered to be as fast, as strong, as agile as a human could be without artificial augmentation, and I'd kept myself in top shape back on Demeter, so as fast as I could was pretty damned fast.

I heard a shot, then another, and angry shouts, but I didn't stop, just cut around the side of the ranch-house, passing by the back door just as one of the guards stepped through it, gun in his hand, visible to me through the night vision filters in my contact lens despite the darkness of the night. I lashed out with my left hand and caught him across the throat with my forearm, sending him crashing backwards through the door. I didn't stop then, either, not even to grab his weapon. Speed was life, distance was freedom.

I was past the house, past the bunkhouses. I considered for just the space of a heartbeat whether I should try to steal one of the vehicles, but I rejected it; it would take too long and it would be chancy whether they had some sort of ID lock or key card. In the same breath, I rejected a run up the wadi because it would be one long straightaway for kilometers and they'd know exactly where to look for me.

Instead, I headed for a path I'd noticed as we'd driven up: a steep, winding packed-dirt path that was the only way I'd seen out of this canyon on foot. It began about a hundred meters from the house, through the thick grass and I felt as if I were a bug on a plate as I crossed the broad, open space. The horses weren't out there at night; the hands must have put them in the barn, or else they went there on their own once the sun went down. Either way, I was alone and I heard no pursuit, just the sound of my own steady footsteps ripping chunks of dirt and grass with every stride.

I reached the path and the nightmare of endless running turned into a nightmare of endless climbing. It was slippery going where the sand and dirt had washed off the slick rock, and I felt as if I was losing a centimeter for every two I climbed. The fatigue hit me then. I hadn't slept for two days now and I'd been working on a massive dose of adrenaline that was starting to run low. My thighs burned with the effort and I had to lean forward and use my hands at some parts of the climb.

Did they know I was here? I wondered, but I couldn't look around to find out. It would slow me down, and in the end, what did it matter? I had the choice to fight, run or give up. I felt a twinge of guilt at making that decision without regard for Captain Yassa, but it hadn't been made on a conscious level and it was too late to change it now.

They couldn't have drones, I knew, not with all the EM interference. That was something. They'd have to send human eyes to find me, and I was betting I was better at this than any of them. I just had to keep going, get far enough away, find a place to hold up through the night, and then I could take the time to think about my next move.

In minutes, I could see the top, could feel the wind picking up as it swept down across the plains over the lip of the box canyon. I gritted my teeth and dug in with hands and feet, just for a few more meters. And I was there, standing above the canyon, looking down into the depths of it at the glowing lights of the ranch. No one was following me. That was strange, unless…

I looked around and had just noticed the glint of the lights from below on a line of metal stakes sticking out of the ground when something was screaming inside my head in a banshee wail of pain and confusion, and everything went black.

14

The first clue I had that I was still alive was how badly my head hurt. I'd had a bad concussion before, bad enough that only several hours in an auto-doc saved my life, but this wasn't like that; this was like someone had stuck red-hot needles through my ears and into my brain. I pressed my hands against my head and moaned softly, not wanting to open my eyes yet.

"Sonic stun field."

I pried one eye open, the right one with the night vision lens, and saw that I was somewhere dark, with sandstone walls close around me and the barest hint of light leaking through from somewhere behind. Crouched beside me was a hulking figure with bare metal glinting in that light on the side of his head.

"Kane?" I rasped. I rolled over onto my side, getting an arm underneath me as I slowly and painfully rose to a sitting position. "I thought they got all of you."

"Got the others," Kane told me, face impassive. "Sonics, like the fence you hit back on the path. Sonics don't get me."

I understood. He probably didn't have physical ear canals anymore.

"Where are we?" I asked him, looking around. "Is this a cave?"

"Three kilometers from the fence." He was frowning now, and I sensed it was because he was being forced to talk too much. "I watched. Saw you get hit, took you here."

"How long was I out?" I wondered. I didn't have my 'link.

"Three standard hours," he snapped off.

It was about dawn. *Shit.* That meant Yassa hadn't made it out. It also meant they'd had plenty of time to comb the hills above the ranch.

"Have they been searching for us?"

He shook his head. That meant they either thought we'd gone down the wadi or else they didn't think it was worth it to look because we were dozens of kilometers from town and couldn't possibly get back on foot.

I took a deep breath and steadied myself. I was thirsty, and my head was still throbbing. I came up to a crouch and duck-walked to the front of the cave. It was about three meters deep and wide, and maybe a meter and change high. Outside, I could see the primary star piercing through the cloud cover near the horizon, sending a faint orange glow through the pervasive grey, and the wind was just a faint whistle that moved clouds of sand across the bare, polished rock that stretched out over my whole field of view. It would pick up later; it would howl across the plateau and scour it like a sander.

I scooted back out of the opening, feeling exposed. It might not have mattered, since they weren't searching and couldn't use drones, but it made the hair stand up on the back of my neck to be out in the open.

"I need some water," I muttered, cradling my head in my hands.

"Back here," Kane motioned towards the back of the cave.

I moved back on hands and knees as the ceiling grew closer and closer to the floor, until I began to hear the faint dripping. At the very furthest corner of the cave, at a spot where it was less than half a meter high, was a hollowed-out bowl of rock with a small pool of water fed by a slow but steady drip from out of the wall.

I swallowed down several handfuls and gradually, the pain in my head began to fade. I pushed myself back up to where I could sit down comfortably, up near the entrance.

"My great grandfather," I said half to Kane and half to myself, staring out at the morning, "thinks I'm trying to plot against him, to keep him from using the artifact as a weapon against the Corporates." I shrugged. "And maybe I am, now. The man I knew when I was growing up wouldn't take a risk like this."

"People change." The two words seemed to contain more feeling than anything Kane had ever said to me. I didn't look back at him, though; I felt like it would make him uncomfortable.

I was going to have to take a risk myself. There was only the two of us, and we couldn't stay here very long.

"Kane," I asked him, "do you think you could make it back to the spaceport on foot?"

It was a longshot. I knew I couldn't do it, not against the hurricane-force winds, not for the ten or twelve kilometers of open ground he'd have to take to bypass the road through the wadi and avoid the guard gate there. It would take me days, and I'd die of hypothermia. But I didn't have an isotope reactor implanted in my gut and a pair of bionic legs that never got tired.

"Twenty-three standard hours," was his answer. I didn't ask if he could find his way. If he thought he couldn't, he wouldn't have just volunteered. "Still got the air defenses."

"Twenty-three hours." I nodded. "In twenty-three hours, I'll have them down." He didn't say anything, and I looked over to see an expression of doubt on the human side of his face. "If I don't," I clarified, "you can take off, sell the ship and use the money to do whatever the hell you want to yourself."

He didn't have to think about that for very long. "Need the codes."

I looked him in his green eye, trying to read his expressionless face. The ship was only authorized to admit me or Yassa. It had seemed like a prudent decision not that long ago, when I had no reason to trust him. I still didn't want to trust him; my track record for that had been spotty lately.

"There's an override." The words seemed to be coming from somewhere else, from someone else, because I didn't want to say them. "I set it for an emergency. Type in the numeric 11-4-30, then it'll ask for a spoken password. It's 'Sophie.' That'll get you in."

"And do what?" It wasn't a bad question. I wished I had a good answer for it.

"The ship's armed. If I don't contact you and say differently, start hitting the ranch house when you're in range. And take out the main barn, bury it in the rubble." I snorted. "Then you can land and see if any of us are left alive to haul out."

He didn't question my judgment the way almost anyone else would have. At the moment, I appreciated that. Instead, his question was more of a practical nature.

"Leave at sunset?"

I nodded. "Sunset."

It was hard to walk, hard to stand, and even hard to *see*. The wind battered me as if I were trying to walk into the ocean against the incoming crash of waves, and I leaned into it, sheltering my eyes with one hand. Particles of sand abraded my exposed skin and kept trying to work their way into my eyes and mouth; I wanted to squeeze my eyes shut, but I had to keep my right one open to see where I was going and I wished it would just rain since that would be less painful than the sandblasting.

Kane had left an eighteen-hour day ago, but I'd waited till now to head back towards the ranch because no matter what happened, it wouldn't take me twenty-three hours to shut down the defense systems. It technically wasn't sunset yet, but it was dark enough that it didn't really matter. I was starting to envy the cyborg at this point, and I was half-sure I'd gone off on a tangent and would never find the canyon when I very nearly tumbled over the side.

Squawking involuntarily in a tone high enough that I was very grateful no one else was around to hear it, I fell to my hands and knees and dug my fingers into the crumbling sand at the edge of the cliff. Stretched out below me, I could see the lights of the ranch gleaming upward, astonishingly bright and yet quickly swallowed up in the haze and dust hanging over the canyon. Once I had my breath and composure back, I did my best to look up and down along the canyon wall. I couldn't use the path back down because of the sonic trap they'd installed there, which meant doing this the hard way.

There. Down another fifty meters or so, there had been a collapse of part of the canyon wall, and it had left an angled, sandy slope down the side. I couldn't have climbed *up* that, but I might be able to travel down it. I moved slowly across those fifty meters, hunched over, trailing my right hand on the ground and keeping my eyes on the edge. It took what seemed like hours and when I reached the collapsed section, I nearly balked at how steep and unstable the edge looked.

This would be a damned silly way to go, and I had to remind myself that luck wasn't something you could count on. I'd survived Demeter, but that didn't mean I was going to keep rolling sixes. I could fall off the side of this cliff and Sophia would never even hear how I died. I winced as I thought of her waiting for me back on Demeter, going nuts worrying. Of all the things for which I was currently feeling guilty, leaving her to be part of this stupid shit ranked pretty high. She'd offered to come, very nearly *forced* me to let her come, but I'd reminded her that there wasn't anyone else who could do her job if she left. I was glad she wasn't along because it was bad enough worrying about people I didn't even like that much who were counting on me to save their asses.

Sighing out a breath I couldn't hear over the wind, I lowered myself down from the cliff edge to the platform of collapsed sandstone over two meters below. My boot soles slipped on the wet, bare rock and I yelped again as I grabbed at finger-holds and barely kept myself from tumbling down the slope.

"What the hell are you even going to do once you get down there?" I muttered aloud, trying to distract myself from the climb. "You don't have as much as a fucking sharp stick and there's got to be thirty people down there." True, only about half of those were armed guards; the rest were ranch hands, but they'd probably fight if Gramps told them to.

Foot and hand on a hold before I moved. Down a meter, down two meters...

"Have to get a weapon," I grunted, then swore as I nearly tore a fingernail off trying to gain purchase on slick rock. But did I want to kill anyone? They hadn't killed any of us yet, as far as I knew. Did I want to cross that line, and maybe give Constantine ammunition to convince Gramps he should take off the kid gloves?

Loose sand and I was sliding, falling, biting off a scream, sure I was dead. Then my foot caught on something and wrenched my leg upward and I lunged forward desperately, grabbing at sand until I found a rock and pulled myself back up. I sucked in air, feeling sweat trickling down my back under my fatigue shirt and jacket, my arms and legs shuddering with the strain.

"Damn it, damn it, damn it," I panted. Getting tired, had to get down before I fell down.

I twisted my head around and looked beneath me. Maybe another twenty meters, still far enough to kill me nice and dead. There was a fairly flat platform maybe three meters down, though, and then the base of the cliff fanned out into a cone of dirt and sand. I kicked away and clenched my teeth, bending my knees to absorb the impact as I hit. I slammed my shoulder into the side of the cliff and grabbed at it with battered fingers, steadying myself.

I maneuvered onto my butt and slid down the last few meters, feeling the wet sand and dirt cold under the seat of my pants. I hit the bottom, taking a deep, shuddering breath and enjoying the feel of the ground firm under my boots for just a moment.

That had been so much harder than I thought it would be.

I felt a wave of weakness, heard my stomach rumbling and realized I hadn't eaten since the day before yesterday. I forced the thought down and tried to focus.

The barn was between me and the ranch house, the lights from it a halo around the metal structure. I was about to push myself up and make a quick run for the barn when I saw a flicker of shadow between it and the house, and I froze, trying to blend into the side of the canyon. It was a single figure, a man dressed in dark clothing. It had to be one of the guards; there was no reason for any of the ranch hands to be out this late. He moved farther to my right, past the edge of the barn, and I saw a long gun of some kind cradled in his arms.

They were ready for trouble. And if I knew Gramps, he wouldn't have people patrolling alone. Sure enough, it was only a few seconds before I saw the second guard, a woman, trailing about five meters behind the first, also armed with a rifle or carbine. I slowly and carefully slid forward, easing down on my belly to minimize my thermal profile in case they had enhanced optics. My fatigues were designed to be resistant to night vision gear, but my head wasn't.

They were circling the barn and I had a sense that their circuit was going to take them all the way around the edge of the canyon. The question was, would they see me before I could get to them? I couldn't run now; I was locked in to this position. If I tried to exfil, they'd spot my movement and either start shooting or call for help. No radios, though, and they were outside the buildings, so no hardwire comms either. If I could take them out, no one would realize they were gone for a good while.

I realized with a start that I'd just decided to kill them. One guard, I might have been able to subdue silently without killing him; but with two in the patrol, I'd have to kill at least one and probably both. It didn't bother me on a moral level. These people weren't innocents, and I knew most of them had come in with Constantine. They'd supported him while he'd bullied and abused the shop owners in Freeport. But it was crossing a Rubicon with Gramps, and despite the conviction I had that he wasn't the same man I'd known, I didn't want to be put into a position where we'd be trying to kill each other.

The man in the lead walked right past me only a few meters away, never looking down, only out in front of him. My old instructors at Recon Selection would have torn him a new asshole for being that sloppy. I let him pass, my head down, the whites of my eyes mostly facing the ground, sensing rather than seeing the woman trailing him as she walked by me.

Was she a bad person? Did she have a father, mother, or children somewhere wondering where she'd gone and what had gone so wrong with her life that she'd had to run away from them?

Those thoughts fled from me as I moved into action, pushing up from the ground and pouncing on her from behind in one, broad step. My right arm snaked around her throat and my left hand grabbed my right wrist, squeezing hard just before I threw her off her feet backwards. She went down hard and I landed on top of her back, planting a knee there and then twisting backwards with all the weight and strength of my upper body, jerking back on her neck until I heard the muffled crack, felt it through my arm and had to shut off the sickening twisting in my gut.

The one in front had kept walking, seven or eight meters ahead, until he'd heard the thump of her body hitting the ground beneath me. He'd stopped then, starting to look around, unsure where the sound had originated.

"Lara?" I heard him start to say, just before Lara's neck broke and she went limp.

I wanted to grab her gun, but there wasn't time. Instead, I let her limp and lolling neck fall from my arm and I charged at him. His eyes finally settled on me, on the totally unexpected threat and the gruesome sight of his comrade lying dead; I couldn't see them go wide because they were hidden by his night vision glasses, but I saw his jaw go slack and I saw the muzzle of his rifle begin to swing around.

Seven meters. That's what I'd been told in Force Recon training: if there was a threat within seven meters of you, human or Tahni, and you didn't already have your gun pointed at it, safety off, you probably wouldn't be able to get off an accurate shot before it reached you. We'd gone over that scenario in shoot-houses a few times and I'd gotten to where I could manage a shot even under seven meters, but my reflexes were pretty far above average. This guy wasn't even average.

I slammed into him with a full body block, smashing the receiver of his rifle into his face as I took him to the ground. He spluttered, tried to shout, but I had one hand pushing the gun against his face and the other wrapped around his throat. He had one hand trapped beneath the gun and was trying to hit me with the other, trying to grab at my eyes. I freed up my left leg and pistoned my knee up into his groin.

The sound that escaped past the vice grip of my hand on his throat was a hoarse ululation of agony, and the strength went out of his hand where it was trying to wrap around my face. I ripped the rifle free of his hands and smashed the butt downward into his face. There was a crunch of breaking bone, and the beginnings of a scream before I brought the rifle down a second time, then a third, into his throat, his temple, his skull. Over and over until he wasn't making any sounds, until he wasn't struggling, or moving or breathing.

Then I rolled off of him, wiping the blood out of my face, spitting and coughing at the taste of it in my mouth, trying not to puke at the coppery taste and the smell of the dying. Jesus, would I ever be *done* with this? Was this really the only thing I was good at?

I clenched my teeth against the rising bile and the adrenalin-fueled shudders and began stripping the corpses of anything useful, working quickly to avoid anyone else wandering out there and noticing the movement. Their rifles were an old design, a century out of date. I'd never seen one outside a museum but they were childishly simple and easy to fabricate out of local materials and, more importantly, so was their ammo. They fired rocket-assisted rounds like my pistol, but these were totally unguided and you couldn't control or adjust the warhead, or the range. A small, caseless charge kicked them out at a high enough velocity to kill point-blank targets until the rocket motor could take them up to their maximum speed. The sights were rudimentary, but they could be synced with the night vision glasses the guards had been wearing.

I slung one over my shoulder and held the other in the crook of my arm as I pulled spare magazines from their tactical vests and stuck them in my thigh pockets. I grabbed the woman's night vision goggles; the man's were smashed into fragments. She'd had a knife as well, and that went into my jacket pocket. The man had been wearing a black, brimmed hat; it had come off when I'd hit him and I grabbed it and pulled it onto my head.

I wanted to keep searching them, but time was ticking down in my internal clock and I knew I had to move. I rolled both of them onto their stomachs to reduce their heat signature and reflective surfaces, then sprinted across the open ground to the barn.

My shoulder hit it harder than I'd intended and I winced at the solid thump it made. The livestock doors were closed, but there was a side door open, a smaller one for workers, and I could see that it was dark inside. I edged through it, pushing it shut gently behind me, hearing the click as it closed. I waited there for a moment, scanning around with my night vision lens but seeing and hearing no one.

The floor was bare concrete, the interior walls cement block, and I could see the bales of hay piled from floor to ceiling just this side of the main doors. Somewhere deeper inside, a horse snorted and another whinnied softly in reply. I brought the rifle to my shoulder and stalked slowly and carefully down the center aisle, everything lit an incandescent green through the infrared filter of the cheap night vision glasses.

I could see the swaying motion of the horses pacing restlessly in their stalls, could see the glowing glint of the eyes of a barn cat where it sat watching on a stall divider, tail swishing fitfully, but of people there was no sign. The elevator to the lab was unguarded, and why wouldn't it be? Those doors would take kilos of hyper-explosives to breach, and they'd only open willingly to Gramps.

I left them and moved towards the front exit, still trying to gather the threads of the plan hanging loose in my head. I needed to get to the others and get them out, get them armed and take out the laser defense net so Kane could bring the ship in and we could get the hell out of here. I didn't have anything more detailed than that because I didn't know anything else. I didn't know if they were still being held in the same building, didn't know if they'd be conscious, didn't even know if they were still alive.

I should have been panicking. If I'd had any sense at all, I would have been panicking. I was probably going to die, and as I wracked my brain trying to figure out which bad decision had led me to this, I thought at first that it had been when I'd agreed to take Yassa to Gramps to warn him about the weapon. But then I realized that he'd already had the others rounded up by that point, probably before I'd even had a chance to talk to Yassa. Maybe he'd have let me roam free a bit longer or maybe not, but he never intended to leave anything to chance from the minute he'd found out why I was on the planet.

Which meant the bad decision that had started all this in motion was trusting Gramps with the truth in the first place. There was something liberating in that. If I couldn't trust Gramps, then I'd have to treat him like an enemy. And if there was anything I knew, it was how to deal with the enemy.

15

I could see the storage shed from where I crouched in the shadows inside the front entrance to the barn. I was about two meters back from the door, staying out of the harsh glare from the floodlights on the back of the ranch-house maybe fifty meters away. There were two guards in front of the shed, and I recognized them from the truck ride out here: Julio and his partner, decked out in armored tactical vests and carrying rifles. They milled around, appearing and disappearing from view as one or the others would lean against the side of the shed or walk around the side.

Why only two, I wondered. If they were still holding everyone in the shed, why wouldn't they have the building surrounded, just in case? Hell, why wouldn't they have every available gun out waiting for me?

Because you've been gone nearly two full days, I reminded myself. *They think you're either dead or on the run, and they've probably searched this whole place from bottom to top four times, if I know Gramps.*

I sat still for a moment and tried to think the way he did. He'd sent people to check for me at the sonic fence, and when they hadn't found me there and hadn't found me hiding on the grounds in the canyon, he must have assumed I'd gone down the wadi, maybe climbed up the side to hide from their vehicles. They might still be looking there, for all I knew. He had a lot of men here, but he didn't have an unlimited number, and they had to eat and sleep too.

Unless he'd had time to call in extra people from town...

Shut up, I snarled at myself. That line of thought led to paralysis by analysis.

I had to take a risk.

I thought about just sniping both guards from here. It would be a tricky shot because they were walking back and forth, screened by the side of the shed about half the time, but if I timed it right, I might be able to get both of them. But these rifles weren't exactly silent, or low signature, and Gramps probably had security cameras at the back of the house. Maybe no one was watching them right now, but if anyone heard a shot, they'd start checking them. People would come, and I didn't have enough firepower to take on all of them.

That left only one thing to do, and it was stupid and ballsy enough that it just might work. I straightened up, pulled the brimmed hat low over my face and walked out the door, carrying my rifle loosely, casually, my gait slow and unconcerned. I was less than ten meters from the shed when they noticed me, and I could see the one I'd punched squinting against the glare of the floodlights as he looked my way. He still had a nasty-looking bruise on the side of his face.

"Ben?" He asked doubtfully. I didn't know who Ben was. Maybe he was the guy I'd taken the hat from.

"Julio," I grunted quietly. His piggish face relaxed a little as he received confirmation that I was who he'd thought I was, and his brain filled in details he couldn't make out yet.

Five meters.

The thinner guy, the one who wasn't Julio, turned towards me a bit more and frowned.

"Hey..." He started to say something, and I had the sense that it wasn't going to be anything I wanted to hear.

I was at three meters when I levelled the rifle at them and they both froze, stock-still, confused.

"What the fuck?" Julio blurted. "Watch where you're pointing that!"

"Sling your weapons," I told them. "I don't want to have to kill you, but it won't keep me up nights if I do."

Julio gaped at me, only just then realizing who I was.

"If you shoot us," the other guy said, not obeying but not pointing the gun at me either, "you'll have everyone out here looking for you." He was trying to sound defiant, but the tremor of fear in his voice spoiled the moment.

"I'd rather not have that happen," I admitted. "But I'll take my chances if it does." I let the corner of my mouth turn up. "I can guarantee neither of you will be around to see whether or not they kill me." I jerked my head toward the door of the storage building. "Or, you sling your weapons, open up the door and we all go inside. I tie you up, leave you there alive, and unharmed, and I'm somebody else's problem." I shrugged. "They'll probably get me anyway, right? But you two will be safe."

I tightened my grip on the rifle and put the slightest pressure on the trigger pad. If one of them made a move, I thought, maybe I could shove the muzzle up against their body to muffle the shot.

Julio was sweating, and the other guard, who I was starting to refer to in my head as "not-Julio," was glancing furtively back and forth between the two of us; I thought he was wondering if he could count on Julio to back him if he tried to take me on. I had a sense of shifting probabilities, a feeling of the balance of the situation changing that maybe came from the Marines or maybe from my more recent experience as a cop. I acted, taking another risk.

I crossed the distance between me and not-Julio in a step, then bent at the knee and swept his legs out from under him with a swing of my calf across his ankles. He went down on his back and I pinned his rifle against his chest with the sole of my boot, still pointing my own weapon at Julio, who'd taken an instinctive step back. The one on the ground wheezed as I pushed the breath out of his chest, putting more of my weight onto the foot against his rifle's receiver.

"Julio," I said quietly and calmly, "sling your weapon and open that door before I lose my fucking patience."

Julio gave a jerking, hesitant nod, and slowly and carefully took his hand off the rifle's pistol grip, using the fore-end to move the weapon to his shoulder, and raising his hands palms up. I motioned towards the door again and he slid over sideways towards it, still facing me. He reached over and threw the bolt back, the sound solid and metallic, then gave it a solid push. The door swung open with a squeal of protest, and I found I was holding my breath, hoping desperately that they were still inside.

"Munroe?" I heard Bobbi Taylor's voice and felt the breath hiss out of me. "Is that you?"

She was curled up in a corner, arms hugging her knees, and propped against the wall next to her were Victor and Kurt, and all three of them looked like they'd been worked over; fresh bruises marked their faces and arms and their fatigues were torn. Ibanez and Sanders had been huddled together in the opposite corner and both looked scared, though Ibanez was doing a better job of hiding it. I wanted to ask them what had happened, but I forced myself to concentrate on the business at hand.

"Inside," I told Julio, motioning with the barrel of my rifle. He stepped hesitantly through the opening and Bobbi unfolded from her spot in the corner and jumped up to meet him, a look of determined fury on her face and her fists balling up. "No," I said sharply. "Just take his gun and get him tied up."

She looked like she wanted to argue with me, but she grabbed the rifle off his shoulder, and then pushed him back against the far wall. With Julio disarmed, I reached down, grabbed the rifle off of not-Julio's chest, and used the sling around his back to yank him up off the ground. He squawked in discomfort but managed to get his feet underneath him. I pulled the rifle off of him and used its muzzle to shove him none-too-gently into the storage building.

The others were had come to their feet now, and Victor and Kurt took not-Julio by the arms as he stumbled inside, following Bobbi's example and patting him down for weapons.

I took a careful glance around outside before I pulled the door partway shut and moved into the shed. Bales of hay and tubs of soy and spirulina were piled into the center of the room, and stray bits of dried grass littered the bare cement of the floor, but there was nothing handy that I could see to use to tie up the two men.

"Here," I handed Victor not-Julio's rifle, then tossed the one I'd been carrying slung over my shoulder to Sanders. He caught it almost gingerly, but seemed to come to himself as he began checking the load and the safety.

I saw that Bobbi and the two brothers had stripped the tactical vests off the prisoners, so I pulled out the switchblade I'd pulled off the woman I'd killed and passed it to Carmen Ibanez.

"Cut their shirts into strips," I told her, "and use them to tie them up and gag them. Hurry."

I turned to the others and motioned to the tactical vests that Bobbi and Kurt were holding. "Sanders, Bobbi, put those vests on, and their night vision glasses, and get outside, just in case someone happens to be watching from the house."

They wouldn't pass more than a cursory examination, but it was better than nothing, and they sure looked a hell of a lot more likely than the giant Viking Brothers.

Once the two of them were posted outside the door, I went over and supervised Ibanez and the Simak brothers ripping the guard's shirts apart and binding them tightly. Julio seemed relieved that I was keeping my word but not-Julio was angry and frustrated almost as much as he was afraid.

"Where's Captain Yassa?" I finally allowed myself to ask, worried I already knew the answer.

Victor and Kurt shared a look. Then the older brother swallowed hard and answered.

"We haven't seen her since they took her out of here yesterday morning," Victor admitted.

"What?" I blurted, shocked. "She was in here? She was alive?"

Ibanez frowned at the question. "Yes, of course. Why wouldn't she be? She thought they killed you." She looked at Victor and Kurt. "I was pretty sure they were going to kill us all."

"Who beat you two and Bobbi up?" I asked Victor.

"Constantine," the man snarled, yanking on the knot he was using to tie Julio's hands and drawing a gasp from the man. "We tried to get in the way when he took Yassa out, and he took all three of us on himself, didn't even let the others in."

"You're lucky he didn't rip your fucking hearts out," Ibanez growled at him. "Or just have you shot. Fucking idiots."

I couldn't help but stare at Ibanez; I hadn't heard her speak a cross word to anyone the whole time she'd been on the team. She was scared and angry.

Victor was about to put a gag on Julio, but I stopped him with a hand on his arm.

"Julio," I said, moving around to look the man in the eye. "Where did they take the woman? The one who was with me?"

"Constantine has her somewhere," he said, shaking his head. "I haven't seen her since he hauled her off. He has her somewhere in one of the rooms we don't go into, like Abuelo's office, or maybe the basement." Not-Julio glared at him, but didn't say anything, probably because he was already gagged.

"Constantine has her?" I repeated, frowning. "What about Abuelo? Where's he?"

"I haven't seen him either," the man admitted. "Not since you got away." He made a face. "Honestly, things have been kind of... strange lately with the Boss."

I nodded to Victor and he slipped the gag over the man's mouth and tied it tight.

"Munroe," Kurt asked me, giving me a look I'd seen before way too many times, a look like he wanted me to give him all the answers, "what the hell are we going to do?"

"Come on," I said, waving towards the door.

The three of them followed me out to where Bobbi and Sanders were keeping watch. I shut the door behind us and slid the bolt home, locking it. My eyes darted back to the house; I winced at the glare from the lights there. It was the dead of night, but I was sure someone was going to wander out of it any second.

"Kane is on the way to Freeport to get the ship," I told them quickly, very cognizant of how exposed we were out here. "We have to shut down the laser defense systems before he takes off, or else he's heading off-planet and leaving us behind."

"What?" Sanders blurted, wide-eyed.

"Shut up," I snapped impatiently. "We have just a few hours before he gets there..." I shrugged. "*If* he gets there. We have to get it done and then stay alive till then."

"What if he doesn't come at all?" Ibanez wanted to know.

"Then we kill everyone and take the trucks," Bobbi said savagely, angry for the same reasons that Ibanez and Sanders were scared.

"Our first priority is finding Captain Yassa," I told them. "We're going inside and we shoot anyone we see. I've got point. Bobbi, you bring up the rear." I glanced at Ibanez, who was empty-handed. "First one we shoot that has a gun, someone get it to Ibanez."

I was being reckless by taking point, especially since I was technically the officer in this mission, but I had a sense of how to handle this and there wasn't time to explain it to them. This whole thing was a shit sandwich, but the hell if I knew any other way I could have done it.

I headed towards the house, up into the central courtyard, again striding carelessly like I owned the place. If they knew we were here already, they'd be shooting at us, so I figured it was smartest to assume they didn't know. The courtyard was lit up almost daylight bright by the floodlights, but there was no one there. I walked straight up to the front door of the ranch house and yanked it open, shoving the barrel of my rifle ahead of me.

The entrance hall was vacant and dark and nothing moved. I felt a twinge of hope fluttering inside my stomach at the idea that maybe this would be easy; maybe everyone was asleep except the guards who'd been on duty. Maybe we could just waltz right in, find wherever the control center was for the defense lasers, find Yassa and then hold up somewhere defensible until Kane arrived.

Yeah, and maybe the Predecessors would fly in on their winged unicorns and spread love and happiness and give everyone their own pony. Nothing was *ever* that simple or easy.

"What are you guys doing in here?"

The voice came from the hallway junction on the other side of the living room, way too loud and way too authoritative for my taste. He was dressed in the same dark colored fatigues and tactical vest as the other security personnel but he had a holstered handgun instead of a rifle and had an air of authority about him that matched his middle-aged features.

"I said I wanted patrols all night..." He stopped, frowning. "Ben, is that you?"

Ben must have had one of those faces.

"Yeah," I said, walking closer, still casual. I kept my voice hoarse and quiet. It was dark in here and he didn't have night vision glasses; maybe the guy wouldn't realize what was going on. "We got called in by the Boss."

"What the hell's wrong with your voice?" Then he stopped walking forward and noticed Victor and Kurt; they were hard to miss, as big as they were, and there wasn't much you could do to hide that. I saw the realization in his face, followed quickly by panic, and his shoulders shifted, his right hand making a desperate grab for the handgun holstered at his hip.

I was right about at that magic seven meters again, and I felt a confidence surge through me that I could reach him before he could draw that pistol. I'd taken two steps toward him, leaning forward and ready to lunge, but I stopped abruptly because his head exploded. The report of the rifle going off was a double thunderclap behind me, the flare of the rocket-assisted rounds a red streak through the darkness of the living room that had come way too close to me.

I spun around and saw Sanders' rifle at his shoulder, a thin haze of white smoke dissipating from the barrel vents, a tremor in his cheek. The man he'd shot slumped to a floor now stained red and littered with pieces of skull and brain, and Sanders looked very much like he wanted to puke. That was probably, I realized, the first human being he'd ever killed. At least he hadn't frozen up.

"Shit," I muttered. So much for sneaking around. "Bobbi! Take Victor and Kurt and go left; find Yassa and find the control center for the lasers. Ibanez, Sanders, follow me!"

I heard voices coming down the hallway in front of me, sleepy and questioning, and I trotted past the dead body and put my shoulder against the wall. I felt things crunching and mushing under my boots and I tried not to think about what they were. Out of the corner of my eye, I saw Sanders take up a position to my right, crouching low against the wall on his side, while Ibanez knelt over the dead body and stripped the gunbelt from it, strapping it around herself and cinching it tight before she pulled out the handgun and checked its load.

"Go," she urged me, coming up behind me, the pistol held at low ready.

I shuffled down the hallway, keeping my left shoulder against the wall. This way led to the den, the bar where Yassa and I had been sharing a drink when she'd told me about Cowboy. I didn't know what else was down here, except for the dining room at the very end, so I had no idea which door opened or whom it belonged to, but I did see the light flash on inside the room, a flare in my borrowed goggles, and I threw up a fist to stop Sanders and Ibanez.

"What was that noise?" It was a woman, dressed in loose fitting pants and shirt that might have been what she slept in, and I could see that she was unarmed. "Is someone out here?"

I thought I remembered seeing her at dinner, but I hadn't been introduced. I'd had a sense she was involved with running the ranch, but she definitely wasn't one of the hired muscle.

"It's okay, ma'am," I told her, waving confidently. "We have it under control. Just stay in your room for now."

She squinted down the hall at me, her night vision ruined by turning on her own lights.

"Who is that?" She asked.

"It's Ben," I attempted, waving again and pulling the hat down a little over my face.

"Oh, all right," she said, nodding and retreating back into her room, closing the door.

Sanders stared at me and I shrugged and kept moving. Ben was so popular, I kind of wished I hadn't had to kill him.

The next door past the woman's bedroom, I knew, was the den, and at the end of the hall I could see the short staircase that led down to the darkened hollow of the dining room. The only door left to check was set in the wall opposite the dining room, and I remembered from passing it earlier that it had been fitted with a biometric lockplate.

Approaching it now, I could see that it was yawning open and inviting and setting off all my internal alarms. I stepped across the hall, motioning for Sanders to watch back the way we'd come while Ibanez covered the dining room. Inside the door was a set of stairs heading downward, and I remembered Julio mentioning the basement, and that it was usually locked. A faint light filtered up from whatever was below, but no sound betrayed what waited down there.

"I'm going down," I told them, speaking quietly. "Sanders, keep a lookout up here. Ibanez, you're with me."

Sanders looked like he wanted to argue about it, but I didn't give him the chance; I just stepped onto the cement staircase, grateful it wasn't wood like most everything else in the house. My steps on it were light taps rather than the creaks they could have been, but they still seemed thunderous in the absolute silence from below. The staircase curved with the wall, following some natural bend in the foundation of the house, and as it did the light grew brighter and more focused.

It came, I saw as I descended, from a 2-D flat-screen monitor affixed to the far wall, long obsolete like most everything else in the Pirate Worlds. An error message flashed across it, obvious even to someone as barely technically literate as me.

"Connection not available," it repeated over and over. "System not responding."

Sitting on a chair bolted to the floor in front of a control panel was Gramps, his face ashen, his hands flat on the console in front of him. I stepped across the room, my rifle trained on him.

"Keep your hands in front of you," I warned him.

His eyes snapped around and he nearly lunged up out of the seat before he saw the muzzle of the rifle yawning in front of him. There was a desperation in his look that I'd never seen before, and maybe relief and definitely rage. I didn't see any obvious weapons on him, but I didn't lower the gun; he was old and devious enough to have one or two concealed on him.

"What the hell did you do, Tyler?" He demanded. "Do you have any idea what you've done to us?"

"What did *I* do?" I balked at him. "What the hell are you talking about? You betrayed me, Gramps. You were ready to lock me up; you're no better than my mother!" I realized I was yelling and reined myself in, trying to bring my temper and my breathing under control. I took a step closer to him. "I saved your life once. Tell me where you have Captain Yassa before I change my mind about that."

"It's not about *me*, you selfish prick!" He exploded, coming to his feet. "When the other cabals realize our defenses are down, they'll come in and steal everything they can and destroy what they can't!"

I felt my face screw up in confusion and I felt the muscles in my arms shuddering as I fought to keep myself from butt stroking him with the rifle.

"What the hell are you talking about?" I repeated. "I've been hiding in a cave for two days, when the hell would I have had a chance to shut down the defense system?"

That took him back a step and the look on his face matched the one I felt on my own. Then it hardened into utter rage.

"Constantine," he growled. He stepped forward again and I brought the rifle back to my shoulder. "You wanted to find your

Captain Yassa," he said impatiently, waving up at the stairs. "I'll take you to her."

I was debating whether or not I should hit him in the face and tie him up when I heard the gunshots echoing faintly down the stairs. I backed away from Gramps and looked up towards the entrance.

"Munroe!" Sanders ran down to where the wall curved, stopping when he could see me. "There's a fight going on at the other end of the house! It's gotta' be Bobbi!"

Gramps looked at me questioningly and I swore under my breath and motioned to Ibanez. "Let him go up. You two, follow us."

Ibanez looked at me doubtfully, but she moved out of the way and let the two of us by. I had to jog up the steps to keep up with Gramps, but once we hit the door, I shoved past him and ran towards the sounds of gunfire. I saw the tiny flares of rocket-assisted rounds smashing into the walls of the living room as I crossed it, then in the darkness of the connecting hallway I could see a dozen fireflies as answering fire headed into the enemy, coming from doorways on either side of the hall.

"Friendly coming up behind!" I shouted hoarsely. "Don't fucking shoot me!"

I could see more details as I got closer. There were at least five or six of Constantine's men barricaded in a doorway at the end of the hall, blocking it with an overturned metal storage cabinet to provide cover. It had a couple dozen holes punched in it and they were still alive, so I assumed it was filled with something thick enough to stop the incoming rounds.

I opened up with my own rifle as I ran, targeting with the reticle projected onto my stolen night vision goggles. One of the figures in the door spun away, holding an arm and cursing, and the others ducked down, giving me the opening to slide into the doorway on the right along with Bobbi Taylor, Ibanez pushing Gramps in behind me. It was his office, the one I'd been in with Yassa a couple days ago. Across the hallway, I could see Sanders huddled behind the

Simak brothers in someone's bedroom, swapping out magazines from the spares we'd doled out.

"They popped out of that room down there a couple minutes ago," Bobbi told me, flinching unconsciously as more return fire smacked into the doorframe beside her. "We've been holding them off, but we don't have enough ammo to assault."

"What's down there?" I asked Gramps as I checked the round counter on the side of my rifle and saw that I had 30 shots left in this magazine.

"The armory," he told me and I sighed. *They* weren't about to run out of ammo, then.

"Of course it is," Ibanez muttered, looking with disdain at the handgun that was her only weapon.

Gramps pushed past me, getting closer to the door.

"Constantine!" He shouted. "Constantine, can you hear me? It's Torres!"

The firing died down a moment and I heard mutterings and rumblings from inside the room. Finally, after a long moment, the enforcer's smooth and deep voice answered.

"What do you want, Grandpa?" There was disrespect in the tone, not at all the subordination that would have made me feel so much better.

"I think you know damn well what I want, Constantine!" Gramps was bellowing now, spittle flying from his mouth, as close to completely out of control as I'd ever seen him. Scared Gramps was so much more terrifying than even just-betrayed-me Gramps. "The fucking defense system is down!"

"Oh, that," Constantine replied casually. "I apologize, did I forget to mention that I had a better offer?"

"The Corporate Council paid you off, too?" Gramps's voice was incredulous, his eyes wide.

Constantine laughed at that, a derisive snort. "You see the damn Corporates under every rock, Grandpa. You were almost too easy to manipulate; it was disappointing. No, it was someone much closer to home: the *Novoye Moscva bratva*."

"The what?" Ibanez muttered. I'd heard of them, though.

"They're a Pirate World cabal," I told her quietly. "Emigrants from old Russia, what was left of it after the Sino-Russian War. They're mostly over on Peboan, a few light years from here."

"They've been trying to take over Crowley's operations since I killed him," Gramps said in a low growl. "Damn it. I knew Constantine was a bastard, but I didn't realize he was such a *stupid* bastard." Then louder, shouting again. "What are they offering you, Constantine? I'll double it."

"They're giving me your job, old man." That laugh again, mocking. "Mr. Munroe, do me a favor and take a look down the hall. I guarantee your safety."

I sneered at that, instead stretching my rifle out around the door jam and using the connection between its sights and the glasses I'd been using. Constantine was standing just behind the storage cabinet, flanked by two of his men. His right hand was wrapped around Brandy Yassa's throat. She'd been worked over; her face was bruised and blood trickled from her nose and a cut above her eye, but her expression was still defiant. Her hands were flex-cuffed in front of her, but given that Victor and Kurt hadn't been able to take Constantine, I don't know that it made any difference.

"Drop your guns," Constantine said, "or I'll snap her neck."

16

I wanted to yell for him not to do it, wanted to step out and surrender, but I knew just how much good that would do.

"You know who I am, Constantine," I told him, pulling the rifle back, not wanting to see any more. "You know where I've been. She's my friend, but I've seen friends die before."

"I apologize for sounding so melodramatic," he said, actually sounding contrite. "Here's the thing, though, I need something from you and your old grandpa, and I need you alive to get it. So, I'll make you a deal. Your people can go. I have the ID cards for the vehicles in here. I'll give them the key to the rover and they can take off, head back to town. But *you* stay here."

"Don't do it, Munroe," Bobbi hissed at me. "You can't trust him."

I could see Victor shaking his head from across the hall, while Kurt and Sanders just watched, wide-eyed.

I closed my eyes, mind working feverishly.

"Toss the key card down the hall," I said to him. "Let the others get out. Once they're gone, I toss out my weapon. Then you let Yassa go after them. Once she's had time to get out, I'll step out of this room."

"He'll kill you," Bobbi said fiercely, pushing against my shoulder in frustration.

"Not before he gets what he wants," Gramps said grimly, eyes hooded.

"You're pretty intelligent for a Marine," Constantine said. "All right. Everyone, hold your fire, let them go." There was a pause and then I saw a small, round code card spinning across the floor outside the hall. "There's the key to the rover."

"Kane should be here soon," I said quickly to Bobbi. "Get out of that canyon as quick as you can and see if you can get a signal to him. If you can do it without getting killed, come back and get us. You're in charge, Bobbi," I added.

She nodded, not speaking, not even looking at me, her expression full of rage and frustration. Ibanez put a hand on my shoulder.

"We'll come back for you," she promised.

"Go," I told them, nodding out at the hallway. "Hurry, before he changes his mind."

"Move it!" Bobbi snapped at Sanders and the brothers, waving them ahead of her. "Get going, now!"

Ibanez followed her out, and I could see Bobbi backing up, covering them with her rifle as they retreated from the hallway. I watched them as best I could, waiting a full thirty seconds before I heard Constantine calling to me.

"Your gun," he said.

"Cut her hands free," I told him. I gave it another ten seconds, then looked at Gramps and tossed the rifle out the door. It clattered to the wooden floor with a solid, metallic sound and I pulled the goggles off, dropping them to the carpet in Gramps' office.

There was no sound for a moment, but then I saw Yassa coming slowly past the door, rubbing at her wrists. She looked at me, the pain in her eyes having little to do with the bruises on her face.

"I'm sorry, Munroe," she rasped through swollen lips.

"Go," was all I said. I wanted to tell her to go to Demeter and tell Sophia that I loved her, but that was stupid. She already knew that. Just like she'd known I didn't have any choice but to go on this mission.

Then she was gone. I wanted to run after her, to take my

chances, but I knew that was suicide. They were watching; they'd shoot me before I got a meter. And even if Constantine needed me alive, that would stop them from putting a few rounds into my legs and taking the chance they could get the bleeding stopped in time.

"That's long enough, Munroe." It was Constantine. He was outside the armory, I could tell from the sound.

I looked Gramps in the eye, reading nothing in that dark gaze, then I put my hands behind my head and did something I'd sworn I never would. I surrendered.

"Get on your knees."

I apparently didn't do it fast enough because hands forced me down and only the pads built into the knees of my fatigue pants kept me from cracking my kneecaps on the hardwood floor. The muzzle of a rifle hovered centimeters from my face as my hands were pulled roughly behind me and my wrists were flex-cuffed together tight enough to pinch into my flesh. Then I was patted down, my jacket lifted up and spare magazines pulled from my thigh pockets.

They even took the knife, I lamented as they yanked me up to my feet. I wasn't sure how big of a difference that switchblade would have made, but I was sad about it anyway.

As I was yanked to my feet, I saw others in Constantine's group of loyalists binding Gramps' hands behind him, and I noted that they found the compact pistol he'd had concealed somewhere under his loose, grey shirt.

Knew the old bastard had a gun, I thought with a quiet snort.

Then Constantine was in front of me, looking very satisfied with himself, like a man who'd bartered a good trade and knew it.

"What do you want from me?" Gramps demanded.

Constantine smiled, then he punched the older man in the face. Gramps went down, unable to balance himself with his hands bound, and fell heavily on his shoulder, blood pouring out of his nose. The enforcer had used his flesh-and-blood hand, I noted with a sigh of relief. Otherwise, Gramps wouldn't have gotten back up.

"That's the first thing I wanted," Constantine said genially. "And by God, I've wanted to do that from the very first day you took over, you imperious, overbearing, old piece of shit. Do you really think any of us gives a shit about your fucking United States Marine Corps or fighting the fucking Chinese in Taiwan? I wish your damned family wasn't so rich, then you'd have died a hundred years ago, and I wouldn't have to put up with your bullshit."

Gramps got his feet beneath him and struggled back up to stand in front of Constantine, his look defiant and somehow dismissive.

"Got that out of your system, have you?" He asked, spitting blood on the floor.

"Watch your mouth, old man," Constantine warned him, "or you'll find out how hard I can hit you with my *other* hand." He raised his gloved right fist in front of Gramps' face. Then he turned to one of the goons guarding us, a short, broad-shouldered woman with a keloid scar down the side of her face. "Take them out to the barn."

It was raining lightly and I felt the wind-driven droplets slap at my face as we walked out the front door of the ranch house and into the night.

"Why the hell would anyone *want* this place?" I muttered. I was talking to myself, but Constantine heard me, and looked at me sharply.

I thought for a second he was going to hit me, but instead he chuckled quietly.

"You ever hear of Milton, Mr. Munroe?" He asked me. "*Paradise Lost*?"

In fact, I had. I hadn't gone to the Corporate Management University the way Mom had wanted, but I'd still kept trying to learn, even when I was in the Corps. And Sophia insisted I read the classics, which I sometimes appreciated and sometimes didn't.

"Better to rule in Hell than serve in Heaven, Constantine?" I looked at him sidelong. "Are those the only choices?"

"For a man like me," he allowed. Then he smiled, a twisted, brutal smile. "And men like your great-grandfather here, I think."

"I never had a choice," Gramps declared, and I looked at him with a sudden shock of guilt as I heard the bitterness in those words.

Then we were in the barn, and the guards in the lead hit the control to switch on the lights.

"Far-sighted of you installing independent power out here," Constantine said to Gramps, waving at the lights. "It would have been inconvenient if I'd switched off our own juice when I had my people shut down the fusion reactor."

The horses reacted to Gramps' presence, sticking their heads over the tops of their stalls, looking for a slap on the neck or a treat, if they were anything like the ones he'd kept in Utah. He stared at them as he passed, and I could read the thought in his eyes: who was going to take care of them now?

Then we were at the doors to the lift, sullenly promising and darkly threatening.

"Open them," Constantine told Gramps.

"You want to give what's down there to the *bratva*?" Gramps demanded. "What do you think they'll do with it?"

"What the hell do I care?"

Constantine slid his pistol out of its thigh holster and I got a good look at it for the first time. It wasn't anything as prosaic as the locally fabricated stamped metal slug guns the others carried, or even the variable ammo pistol I'd brought with me. It was a pulse pistol, a laser weapon that you didn't see outside Space Fleet very much. Ammo for it would be expensive as hell out here, but I guessed it was more of a status symbol for him than anything else.

"You're going to kill me anyway," Gramps said, ignoring the threat.

"Yes, I certainly am," Constantine agreed genially. "And even if I weren't, Popov and the *bratva* would soon enough, though probably not as gently. But I don't have to kill *him*."

He raised the pistol and leveled the emitter crystal at my head. It was odd, like having someone point a holographic camera at me instead of a weapon, but I knew that one shot could blow my head apart like an overheated egg, turning my blood and cerebral fluid to superheated vapor.

"I most certainly *can* kill him," Constantine amended, "but I don't especially *want* to, not the least because, unlike you, old man, he actually *did* something in the war that made a difference, and I respect that. And unlike you, he doesn't have to be here. The choice is yours. Open the damn door, disarm whatever bloody-minded traps you have set and tell your pet scientists down there to keep doing what they're doing but do it for me and Popov."

Gramps said nothing, looking away sullenly, almost petulantly, his incipient growth of beard stained with his blood. Was it really that he'd changed so much, I wondered, or had I built him up too much in my memory because he was all I'd had?

I was looking at Gramps when the gun went off with a thunder-crack and a blinding flash of ionized air heated to plasma by the laser pulse. I felt a searing spear of pain in my side and I spun to the ground, crying out involuntarily. Loose strands of hay were burning on the floor behind me, and a haze of smoke drifted up towards the roof of the barn. Teeth clenched against the pain, I forced myself to look down and saw that my armored jacket had taken the brunt of the shot. It was scorched and blackened and cracked, but the pain on my side was mostly from the flash burn; the shot had been aimed to graze and it hadn't penetrated.

"Did I mention there was a time limit on this offer?" Constantine asked, his voice still pleasant and casual, in stark counterpoint to the glowing emitter of his pistol, still radiating heat that I could feel a meter away.

Gramps was looking down at me, his face drained of color, sweat dripping down his forehead, his shoulders held by two of the guards; I had the sense he'd instinctively tried to run when the laser discharged. Constantine grabbed him across the cheeks with the splayed fingers of his bionic hand and gently turned his face to make him meet his eyes.

"Popov and his ships will be landing within the hour, you see," the enforcer went on, and the look on his face changed from his forced cheerfulness to something closer to the rage I knew he was actually feeling. "And as a demonstration of my competency and usefulness, I fully intend to have your little mad scientist lair open and ready for Mr. Popov to inspect. If I don't, I won't be happy. And if I'm not happy, then I will dutifully step aside and let Mr. Popov's very well-trained and experienced interrogators go to work on both of you."

I watched my great-grandfather's eyes, wondering if he was so attached to his dream of revenge that he was going to let both of us die before he gave it up. I didn't get the chance to find out. The scream of turbojets rolled across the floor of the canyon, shaking the aluminum walls and sending the horses into a frenzy of stamping and bucking.

Constantine sighed as he let loose of Gramps' face and shoved his laser back into its holster. He glanced back over his shoulder at the unmistakable sound of landing jets coming from the fields in front of the ranch house.

"Too late," he said, his tone light but the frustration evident in the set of his face. He motioned towards me. "Get him up and bring both of them along. Time to meet the new boss."

Two of his people grabbed me under the arms and yanked me up to my feet and I gasped as pain flared anew in my side. I tried to push it down, knowing that much worse was coming. I had no choice now; I had to try to fight and run because getting shot trying to escape was the better option. At least I'd got the others away from here; I was counting on Kane to find them and get them out of here, because he definitely wouldn't be in time to save me.

I knew something was off when we emerged from the barn. I could see the ships from there, three bulbous, lifting body shapes matte black and sucking up the light from the house, steam billowing off their metal hulls. Those weren't some up-armored cargo shuttles slapped together by the Russian mob out in the Pirate Worlds, they were military assault shuttles.

"...the fuck?" I could hear Constantine muttering, and I knew he was having the same thought I was, and I could feel our pace begin to slow as we reached the courtyard between the house and the outbuildings.

Dark shapes moved through the night around the ranch house in tactical formations, faceless in visored helmets, wicked-looking pulse carbines carried at the low ready position. They flowed like a swarm of deadly, black-armored insects, some of them splitting off to enter the ranch house and the rest spreading out to surround us,

At least two laser emitter cones targeted each of us, and the four guards Constantine had brought with him were glancing back and forth nervously, not dropping their guns yet but taking care not to move the muzzles upward. The armored figures parted and a woman in a tailored uniform stepped through, her brown hair pulled into a bun, her face knife-edged and severe. She had a pistol holstered at her waist but she didn't bother to draw it; she didn't need to.

"You're Constantine Terranova," she said to the enforcer, looking him up and down.

"You work for Popov?" The man seemed lost, and didn't look happy about the unfamiliar feeling.

The woman laughed sharply. "I'm afraid not. Mr. Popov received a better offer. My name is Trina Wellesley and I work for the Corporate Security Force."

I grunted deep in my throat, feeling like I'd been kicked in the balls. She looked at Gramps and I with a glint of curiosity in her eye before turning back purposefully to Constantine.

"We're here to take possession of the artifact."

17

"What about my deal?" Constantine demanded, greed and anger warring visibly with fear and uncertainty in his tone and his face. I stared at him in disbelief. He'd been DSI, he should know who these people were and what he was dealing with.

"Your deal is quite clear-cut, Mr. Terranova," she said, sounding almost surprised at the question. "You give us the artifact, we leave, and you get to stay alive." She arched an eyebrow. "Towards keeping that latter part of the deal, perhaps you and your friends should disarm before my people start getting nervous."

Constantine mulled that suggestion over for the space of two or three uncomfortable seconds, then he nodded to the guards. They seemed almost grateful at the chance to drop the rifles, but Constantine himself was slow and reluctant to unfasten his gun belt and hand over his weapon. The CSF mercenaries took charge of the guns quickly and efficiently, and the laser emitters moved from targeting our heads to a general port arms.

Wellesley smiled thinly. "The artifact, Mr. Terranova," she reminded him. "I'll need you to take us to it."

"It's under the barn," he said, motioning behind us. "But the entrance is sealed with a biometric lock. To get inside, you're going to need him." He indicated Gramps, who looked very much like an elk calf who'd just noticed the wolves.

"Well, by all means," she said, stepping forward and laying a hand possessively on Gramps' shoulder, "let's get started."

I think he was too stunned to resist as she led the two of us back inside, trailing a half dozen of her CSF troops. The others stayed with Constantine and his guards. As we walked, I heard the distant sound of pulse carbines firing, probably from in the house. That roused Gramps from his stupor and he turned on the woman.

"Who are they shooting?" He demanded inanely, as if she'd know.

"Why, anyone stupid enough to make themselves a threat to us," Wellesley answered readily, and I could tell she felt not the least bit of guilt. "Don't you be that stupid, Mr. Torres. I know Ms. Damiani would prefer I bring you back alive, but it's not a requirement."

"You…" Gramps licked his lips as if they'd gone dry and tried again. "You work for Patrice?"

"I work for the Corporate Council, Mr. Torres," she corrected him. "Please keep moving."

Shit. Shit, shit, shit, shit, shit. She worked for Mom. Now, for the first time in this whole business, I felt truly afraid. Dying didn't scare me, not after Demeter. Mom scared the hell out of me.

The elevator seemed less intimidating now, perhaps because everything else seemed even worse. Wellesley pushed Gramps towards the ID plate and then motioned to one of her troopers to come forward.

"Have a look at this lock for me, Captain Petrelli," she said.

The armored figure could have been a slender man or a burly woman, and it was impossible to tell with the featureless helmet and bulky body armor, but I went ahead and labelled the Captain a man in my head for convenience. Petrelli slung his pulse carbine and pulled a small computer module from a pouch at his belt, holding it against the ID plate for a moment before turning back to Wellesley.

"It'll take some time, ma'am." The voice coming over the

helmet's external speakers was deep and I thought I'd been right. "We have the right equipment in the shuttle, though. Maybe an hour."

"There you go, Mr. Torres." Wellesley turned back to Gramps, lip curling in something more a snarl than a smile. "I'll get in one way or another. If you save me an hour, I guarantee you that I won't have my troops execute the team of scientists you have down there."

Gramps didn't look at her and he sure as hell didn't look at me. He just held out his hands. Wellesley nodded to Captain Petrelli and the man produced a small utility knife from a pocket and sliced through the flex cuffs. Gramps shook feeling back into his hands for a moment, then walked over, and slapped his palm against the ID plate, then typed in the code.

"There, that wasn't so hard." God, she was a talkative bitch. She reminded me of Mom.

It felt like the lift took forever to reach the bottom this time, as if the machinery knew why we were there and was dreading it as much as I was. When the doors swung open, the entire staff was lined up waiting, all six of them, and at the sight of the CSF mercenaries most of them raised their hands hesitantly.

"I see word of our arrival has preceded us." Wellesley's voice was droll, but it trailed off as her eyes went to the pod. Even she was struck dumb for a moment by the sheer alien strangeness of it. "Holy shit," she mumbled, walking slowly and deliberately towards it.

Gramps walked over to Dr. Erenreich and I started to follow him, but then turned back to Captain Petrelli.

"Is there any chance I could get these cuffs off?" I asked him.

The officer regarded me silently from behind the darkened, featureless visor for a long moment, and I thought he was going to ignore the question. But then he turned to where Wellesley was still walking towards the thing.

"Ma'am." His voice was tinny and scratchy over the helmet speaker.

"What?" She didn't turn around; she couldn't take her eyes off the artifact.

"Do you want Mr. Callas' hands freed?"

Shit. They knew exactly who I was. I'd been afraid of that, too.

"Go ahead," she waved a hand dismissively. "Do keep an eye on him, though. I'm told he can be quite resourceful."

Petrelli motioned for me to turn around and I felt a tug on the cuffs as he cut through them. I felt the pins and needles in my hands as blood flow returned and I rubbed and shook them, wincing.

"Thank you," I told Petrelli. He didn't respond, but I hadn't really expected him to.

I shrugged and followed Gramps over to where Erenreich was standing, next to the other researchers. She didn't have her hands up, but she was keeping them out in the open and not making any sudden moves. In her shapeless, brown tunic and loose-legged slacks, she looked as if she'd been woken from a sound sleep. She might have been; I saw curtained off sections at the other end of the chamber that were partially open to reveal folding cots. All of them probably slept and ate down here most of the time.

"It's...moving somehow," Wellesley said from over at the pod, her palm resting on its curved surface, touching it like an expectant mother might touch her stomach. She looked back at Erenreich. "It feels like it's pulsing. How long has it been doing that?"

I purposefully did *not* react to that, though I wanted to. Pulsing? When the hell had it started pulsing?

"A few hours. It does it every now and then for a few hours at a time, then stops." Erenreich was lying through her teeth, and I hoped it was more believable to Wellesley than it was to me. "We still don't know why."

"Of course you don't," Wellesley sniffed with disdain, turning back to the pod. She couldn't seem to keep her hands off of it. "The idea that a bunch of misfits and exiles with black market equipment could achieve anything in this toxic shithole is ludicrous."

"What did you do, Heather?" Gramps said so soft and low I nearly missed it, even from right next to them.

"When I saw them coming on the security monitors from the house," she murmured just as quietly, "I hit the pod with a massive dose of microwaves. It's been doing that," she nodded at the faint respiration that seemed to be coursing through the thing, "ever since."

"You could destroy the fucking planet," I hissed at her, disbelief crawling over the nape of my neck.

"And what do you think *they'll* do with it?" Erenreich growled in return, eyes flickering towards the CSF troops, silent and unmoving.

"This thing won't fit in that elevator," Wellesley realized abruptly. She looked to Gramps. "How did you get it in here?"

"It was excavated with heavy machinery," Gramps said.

"We'll have to bring some in from Freeport," the woman mused, seeming a bit put out by it. "Damn, that will keep us here for days."

"We could level the barn with the ship's weapons," Petrelli suggested, "then expand the elevator shaft with hyperexplosives." He shrugged beneath the armor, the motion barely visible. "It'll be messy, but we could do it in a day."

"Excellent idea, Captain." Wellesley's expression brightened. "You're definitely earning a bonus this quarter. Get someone on it." She turned to Erenreich. "I'm going to need every bit of research you have on this thing. Upload it to a data crystal; I'll check it before we excavate. If I decide you're holding out on me, all six of you will be coming with us to a CSF holding facility, and once you're there, I wouldn't count on ever leaving it again."

"You'll get it," Erenreich promised her. She turned to a pale, emaciated little man with crazy eyes. "Gino, go back up the data as quickly as you can."

Gino nodded and shuffled cautiously over to a data storage bank, looking back with every step as if he expected to be shot down before he got there.

"Leave a guard with this one," Wellesley told Petrelli, indicating Gino. "The rest of us are heading upstairs. There's no need to keep Mr. Torres and Mr. Callas waiting around here when Ms. Damiani is so eager to see them again."

She seemed so cheerful about it that I wanted to put my fist through her teeth. On the other hand, I didn't really want to get stunned or even shot, if they were in a bad mood, then stuffed into a hibernation tank for the rest of the trip, so I kept my fists and my anger to myself. My insides were churning, though, as we rode back to the surface. Mom had promised to have me psych-probed, and I had no reason to doubt she'd do it. With enough drugs and brainwashing, I wouldn't even remember my old life or that I'd ever felt any other way than totally devoted to her.

Of course, for that to happen, I'd actually have to live to get off the planet. There was always the chance that the fucking artifact was going to blow the whole place up before I had the chance to get turned into a zombie. I was having trouble deciding which of those two I'd prefer.

"Get the explosives planted as soon as possible, Petrelli," Wellesley was saying when I could pull my head out of my ass long enough to listen. "I don't like being blind, and we're pretty much blind on this planet. We can't even maintain a consistent line to the lighter unless it's directly overhead."

"Yes, ma'am."

My ears picked up at that. I knew what a lighter was historically, though I'd never seen one: a cargo ship armed and armored as a makeshift combat vessel. Nothing that would last a minute against a Fleet cruiser, but it would outclass anything the Pirate World cabals could produce. Its biggest weakness from Wellesley's point of view was that it wouldn't be well equipped for orbital fire support; the sort of weaponry that could pierce planetary cloud cover with enough precision to respond for a call-for-fire wasn't something you could stick in a bolt-on weapons pod. It had to be built into the original design for the ship. But they did have those assault shuttles, which was probably more than they needed.

The horses were restless as we walked by them again and Wellesley paused to run a hand across the muzzle of an Arabian as we passed.

"Make sure to let the horses loose before you destroy the building," she instructed.

I glanced at her in surprise, half-expecting her to make some snide remark and dispel the sudden air of humanity that the command had given her, but she said nothing more about it.

Nobody's a bad guy in their own head, I reminded myself. It didn't make her any less dangerous, and it didn't mean I wouldn't kill her if I could.

Outside, there was a flurry of activity as bound prisoners were hustled out of the bunkhouses and forced to their knees in neat and orderly rows out in the courtyard. Other CSF troopers were hauling heavy-duty polymer cases off one of the assault shuttles, the faces of the containers marked with the universal sign for caution and the military symbol for explosives.

Ten cases altogether that I saw, each big enough to hold at least ten kilos of hyperexplosives.

Jesus, I thought, feeling an eyebrow shoot up in appreciation. *That'll do it, all right*. That was enough HpE to blow a hole in the valley floor fifty meters wide or, if you set it for directional blasts, a hundred meters deep.

We were being marched towards one of the shuttles and behind us, I could hear the whinnying and snorting of the horses as they were chased out into the pasture to a chorus of shouts and yells from Petrelli's underlings. I wondered how much good it would do, and how long the animals would survive without Gramps to take care of them. Horses were fragile beasts even on Earth, and this place was much less hospitable.

I tried to chide myself for worrying about the damn horses instead of watching for a chance to escape, but I honestly didn't see it happening. These guys were professionals, not just hired thugs like Constantine's people. Maybe they weren't as STRAC as a Force Recon platoon, but they were a damn site better than the next best thing around at the moment. Oh sure, I could take one of them down and get his gun, maybe get out past the house, but they had the assault shuttles and I wouldn't be hiding in any fucking cave this time.

We were about twenty meters from the open belly ramp of the nearest shuttle when Petrelli abruptly halted and turned to Wellesley.

"Ma'am," he said, urgency coming through the exterior speaker, "the lighter just contacted the shuttle via a tight-beam laser; it's detected a thermal signature coming this way at high speeds…"

A bolt of lightning split the sky and struck the assault shuttle farthest from us, about a hundred meters away, just aft of the cockpit. My vision filled with afterimages and then went completely white as a hemisphere of glowing plasma engulfed the ship and a concussion wave threw us to the ground. A roaring filled my ears and my head and a blind panic filled my gut and for long seconds, I couldn't breathe. I fought to suck in a mouthful of air, pushing against the pressure on my chest, clutching at the ground with desperate fingers.

I heard turbojets screaming overhead and then another lightning strike, what my battered brain was coming to understand was the proton cannon on a starship firing, speared into the ranch house and concussion struck again, this time from behind. I was already on the ground, my hands over my head, mouth open when it passed over me but it tumbled me sideways and I was on top of one of the CSF troops, his pulse carbine digging into my chest. My hands found the butt of a pistol, holstered on the trooper's chest, and I jerked it free as he threw me off.

He was coming to a knee when I fired, aiming instinctively, pointing the gun like a finger. I'd never fired a pulse laser before and it felt strange; it shuddered rather than recoiling, as a small hyperexplosive capsule ignited inside its chamber and pulsed that heat energy through a semiconductor rod, focused by the emitter crystal. A flash of ionized air connected us for a fraction of a second, and then the visor of the trooper's helmet exploded from the inside as brain matter and cerebrospinal fluid vaporized and took the path of least resistance.

I rolled into a crouch, then got knocked back down as the barn went up this time. Corrugated aluminum walls were blown outward by superheated air and the ranch house exploded into a fireball as that rush of air fed the smoldering kindling. Flames licked up into the night from three sides and smoke and steam and clouds of debris floated across the canyon floor in a vision of hell from a poem of centuries past.

The barn, I realized. *The house, the barn...I'd told Kane to hit the house and the barn.*

That was him up there, in the *Wanderer*, come back to get me. I had to get out of here. I pulled myself up onto my hands and knees and looked around quickly, saw Gramps struggling up to his knees in the middle of two of the CSF troopers who'd been guarding us. I shot them, one round each, one in the head, the other in the chest, then I was up and grabbing Gramps by the arm, pulling him away and starting us both running for the pasture. We had to get somewhere where Kane could land and pick us up.

We'd made it maybe ten meters before they started shooting. The only reason we weren't killed immediately was the fire washing out their night vision and the smoke clouding the targeting systems in their helmets, but a swathe of laser pulses smacked into the ground less than a meter from my right foot, spraying me with a hot wash of steam from the water vapor in the dirt. Gramps stumbled and went down and I skidded to a halt beside him, turning back and raising the pulse pistol, wishing I could link my contact lens ocular to its unfamiliar sights.

Two of the Corporate mercenaries had gotten to their feet and were running our way, and I was trying to aim for the closest when he jerked backwards at an impact against his chest, blood spattering from between his shoulder blades as something fast and powerful and armor-piercing cut through him. The other took a round through the visor before the first had hit the ground and that's when someone on the other side figured out what was going on.

"Incoming!" Petrelli was yelling, probably intended for his

troopers' internal communications, but he'd forgotten he still had his external speakers activated. "Get to cover now!"

I picked Gramps up by the arm and took off again, in the direction the shots had come from, knowing exactly who had fired them. Those hadn't been the rocket carbines my people had taken with them; those were Gauss rifle shots, and the only Gauss rifles I knew of were the ones in the arms locker on the *Wanderer*.

18

"Munroe!" I heard Yassa's voice before I saw her sprinting across the pasture towards us, the rest of the team spread out in a V formation behind her. They were dressed in the combat armor we'd brought with us and looked a lot less ragged than the last time I'd seen them, and every damned one of them was still alive.

"Kane found you!" I yelled inanely, stumbling toward them. "Holy shit, Kane found you!"

She didn't respond, just grabbed me by the sleeve and pulled me down into the prone, hugging me around the shoulder at the same time. The wet grass bent pliantly under my knees and the ends of it teased at my face. Gramps collapsed next to me, horror and pain etched in his face as he watched everything he'd built up over the last six years burning to the ground before his eyes. I felt bad for the old man; I would have felt worse if he hadn't been ready to betray me to Constantine a couple days ago.

Yassa had been carrying a spare weapon over her shoulder and she shoved it into my hands, along with a bandolier of loaded magazines, and nothing had ever felt quite as good to me as the weight of that Gauss rifle. I offered the pulse pistol to Gramps and he took it automatically, with instincts so deeply ingrained that they overcame even his current anguish.

"We're here, Boss," Yassa yelled into my ear over the roaring of the fires as I slipped the bandolier over my shoulder. She shoved a 'link into my hand and I took it, realizing she must have grabbed mine off the ship. I slipped in the ear bud; it would, at least, be good for short-range communications, if nothing else.

"Kane is going to circle back around and give us some air support, then he'll pick us up back closer to the canyon wall!" I could hear her through the ear bud now, clearer than over the din outside. She jerked a thumb behind her. "We need to move back another hundred meters and set up a perimeter for his LZ."

"Hey!" That was Sanders, moving up beside us in a high-crawl, the grass still reaching nearly to his shoulder. "Something's happening over there!"

He pointed over to where the shredded remains of the barn burned furiously, fueled by hay and fertilizer, about a hundred meters from us. It was hard to see in the glare from the conflagration at the ranch house, but I could tell that the wreckage was stirring, throwing showers of sparks and jets of black smoke where the sheets of aluminum twisted and shifted.

"What's in there?" Yassa wondered, frowning in confusion. "No one could be alive in that fire."

An actinic flare of light exploded through the wreckage, brighter than the fire, brighter than the unclouded sun that I hadn't seen in days, and my first thought was that there'd been a hydrogen fuel cell in the barn that had blown. But it was too bright for that, too bright for anything natural. I looked over at Yassa and saw her face going pale. A second blast shot out at about a sixty-degree angle from the first, like something using a piece of a star as a shovel to widen a hole.

"Oh, sweet Jesus..." Yassa murmured, eyes widening. What did she know, I wondered, that the rest of us didn't?

"Is this the artifact?" I said, grabbing at her shoulder to get her attention. "Do you think this is it activating? Is it about to blow up?"

"I don't know," she admitted, "but I get the feeling this is much worse than just a bomb, Munroe."

There was a dark gap where the middle of the barn had been now, like something had swallowed up the wreckage there, and as we watched, something came out of it, something very, very big. It was lit up by the fires, but the black, chitinous surface of the thing almost absorbed the light, swallowing it whole.

What I *could* see... At first, I wanted to say it was an insect, but that was more a trick of the mind, trying to force something unknown into the familiar. Its body was segmented, armored, maybe less like a beetle's than a scorpion's, with curved, chitinous plates that covered its joints, and it moved on two sets of legs, the rear larger and much more muscular than the front. Above the front set of legs, the body curved upward in an almost centaur-like segmentation, with a pair of manipulating limbs at the shoulders that ended in wickedly articulated claws. The head was flattened, almost wedge-shaped, with any eyes or ears concealed deep within the armored shell.

It was alien, more alien than anything Tahni had ever been, but that wasn't the most disturbing aspect of it. It was monstrous, *evil* on a gut level that had no time for ruminations on how different cultures and species might have different ideas of morality and ethics. But even that wasn't the most disturbing thing.

The most disturbing thing was the massive energy weapon mounted on the armor of its left shoulder, meant to be manipulated by the arm on that side. I could have believed that the thing was an animal, or even perhaps a mindless automaton except for that one piece of high technology sitting there obscenely connected to the rest of what looked very much like a living thing.

"What in the living fuck is that?" Victor blurted, bringing his Gauss rifle around to aim at it.

I was about to caution him not to shoot, but the CSF troopers were closer and just as freaked out. I could barely see them in their dark camouflaged armor running past what was left of the barn, but I saw the plasma flare discharging off their laser pulses as they opened fire on the thing. There was a shimmering where the lasers hit, like a heat mirage in the desert, but nothing that showed any real effect on that biological-looking armor, even when the shots impacted the massive head.

I thought the monster would shoot them, then, but instead it scuttled forward with deceptive speed, crossing the dozen meters between it and the closest of the troops in the space a breath and catching the luckless mercenary in the claws at the end of its left hand. That was when I got an idea of the size of the thing, seeing it lift the CSF trooper into the air by his waist. The scorpion-thing was at least three meters tall at the shoulder, and probably five from the tip of its head to the tip of its articulated tail.

Laser pulses spalled harmlessly and impotently off of its armor as it grabbed the man's head in the mandibles under its jaw and ripped it off his body. Blood fountained black in the night and the thing discarded the rest of him almost negligently. Then it waded into a group of four more Security Force troops, crushing one under its front left leg and smashing another to the ground with its forearm, ignoring their weapons fire.

"Jesus," Sanders moaned.

Victor cursed and opened fire. I didn't realize it was him until I looked over at the deep-throated hum-snap of the Gauss rifle discharging over and over. I didn't bother to order him not to; instead, we all joined in the fire, pouring dozens of tungsten slugs at the alien thing.

"Aim for the left shoulder," I snapped. "Everyone! Aim for the left shoulder!"

It hadn't used whatever that weapon was, and I was hoping we could keep that from happening by taking it out ahead of time. I could see the thing flinching, its shoulder twisting away as the slugs impacted, and I thought we were having more effect than the laser carbines. Of course that also meant we were going to garner more attention...

The discharge of the weapon was a hundred times brighter than what had broken through the elevator lift tunnel, unfiltered by dirt and distance, and it ripped the night apart like the very fabric of reality had been sundered. Only the contact lens in my right eye kept me from being completely blinded by the flash; it blacked out automatically while my left eye was swimming in pure whiteness.

How the thing missed us, I'm not sure; maybe our shots had thrown off its aim. Instead of turning the eight of us into atoms, the blast hit one of the bunkhouses and blew a hole through it the size of a cargo truck. The rest of the building exploded outward on either side from the pressure of the superheated air and a wave of heat and force slammed into us from over seventy meters away.

I was already on my belly, but Sanders and Victor had been firing from their knees and the blast knocked both of them backwards with a grunt of pain and shock. The thing steadied itself and began to aim more carefully, and I was a hundred percent sure we were dead until I heard the turbojets again. I rolled onto my side and stared upward, trying to close my left eye to stop the purple flashes over my vision on that side.

It was the *Wanderer*, coming back around, nose pointed directly at the alien creature. I squeezed my eyes shut, knowing what was coming, and still saw the glare of the proton beam through them, heard it concuss the air like a spring thunderstorm. When I opened my eyes again, the *Wanderer* was pulling a tight curve that took it around the edge of the canyon, and the monstrous alien thing that had hatched out of the pod was gone. All that was left was a smoking crater, littered with blackened bits of whatever the hell it was.

I sagged slightly, feeling an overwhelming sense of relief.

"That..." Ibanez was stuttering, her eyes wide and white as she sat back on the dirt, in shock. "That fucking *thing* was a Predecessor?"

"No," Yassa said grimly, shaking her head. "That fucking thing was what *killed* the Predecessors."

"Ty," Gramps put a hand on my arm, his voice shaky, too rattled to remember that Ty wasn't my name anymore. He was pointing towards the barn.

I followed his gesture and saw another of the things scuttling its way out of the tunnel they'd blasted, just as big and black and ugly as the first. It cleared the hole and a second crawled out behind it... and then another...

"Kane!" Yassa was screaming into the pickup of her 'link, as if she thought that would help the little device penetrate the background static here and reach the ship. "Kane, we need your help!"

Whether or not he heard her, Kane was coming back around in a tighter turn than I'd ever seen a ship that size pull. He'd just described an arc away from the canyon wall when the energy beam sliced through the night sky and sought him out like a striking snake. It clipped the *Wanderer*'s port-side delta wing, blowing a chunk off of it in a spray of sparks and vaporized metal and the ship went into a spin.

I felt my teeth clenching against the tightness in my gut, and I knew that I was less worried for Kane, for all that he was one of the crew, than I was for the fact that the ship had been our only way of fighting these things...and was our only way out.

Kane only had one option, and he took it: the belly jets ignited with a roar of white flame and power billowed out beneath the *Wanderer*, fighting with urgent desperation to pull her out of the spin before she slammed into the canyon wall. I wasn't a pilot and I wasn't a ship-designer, but I'd learned a few things from the pilots who'd flown my Recon platoon around, and one of them was why you didn't want to try to break out of a spin with the belly jets. There was only so much stress a ship's hull could take, and putting that high of a G-load on it...

The *Wanderer*'s BiPhase Carbide hull cracked on the stress points near the nose and the ship ripped apart like a child's puzzle, torn into three pieces only thirty meters above the ground. The drive section rocketed upward, the belly jets still burning and the weight reduced, spinning like a top as it arced over the walls of the canyon, beginning to pinwheel as it lost stability. Part of me wanted to keep watching it, and part wanted to watch the cockpit tumbling down to crash near the wall of the canyon, past where the assault shuttles had landed…and a greater part still wanted to stare in horror at the alien things swarming out of the tunnel under the barn.

We were all frozen there for what seemed like long minutes but were probably just a few seconds. Then there was a roar, and a rumble like a distant earthquake, and a flash brighter than the sun and I knew that the *Wanderer*'s engine section had hit. It was kilometers away, on the other side of the hills, but the flare was brighter than a searchlight and I could already see a mushroom cloud climbing into the night sky, glowing with inward light.

What's a little more background radiation on this place? I thought, a bit hysterically.

"The shuttles," Yassa was saying, though I could barely hear her over the roar of the explosion. "We have to get to one of the shuttles!"

I nodded. They were the only way left out of here, the two of them that were still intact.

"Those things…" Gramps was saying, his face slack and grey. "They couldn't have all been inside that one pod the whole time. It's making them."

"The shuttle will have a tight-beam laser transmitter," I said. "There's a kinetic strike package sitting in orbit." I thought of my 'link with the codes for the satellite programmed into it, and patted its shape in my jacket pocket. "We have to bury them in this canyon."

I turned to the others, the plan formulating in my head about a half-second earlier than the words came out of my mouth. "Cap, Kurt, Victor and Bobbi, you're one fire team. We bound by teams, but don't fire unless they're firing at one of us; we don't need to draw their attention. We're heading for the closest shuttle. And watch the Corporates, they'll be thinking the same thing. Yassa, your team moves first."

She gave me a nod, then waved for her people to follow her and took off at a sprint. The rest of us rose to a knee and trained our rifles downrange, and I took a moment to survey the nightmare scene laid out before me. Fires burned everywhere: the shuttle, the ranch house, the bunk houses---both of them now, the other had caught---and the barn. Smoke was twisting in black, spiraling eddies, caught in the gusts of wind that swept down off the rim and curled down into the trap below, and it was beginning to obscure the far side of the box canyon. I didn't know what had happened to the ranch workers the CSF troops had rounded up; they were nowhere around and I didn't see any bodies. I thought maybe they'd all taken off when the *Wanderer* began its attack run. I hoped they'd headed up the road and gotten the hell out of here.

The motion of the bug-like things was furtive and mysterious through the layers of smoke, but the movements of the Corporate Council mercenaries was less mysterious and much more predictable. They wanted the same thing we did: out. And they were doing the right thing, moving towards the shuttles in bounding over-watch formation, just like we were. But they made the mistake of shooting at the aliens.

Their lasers were even more visible in the fog and smoke, flashes of heat lightning in the distant clouds and cracks of tinny thunder. The return fire was more than visible, it was overwhelming, indescribable, the gods of old come to our world to lay down their judgment. I couldn't see what happened where it hit, and the screams of the dying were trapped inside faceless helmets, but I knew nothing we had could stand against their weapons, whatever they were.

Yassa's team reached the first cover, the shelter of a flatbed trailer loaded down with covered bales of hay, and I heard her yell "Go!" in my 'link's ear bud. I echoed the command to my group, slapping Gramps on the arm to make sure he heard me, since he wasn't using one of our 'links. He followed me, clutching the pulse pistol like a totem, and I tried to keep one eye on him and the rest of my team and the other on the multiple threats. The aliens were shadows, for all their gargantuan size, and panic gnawed at my nerve-endings at the thought that one of them might pop out of the smoke and haze right in front of us.

"Munroe," Yassa spoke from twenty meters away but still in a whisper in my ear, "if that pod can manufacture those things, what else do you think it can build?"

"Shit," I muttered in return. "Thanks, Cap, as if I didn't have enough on my mind…"

Ships. She was talking about ships. The pod had made living things, these bug warrior things, out of whatever was inside it. Could it make ships? Could the bug things make them? Could it make more pods?

I shoved those thoughts down as my team ducked behind the trailer beside Yassa's and her team slid out to the other side with ours behind. I fell into a spot at the far right-hand edge of the trailer, near the tow hookup, and Yassa led her people past me, running for the next bit of cover while we kept watch.

I could see the remnants of the CSF force running back our way now, any sense of formation or organization lost in a blind panic. This was bad. The mercenaries didn't worry me, not without any cohesion or leadership. But they kept shooting at the aliens, and that was going to attract their attention back our way…

"We're not going to make it," I heard Sanders say from beside me, his eyes on the bug things as they began scuttling closer, only a hundred meters away now. "They're going to get us before we reach the shuttles."

"You got any suggestions," I snapped back at him, "or grenades, I wish you'd tell me about them."

Yassa reached the burning ruins of the shuttle Kane had destroyed and her team crouched down behind the mostly intact tail section, sheltered by the BiPhase Carbide of the engine assembly. She looked at me as we ran to join them.

"Sanders is right," she said grimly. "We sure as hell won't have time to get it prepped and take off before they're on top of us."

Seventy meters away, an energy weapon vaporized two CSF troopers and several square meters of soil in an explosion of steam. I recognized a ripping, crackling noise to the shot that preceded the blast of its impact, but that gave me no further clue to what it was. There was another sound too, whining high-pitched above the echoes of the blast, and it took me a second to recognize it over the drumbeat of my own pulse in my ears as I ran to join Yassa and her team.

It was the turbines of one of the shuttles spinning to life. Someone was getting ready to take off without waiting for their buddies.

19

"Shit!" I yelled, shoving past Yassa and running out from the cover of the tail segment, heedless of the possibility of incoming fire.

The smoke billowing off the smoldering mid-section of the destroyed boat was like a curtain drawn across the valley, but even as I ran towards it, the hot breath of vertical take-off jets began to disperse it like a giant fan. I held my breath against the wall of heat and toxic fumes that washed over me, squinting as dust and sand scoured at my face.

It was the closer of the two remaining shuttles, maybe fifty meters away, already rising one meter, then two as fire and smoke roared out of its belly jets and I fell to my knees as the hot blast of the exhaust began to buffet me too strongly to stand against it. I yelled a curse that no one could have heard over the roar of its engines, and I wanted to raise my rifle and shoot at the thing, but I realized that wasn't going to do us any good.

The aerospacecraft was nearly a hundred meters up and turning back along the canyon wall towards the barn and I thought maybe I'd misjudged whoever was flying it. Maybe they weren't planning on running, maybe they were going to use the shuttle's on-board weapons against the aliens.

The aliens must have had that thought as well, because the boat had only made it halfway into its turn when they shot it down. I blinked at the flashes, shaking the afterimages of the energy beams from my eyes, squeezing them shut before what was left of the shuttle impacted the canyon wall a couple hundred meters away.

When I opened them again, I saw the last shuttle, our only way left out of here, still sitting isolated and vulnerable almost a hundred meters away. The clouds of smoke had settled back down and I could smell them as they began to roll over me like a cloak, the image of the shuttle ahead of me appearing and disappearing in their black, oily folds.

I barely registered Yassa and the others gathering around me, recklessly exposed but beyond caring.

"I'm going to go draw their fire while you grab the boat," Yassa declared. My head snapped towards her.

"Fuck no, you're not!" I exploded. "Don't even think about it!"

"Use your head, Sergeant," she replied calmly. "You have the codes for the strike package, and destroying these things is more important than any of us."

"I'm not going to let you kill yourself!" I yelled, feeling a red haze drifting over my brain. "You don't have to do this!"

She didn't yell back, just placed her hand flat on my chest for a second and smiled softly.

"Go home to your Sophia," she said. "I've got this."

I wanted to stop her, wanted to jump on her and restrain her, but I couldn't because she was right. It had to be done, and I couldn't do it.

"You need a hand, Captain Yassa?" Gramps asked her, standing straight.

"It would be an honor, Master Gunnery Sergeant Torres," she said to him with a nod.

"Gramps?" I shook my head, uncomprehending.

"This is my mess, son," he said to me, and I finally saw the man I'd known, the one who'd raised me. "I'm going to be the one to clean it up." He smiled at me, just a bit of sadness in it but also something of the savage joy of a Marine heading into battle. "I'm sorry I let you down."

Then the two of them were gone, sprinting into the night, into the haze and smoke, charging towards the sound of gunfire. Something was squeezing my chest hard, but I fought to get words out anyway.

"Bobbi," I said to her, "I'm on point, you run drag. The target's the shuttle. Anyone falls, leave them where they lie and take that damned boat." I wiped something off my face; it might have been rain. "They're giving us a chance; don't waste it."

Wellesley had left a team guarding the shuttles, and at least some of them had stayed at their posts even amid the panic and confusion…probably because they were too panicked and confused to move. I saw them as I cleared the wreath of smoke at a sprint, saw them huddled around the landing gear of the last intact shuttle, only sixty meters more. There was no more cover between us and them, but I thought for a moment that we could cross the distance clean, that their attention was totally focused on the aliens.

We were twenty meters from the rear of the armored aerospacecraft when one of them just happened to turn and see us. I'd had a microsecond debate inside my skull during the run about whether we could get out without fighting, but the decision was made between us without thought. My Gauss rifle had been at low ready, his pulse carbine was slung at high port and we both brought them on-line at nearly the same moment. I waited the microsecond before I saw my contact lens' targeting reticle pass over his chest; he didn't. His shot went wide to my right by less than a meter just before a heavy tungsten slug sliced through his chest.

I heard a yell behind me, but I couldn't look back; there wasn't time. The one I'd shot was wobbling on his feet, dead but not quite realizing it yet, when I switched my point of aim and put a round through the helmet of a CSF trooper who'd been crouched in the lee of a landing tread under the portside wing. Blood sprayed over the slate grey cover of the landing gear strut and he slumped to the ground, and then I was past the whole group and heading for the waiting boarding ramp. There was gunfire behind me and I fought the almost irresistible urge to turn back towards it, knowing I had to get to the cockpit.

The ramp vibrated under the stomp of my boots and I could feel a searing hot knife stabbing into my side from the wound there opening again from the pull on the muscles from heading up the steep metal slope. Exhaustion and hunger dragged at me and I felt incredibly weak, but I kept telling myself that I had this one last run and then it would be over, one way or the other.

The interior lights in the shuttle's utility bay backlit the man jogging towards the ramp, throwing his shadow across me and all I could see was his outstretched arm and the pulse pistol he held. The reticle from my rifle sight bounced around with my steps, and I knew he was going to fire first before it settled down, so I threw myself to the side. A glowing line of ionized air passed through where I'd been just a heartbeat before as he opened fire, and my shoulder slammed into the metal deck plating, my rifle only a meter away from him when I shot.

The slug passed upward through his chest and out the top of his skull before it spent itself inside the bulkhead. He collapsed to his knees, then hit face first beside me, missing the upper half of his head. He hadn't been wearing armor or a helmet, just a set of black CSF fatigues, and I guessed he was flight crew. I didn't look at what was left of him, just grabbed his pulse pistol from where it had fallen, then forced myself painfully back to my feet and slung my rifle over my shoulder. I didn't need to put a slug through the hull or into the flight controls by accident.

I heard footsteps on the ramp behind me as I passed through the rows of acceleration couches where the troopers had ridden the shuttle down from orbit, but I had to just hope it was my guys and keep moving forward to the cockpit. The hatch between the utility bay and the cockpit was propped open, like the man I'd shot had just come out of it, but I could see an arm and part of a shoulder reaching through to grab the handle and shut it.

I snap-shot the laser, squeezing the trigger a bit too long and firing four rounds instead of the two I'd intended. There was less thermal signature here, inside the shuttle with no particulates in the air, just a slight flash and then the arm jerked back and someone screamed and there was an impact of a body against the deck. The hatch had swung halfway shut where the hand had grabbed it, and I kicked it open and stuck the pistol inside.

There was a woman lying on her right side on the deck between the pilot and co-pilot's acceleration couches. She had short, red hair and hazel eyes and she was trying to suck in her last breath with a fist-sized hole burned through her chest. Her left arm ended at the bicep, the bone charred and splintered and the rest of it blocking the cockpit hatch. She had a gun, but it was in the holster at her left hip. I thought she'd been the pilot.

Maybe it was the pain from the wound in my side, or maybe it was the lack of sleep and lack of food, but I couldn't hold back the bile rising in my throat this time. I pulled back out of the cockpit and vomited what little was in my stomach onto the deck beside the hatchway, leaning against the bulkhead heavily.

"Boss, are you okay?"

It was Victor, concern in his eyes as he ran up through the aisle between the rows of seats, Kurt just behind him.

"Yeah," I said, spitting on the deck to clear my mouth. "Get her out of there," I nodded towards the cockpit, "so we can try to get this thing in the air."

Victor grimaced when he saw the woman, but he did what he was told, grabbing the pilot by the legs and dragging her out of the cockpit. She'd stopped trying to breathe, and her eyes were open and unblinking. Kurt picked up her severed arm, his face intentionally expressionless, and followed the trail of blood on the deck out to the ramp.

Before they could get to the end, Bobbi came up, pushing Sanders in front of her as he cursed and fought her.

"Let me go!" He was yelling at her, trying to break free of her grip without much success. "Carmen could still be alive! We could still save her!"

"She's flatlined," Bobbi said, firmly but gently, grabbing him by the jaw and forcing him to look her in the eye. "She was shot right through her neck, Eli. *If* we had an auto-doc or a fully-equipped medical bay and we got her into it immediately, yes, we might save her. We don't have either of those, and she's dead. She's gone."

"Jesus," I moaned, squeezing my eyes shut. Ibanez. They were talking about Ibanez, and she was dead.

I pushed off the bulkhead and stumbled into the cockpit, not wanting to look at them, just wanting to get this thing off the ground and blow this whole damn place up. There was blood all over the control console, enough that it was interfering with the displays. I swore under my breath, pulling off my jacket and wiping it away enough for the holo-projectors to work. There was blood on my fatigue shirt, too, and seeing the charred hole in my side almost made me throw up again.

I fell into the pilot's seat and hunted for the control to start the turbines. This shit was state-of-the-art, not like the century-old crap they had on Thunderhead; haptic holograms with a pretty advanced AI that would fly the ship for me if I could figure out how to tell it what to do. I scrolled through one screen after another until I finally saw the icon for the engines and pulled it up to access the menu.

And it blinked at me in large, red letters: "Access denied. Identity scan unknown."

"Fuck!" I screamed, slamming my fist into the hard polymer of the console.

I heard the shouts then, and a shot. I bolted out of the cockpit, pulse pistol jumping into my hand from where I'd set it next the control panel, and found Sanders writhing on the deck, a ragged hole burned through his shoulder, while Victor and Kurt aimed their rifles towards the top of the ramp.

Constantine Terranova stood there, his pulse pistol extended in his left hand, the cybernetic fingers of his right wrapped around the throat of Bobbi Taylor, holding her in front of him as a shield. Her rifle was on the floor and she was clawing in futility at the hand slowly choking her.

"Everyone throw down your guns," Constantine said, his voice deadly flat despite what looked like a painful and serious burn on the left side of his face. "If everyone stays calm, we can all get out of here alive."

"No one's fucking getting out of here alive, you piece of shit," I snapped at him, feeling almost more annoyed than enraged. "The pilot's dead and we're locked out of the controls. So why don't you let her go and I'll go easy on you and put a round through your forehead before the aliens get the chance to rip you to pieces with their fucking claws."

Victor glanced over at me for just a moment at the statement, like it was an involuntary shocked reaction.

"Well, I'm not fucking giving up, Munroe," Constantine growled, finally, it seemed, losing his composure. "So drop your damned…"

He didn't have the chance to finish the sentence. He jerked and spasmed, the gun falling from his hand as he grimaced in pain. He let loose of Bobbi and tried to reach behind him with his bionic arm, like it was the only strength left to him, but his mouth opened slack, spilling a gush of blood, and his eyes rolled back in his head. Then he fell forward, crashing to the deck with a metallic clang, a huge hole ripped into his back just below his left shoulder blade.

Behind him, Kane shook blood from his fist. The flesh half of his face was charred and cracked, the human eye swollen shut, and his fatigues were shredded and covered in burns and blood. Standing a step down from him on the ramp was Trina Wellesley, her face more shocked and horrified than I'd thought her capable of feeling.

I felt my lips pulling back from my teeth in the closest I was going to come to a smile at the moment.

"Found her out there," Kane said, his voice slurred and mechanical. "Said she could help."

"Get the board unlocked," I said to Wellesley, "and we'll take you out of here." I looked at Kane again and shook my head. "Can you fly?"

By way of response, he stomped past me towards the cockpit,

the Corporate Security Force agent jogging beside him. Bobbi was on her knees, rubbing at her throat and staring daggers at Constantine's corpse while Victor and Kurt had gone to help Sanders.

"Get rid of the bodies," I told them, "and close the ramp. Then everyone get belted in, and get Sanders strapped down, too. We may have a rough ride."

I could hear the turbines spinning up as I made it to the cockpit. Kane was already strapped into the pilot's seat, but he wasn't bothering with the holographic display; he was plugged directly into the control console, his cybernetic eye gleaming. I fell into the co-pilot's seat, motioning a hesitant Wellesley into the navigation position as I buckled the restraints.

The forward viewscreens were active now, and I could see what the cameras and sensors were picking up. The aliens were still over by the barn, firing energy blasts in three directions, all of them away from us. Yassa and Gramps had to still be alive out there, still keeping them busy. But that wouldn't last long. I pulled my 'link out of my pocket and called up the file I'd been given by Cowboy.

I found the communications controls and activated the shuttle's primary tight-beam antenna, realigning it towards the coordinates I read off the 'link. I sent the signal code and held my breath. If Cowboy had been lying, or the CSF had detected the strike package and destroyed it...

No. There was the return signal, beeping cheerfully and flashing green in the communications display. It was a fairly simple interface, and it only took me seconds to figure out. I fed the coordinates of the canyon to the satellite, then told it to launch immediately, which gave us...

"Three minutes, thirty seconds until we're toast," I informed Kane.

"What does that mean?" Wellesley demanded, looking sharply at me.

I didn't answer her, just stared at the main display and watched the bugs. They were all firing at the same place now, the far corner of the barn, their converging energy beams nearly whiting out the view screen. When the glare faded, they all began to turn away from the wreckage…and turn towards us.

"Kane," I bit off, but almost before I said the word, the shuttle leapt into the air, jetting forward the second it lifted off.

I was pushed back into the acceleration couch, the breath going out of me as Kane opened the throttles and rocketed us across the canyon floor only a few meters off the hard deck. Everything seemed to be narrowing to a black-rimmed tunnel in front of me, and I knew I was close to passing out. I tried to clench my stomach muscles, but pain flared again in my side and I gasped with air I didn't have to spare and the blackness swallowed everything.

20

I spasmed against my seat restraints, eyes flying open, and I instinctively knew I'd blacked out from the g-forces. I looked around and saw that Wellesley had done the same and was still out. Kane was stock-still, effectively part of the shuttle's computer system. The rear view and threat readout in the main display screen showed that we were nearly ten kilometers from the ranch house, well out of the firing arc of the aliens.

My eyes danced around the display, hunting desperately for the countdown from the strike package, until I saw a much more dramatic and definitive answer to that question. Streaks of white-hot plasma descended out of the cloud cover like a swarm of meteors, each of the two dozen spears of light actually a three-meter long tungsten rod that weighed hundreds of kilograms.

They struck simultaneously and a dome of fire kilometers high expanded out to engulf the entire canyon in a blast as powerful as a fusion warhead. The glowing hemisphere faded and a mushroom cloud climbed high above the canyon, carrying with it the vaporized remains of Carmen Ibanez, Brandy Yassa and Cesar Torres. They were gone, as if they'd never been.

I leaned forward into my hands, and to my surprise, found myself whispering a prayer for them. Mom had raised me an atheist, but Gramps had been an old-fashioned Catholic, and I'd gone to mass with him many times over the years. I wasn't sure I believed, but I was sure he did, and I was sure he'd want it. As for Yassa and Ibanez, I didn't honestly know, but it wouldn't hurt.

I frowned as I felt the shuttle nosing upward, the thrust increasing as the boat gained altitude.

"Take us back to Freeport," I instructed Kane, my voice rasping and husky.

"No can do," he said. I glanced over and saw him still staring forward, expressionless. "Remote override taking control. Can't fight it."

Trina Wellesley was awake now, and she was smiling thinly.

"That would be the *Medellin*," she told me, her voice in control now, her demeanor calmer. "That's my lighter, in high orbit," she amended. "When I unlocked the controls, I activated an emergency alert. They took control once we were out of the canyon and they're bringing us into a docking orbit with them."

I'd tucked the pulse pistol into a storage pouch in the side of my chair. I pulled it out and levelled it at her face.

"Unless you get back on the comms and tell them not to," I corrected her.

"If you shoot me, Mr. Callas, they'll *still* bring you on board, and when they access the on-board security monitors, they'll see that I'm dead and they'll gas this ship, then hit it with sonics just for good measure. If you're lucky, you'll wake up in confinement. If you're not, you'll never wake up at all."

"You'd still be dead," I reminded her, trying to be as calm as she was, but feeling my lip curl into a snarl. "And we have all the way to orbit to think of a way to stop the shuttle."

"How about I offer you something you want, then?" She nodded back towards the hatch to the utility bay. "Your man back there is badly wounded. If you put down the gun and don't attempt to resist, I guarantee that he'll receive treatment." I opened my mouth to object, but she halted it with an upraised palm. "I'll also guarantee that the rest of your team will be released once we reach

Hermes." She cocked an eyebrow at me. "With Mr. Torres apparently no longer a concern, my job is to bring you back…just you."

I pressed my lips together to keep from cursing reflexively. That bitch knew just what notes to hit, all right. She knew I'd have no problem killing her and taking my chances, but if it meant the chance to keep the rest of the team safe…

I spun the pulse pistol upward on its trigger guard and flicked on the safety.

"I'm not certain how much you know about me, Ms. Wellesley," I said with quiet resignation. "But I can guarantee you something: if you fail to deliver on your part of this deal, don't count on anyone else to keep me from getting to you."

"Once Ms. Damiani gets you back," she countered, "*you* won't know much about you, Mr. Callas." She sniffed. "But your mother would probably frown on me going back on my word to her son, just on principle."

"My mother," I said to her, staring out the view screen as the clouds gave way to the stars, "doesn't *have* principles."

The hull shuddered as the shuttle docked, and I shuddered with it.

"We should have fought 'em," Bobbi Taylor grumbled, anchored by one hand to a strap on the bulkhead by the airlock. The fingers of her free hand flexed unconsciously, as if it longed for a weapon. The Gauss rifles and the pulse pistol were stowed in the locker just aft of the cockpit, at Wellesley's insistence.

"Sanders and I are both shot," I pointed out, my voice sounding distant in my own ears, my head floating as much as the rest of me, and not just because of the microgravity. "Kane crashed a starship and all three of you are pretty beat up. We have a few rifles, no pressure suits, one avenue of egress, and no control over this boat *and* they have gas and sonics and all the time in the world."

As if on cue, Sanders moaned softly, his eyes blinking fitfully. I grabbed him by his fatigue pants' belt and kept him from floating off towards the overhead. Kane was standing behind us, his metal feet magnetized to the deck, and said nothing. He hadn't spoken a word since the CSF had taken over control of the shuttle and I wondered if he had a concussion from the crash.

"You didn't have to do this for us, Boss," Victor said quietly. He and Kurt looked smaller, somehow, bobbing there with no purchase.

"Of course he did," Wellesley commented drily from the front of us. She glanced back at me, with what might have been disdain and might have been...what? Envy? "It's who he is...for the moment."

We were in the belly of the beast now, inside the lighter's docking bay. It was a bulky, bulbous, ugly ship seen from the outside and I felt even worse inside it. The docking collar hummed mechanically as it sealed around the airlock of the shuttle, like a noose around our necks.

There was no pressure equalization to worry about, so the inner and outer airlock doors opened together with a smooth hum of servos. There were a pair of armored CSF troops waiting for us outside the lock, their boots magnetically locked to the deck, pulse rifles cradled in their arms like they didn't think they'd need them. I was suddenly conscious of the blood stains on the deck beneath my feet, and I wondered if anyone in the crew of the *Medellin* had been friends with the people I'd killed, and whether they held a grudge. And then I looked past them and forgot all about it.

Standing behind them, anchored to the deck by the magnetic soles of his ship boots, was Cowboy.

"Howdy Munroe," he drawled. Then he nodded to Wellesley, who looked even more shocked than I was. "How you been, Trina?"

"West," she hissed the word like it was a curse. "What the hell are you doing here?"

"Just safeguarding my employer's investment, Trina," he said with a grin. He turned to the two CSF guards. "Get that man," he gestured towards Sanders, "to the medical bay and see they get him treated right away."

"Yes, sir," a woman's voice answered him from the exterior helmet speakers of one of them, and they moved forward and took the barely-conscious Sanders from my charge. I let him go reluctantly, not so much because I didn't think they'd take care of him but more because I was reeling and at least he was something to hold onto.

"Kane," I said, finally shaking off my stupor, "go with them. Get looked at by the docs."

He didn't argue with me, and I knew that meant he was hurt worse than he was letting on.

"West," Wellesley snapped, pushing herself out into the passageway as the guards retreated with Sanders' limp form, Kane clomping along behind, "you can't just come on board *my* ship and order my people around!"

"Oh, of course I can, Trina," he sighed in mild exasperation. "I just fucking did it, didn't I?"

Behind him, in the security monitors that displayed the lighter's docking bay, I could see West's cutter taking up the other half of the bay, opposite the shuttle, squeezed into a space that had held two of the now-destroyed assault boats.

"What the hell am I going to tell Patrice?" Wellesley demanded, less outraged now and sounding a bit desperate.

"Tell her this is what Andre wants," Cowboy responded with an easy shrug.

I could see her biting back her instinctive response, but I felt a cold tingling in my scalp. Andre? *Uncle* Andre? Was *that* who Cowboy worked for?

Wellesley was rubbing a hand over her eyes, looking gut-punched by the realization that the only thing she thought she could salvage from this clusterfuck was being taken away from her.

"Take these people to the mess, Trina," Cowboy ordered her, waving at Victor, Kurt and Bobbi. "Get them something to eat, then take them somewhere they can get cleaned up. It's a long flight back to Hermes and they all smell like blood and ashes."

Wellesley didn't even bother to argue with him, just pushed off down the passageway towards the hub of the ship, not waiting to see if anyone followed her. Victor and Kurt headed after her immediately, glancing uncomfortably at Cowboy as they did, probably remembering him as a vaguely threatening presence from wartime Demeter.

"So you're Cowboy, huh?" Bobbi asked, looking him up and down as she pulled herself out of the airlock. "You're cute...but that damn money better be in my account when I get back."

"It's there already, ma'am," he assured her, grinning in amusement as she brushed past him, closer than she had to. Then he looked over at me, his expression growing more serious. "Come along with me, Munroe."

He grabbed me by the shoulder and propelled me beside him as his magnetic boot soles kept him on the deck. I let myself be pulled along without a word, numb and drifting, literally and figuratively. I should be furious with him, I knew. I should be raging; he'd known that Gramps was Abuelo, he'd recruited Yassa to...

I blinked. Recruited her to what? Cowboy was a lot of things, but stupid wasn't one of them. He'd have known that Yassa wouldn't betray me, even with the drugs. He'd brought her in to...

"You brought her in so you could tell her the things you couldn't tell me," I said, my voice muted and unemotional. "So that it would come from someone I trusted."

"Even strung out and half-delirious," he said, shaking his head, "you're smarter than ninety percent of the Corporate Council Executive Board." He eyed me sidelong, an appraising look. "Ruthless, too. Not squeamish at all about doing what has to be done. I completely understand why your mother wants you back so badly...and why Andre Damiani would rather you stay gone, for now."

I vaguely realized we were heading for the other side of the hangar bay, to where his ship was docked.

"If Uncle Andre wants me out of the way," I asked him, "why doesn't he just have you kill me?"

We were paused outside the lock to Cowboy's cutter, its curved, delta shape visible in the display screen, and he peeled off a glove and touched the ID plate.

"Because *Monsieur* Damiani didn't get to be the Director of the Council's Executive Board by wasting resources." The lock slid aside and West pushed me into the ship's utility bay. "He just doesn't want you being a resource for his pain in the ass sister."

I caught myself against the padded bulkhead next to a storage locker and stared at him, curiosity warring against resentment, and both fighting a losing battle with fatigue.

"What's the real reason you didn't do this yourself?" I wanted to know.

"I wasn't lying to you," Cowboy insisted, closing the lock behind us. "There's a man down there who knows me. You met him too, once, back on Demeter at the end. He's one of the Glory Boys, so if he decided to pick a fight with me, it's not certain who'd win."

"You told me one lie," I asserted. "You said it was a Predecessor artifact. That damned thing didn't come from the Predecessors."

"No, it didn't," he admitted with a shrug. "But that was information I couldn't admit, or I'd have had to tell you about your Great-grandfather…and then, you might not have done it."

"Just one last thing, Cowboy." I felt like I was slurring my words a little and I concentrated harder, trying to make sure I stayed sharp, because this was an important question. "Did you really want that pod intact?"

"Oh, sure, if you could have pulled it off," he told me readily. "We'd have studied it in a contained lab with a lot of safeguards, just like we have the others."

I nodded, forgetting I was in microgravity, feeling the motion send me drifting. So, the Corporate Council had a bunch of those things stored in labs somewhere, each a little time bomb that could probably take down our whole civilization if we didn't contain them in time. Just one more thing to keep me up at night.

"Why am I here?" I wondered, looking around the ship.

"Come here," he said, waving me towards the other end of the bay.

Tucked in by the bulkhead there was what looked like an auto-doc: a transparent polymer cylinder lined with medical scanners and connected to spherical tanks of nanite-infused biotic fluid that could repair almost anything short of an amputation or major brain damage, given enough time. I pushed off from the storage locker and floated over to it, catching myself against the smooth, curved surface of the thing.

"Why couldn't I use the one in the lighter's medical bay?" I asked, starting to strip off my fatigue top.

"Because this isn't a normal auto-doc," Cowboy told me. I paused with my shirt halfway off, looking back at the thing again, more cautiously.

"This," he continued, walking around the cylinder in the stiffly awkward manner that ship boots forced on you, "is a..." He shrugged. "...an investment by *Monsieur* Damiani. You're already a nearly perfect physical specimen thanks to your mother's genetic intervention. This is something to make sure you stay that way."

"Can you be less specific?" I murmured, pulling off my shirt and tossing it away. It was soaked with sweat and stiff with blood and it rotated slowly away before slapping against the far bulkhead.

"One of the things that makes me and the other Glory Boys what we are," Cowboy elaborated, "is a highly-specialized nanite suite tailored to our DNA, self-sustaining, self-replicating and powering itself from our own blood sugar. It can repair most injuries in hours, assuming you have the raw materials available in the form of body fat or undigested food. It can basically do almost anything an auto-doc can do, but it's *inside* us."

"Holy shit," I said, suddenly alert, my eyes opening wide. "Is that even *possible*?"

"Oh, it's possible," he assured me. "But it's really fuckin' expensive. So expensive that only ten people have ever had the treatment." He nodded towards the auto-doc. "Until now."

I felt my face twist into a mask of disbelief.

"Why?" I restrained myself from shrugging, knowing it would send me floating off again. "Why me?"

"Because you're his damn nephew," Cowboy said in a tone like it was incredibly obvious. "And he put you in a position where you might get killed."

The other shoe dropped inside my head.

"And he's going to do it again."

Cowboy smiled, touching a control and opening the auto-doc chamber with a pneumatic hiss.

"Like I said, you're a smart kid, Munroe."

I felt myself sag. *I'm sorry, Sophia.*

I pulled myself inside the chamber and closed my eyes.

"Let's get it over with."

21

The house was dark when I stepped inside. It was after midnight local time in Amity, and Sophia was always asleep by ten; she had to get up early on work days. I didn't have to turn on any lights, since I still had my contact lens in place. I didn't have any luggage to unpack; everything I'd taken with me had been destroyed either on the *Wanderer* or in the ranch house. The clothes I was wearing had been fabricated on board the *Medellin* while I was in Cowboy's auto-doc.

I found myself experiencing *déjà vu* for when I'd come back to the Marine base on Inferno after the Fleet had finally liberated Demeter. I'd stepped off the shuttle in Tartarus owning nothing but the dress uniform they'd given me on the troop ship.

And look how well that *turned out,* I thought acerbically.

But no, that wasn't fair and it wasn't true. I hadn't been left with nothing then or now. I'd left everything that was important to me here on Demeter, and it was all still here.

Sophia was in bed when I pushed open the door to our room, but she wasn't asleep.

"Hi, Munroe," she said, and I could see her smile as she rose up on her elbow. She was wearing the same long T-shirt she always slept in.

"Hey Sophie," I said, sitting down on the edge of the bed and kissing her. I pulled her against me, clinging to her with a desperation like there was a hole in my chest that only she could fill. "You shouldn't have waited up for me," I chided her gently. "You have to get up early."

I'd sent her an Instell Comsat message from Hermes when we'd dropped off Sanders, Kane and Bobbi Taylor there, letting her know I was all right and would be back in a few days. Victor and Kurt had returned to Demeter with me to visit their family. I'd offered them jobs at the Constabulary and I thought they'd take me up on it.

"I'm the boss, Munroe," she reminded me, chuckling as she ran a hand through my hair. It was a little longer than when I'd left. "I can come in late."

She pulled me into the bed and I barely had time to kick off my boots before she was stripping away my clothes, leaning down to kiss me more seriously. We didn't say anything coherent for a while after that, and we didn't need to.

Forever later, I rested with my arm around her shoulder, her head laying against my chest, the rhythm of her breathing slowly coming back to normal, and we both spoke at once.

"It isn't over, Sophie..." I was saying at the very same moment she said: "Munroe, I want to have children."

I felt my jaw drop open at the unexpected declaration, and saw the shock on her face as well.

"What do you mean?" She demanded, pushing herself up to look into my eyes.

I shook my head, trying to organize my thoughts enough to answer her. "This thing with Cowboy. They're not done with me, Sophie. This is just the first installment of what I owe them, not hardly the last."

"Oh," her voice was small, her eyes narrowing at the thought. "Shit."

"You want kids?" I blurted, still feeling like I'd been kicked in the head. "When did you decide that?"

"A while ago," she admitted, laying her head back down. "I just figured there was plenty of time to talk about it. Then all this shit happened, and maybe...I don't know, maybe there isn't. What do you think?"

I started to answer, stopped, started again.

"Do you think I'd be a good father?" I waved a hand helplessly. "I mean, I had a pretty fucked up childhood."

"You had Gramps," she reminded me. I tried not to wince. I hadn't told her about that, yet. I'd have to, eventually, but that was for the morning.

"Yeah, I did. I guess a kid could do a lot worse for a father." I paused, trying not to think about having to explain to her everything that had happened. "Do you want to get married?"

Back on Earth, with the crowd Mom ran with, marriage wasn't a thing. It was considered beneath our station, something the proles did, like religion and sports. The controlling class did things more logically, signing cohabitation contracts, or reproduction contracts detailing when each biological parent would have custody, who would decide education, philosophy, discipline, finances... But I knew attitudes were different about a lot of things in the colonies, and most people who wanted to have a family got married first.

Sophia took my hand in hers, interlacing the fingers and squeezing it tightly.

"I'd like that," she said softly.

"What about me working for West? It's going to be dangerous."

"It sucks," she said flatly. "I hate it, and I hate the idea of you leaving again and me not knowing if you're ever coming back. If you want to run, you know I'll run with you. I always told you I would."

"How long can we run?" The question was rhetorical. I knew the answer: you couldn't run at all from someone with a reach as long as Andre Damiani. "No, I think I'd rather fight than run."

"Do you really think we can fight them?" I could tell by her tone that she didn't.

"Not yet," I said.

She still held my right hand tightly, but I lifted my left in front of my face and flexed it, almost believing I could feel the nanites Cowboy had given me coursing through my blood.

"They think they're making me their weapon," I told her. "That's the thing about weapons, though; they can be pointed at anyone."

The story will continue in THE MERCENARY.

THANK YOU FOR READING HUNTER!

We hope you enjoyed it as much as we enjoyed bringing it to you. We just wanted to take a moment to encourage you to review the book. Follow this link: THE HUNTER to be directed to the book's Amazon product page to leave your review.

Every review helps further the author's reach and, ultimately, helps them continue writing fantastic books for us all to enjoy.

You can also join our non-spam mailing list by visiting www.subscribepage.com/AethonReadersGroup and never miss out on future releases. You'll also receive three full books completely Free as our thanks to you.

Facebook | Instagram | Twitter | Website

Want to discuss our books with other readers and even the authors? Join our Discord server today and be a part of the Aethon community.

Looking for more from Rick Partlow?

Go to war or go to jail. For small-time street hustler Cam Alvarez, the choice is simple. He has no family, no friends, no place in the world…nothing to lose. When his latest con results in the death of a cartel hitman, Cam opts to join the Marines and leave Earth to fight a vicious alien enemy. Drafted into the Marine Drop-Troopers, Cam discovers there's one thing he's even better at than running street-con games, and that's killing the enemy. Wrapped in an armored battlesuit, Cam finds purpose amidst the horror and destruction of the war, and the opportunity for a new sort of friends and family…if he can break the habits of a life spent alone, trusting no one. And, if he can survive...

Get Contact Front Now!

First contact gone wrong... It was every starship captain's nightmare, and for Travis Miller, it was his own personal hell. He'd done everything by the book, but when the Tahni had attacked him and his crew, there was no choice but to return fire and destroy the first alien vessel humans had ever encountered. Excoriated in the press, his career in shambles, Travis is exiled to a long patrol of the outer colony worlds. Forgotten, except as a bad example...until the Tahni prove him right by declaring war on the human Commonwealth. Now, Travis Miller is the tip of the spear. Humanity's best hope for turning back an overwhelming assault on human space. Because to the Tahni, humans are infidels and this is a holy war...

GET GENESIS NOW!

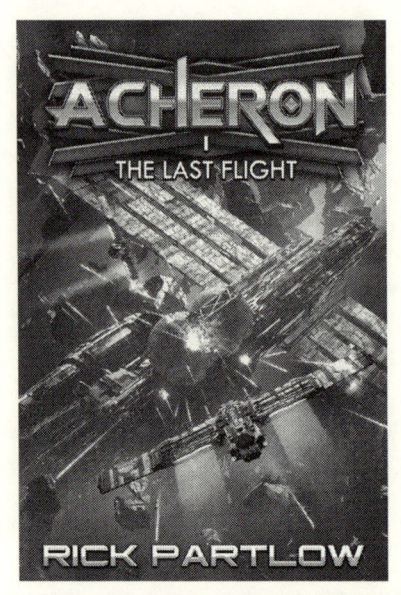

Sandi and Ash never set out to be heroes. She joined the Fleet to please her mother, the Admiral. He signed up to escape the grinding poverty of the Housing Blocks. And the unlikely friends envisioned boring, peacetime careers as shuttle pilots. The Tahni Imperium had other ideas… Caught in the desperate fury of the Battle for Mars, the two young pilots wind up the last defense against an alien armada, but their war is just beginning. Recruited to fly the Fleet's newest weapon in this new war, they take the fight deep into the heart of the Imperium and battle not just against the enemy but against incompetent leadership and ineffectual tactics. Can the unconventional strategies of a pair of hotshot young pilots change the course of the war? And when the time comes that a choice has to be made between duty to command and loyalty to a friend, which of the two will be willing to make one last flight alone…

GET THE LAST FLIGHT NOW!

Looking for more great Science Fiction?

When the rules of war keep changing, fight for each other...
Humanity has been banished to a distant star. Left to fight over resources rationed to them by mysterious machine-overlords known as Wardens. Commander Rylan Holt labors against inter-colony arms trafficking when an informant gives him horrific news. The ruthless cartel boss, Lilith, has stockpiled outlawed weapons of mass destruction. Worse, she claims to have permission from the Wardens to unleash them upon the system. When the battleship *Audacity* speeds to investigate Rylan's discovery, operations officer Scott Carrick finds himself in a trap more deadly than he could have ever imagined. His only hope of escape may lie with their most junior crewmember, a nurse named Aila Okuma, who's never seen battle. As Rylan, Scott, and Aila struggle to survive a war where the rules keep changing, they must answer a terrible question: how do they win when it seems the Wardens intend for everyone to lose?

Get Hellfire Now!

———

A smuggler, a spy, a brewing revolution…and a rogue agent who could destroy it all. Perrin Hightower can fly a run-down freighter through the galaxy's most dangerous wormholes blindfolded, a handy skill in her shipping business…and her smuggling enterprises. Special agent Tai Lawson dreams of leading the Ruby Confederation's spy agency. But when his partner steals a top-secret list of revolutionaries and vanishes, Tai's accused of helping his friend escape. When Tai seeks her navigation expertise, Perrin would rather jump out an airlock than help. But the missing person is her ex-boyfriend—a double agent she thought was helping the revolution. Her name's on that list, and she'll do anything to keep it secret.

Get A Rogue Pursuit Now!

"Aliens, agents, and espionage abound in this Cold War-era alternate history adventure... A wild ride!"—Dennis E. Taylor, bestselling author of We Are Legion (We Are Bob)

GET THE LUNA MISSILE CRISIS NOW!

For all our Sci-Fi books, visit our website.

ABOUT THE AUTHOR

Visit my Facebook Author Page and sign up for my newsletter at:
www.facebook.com/dutyhonorplanet

Or visit my author blog at:
www.rickpartlow.com

Or visit my Amazon author page at:
https://www.amazon.com/Rick-Partlow/e/B00B1GNL4E

Manufactured by Amazon.ca
Bolton, ON